VAULT OF SILENCE

BOOK TWO OF THE HIDDEN WIZARD

VAUGHAN W. SMITH

FAIR FOLIO

ISBN: 978-0-9874694-8-9

For Elli

1

A NEW FIRE

Lara crept up to the edge of the hill and peered over. She could see a large mass of Blighters, all of them hunched over and roaming in no discernible pattern. The terrain was a mix between rocky and sandy, with very little vegetation. She shielded her eyes from the harsh sun as she scanned the entire scene. Her nose wrinkling as she caught the putrid smell coming off them.

"It's as you expected, we have a whole barrel of them down there," she said.

"Blighters?" Alrion said.

"Looks like it. But there are others too. I think we should go around them." Lara swept her head over to take in the view and plot a course around the mob.

"Aren't we close to Brangtur?" Alrion gestured into the distance to emphasise his point.

"Yes, really close. If we avoided them it may take another day to do so safely."

"I don't want to waste the time, and we've dealt with Blighters before. This can be a fun romp." The young wizard had a mad grin on his face, which made Lara annoyed.

"Fun? There's an awful lot of them. I really think stealth is the preferred approach." It didn't make any sense to willingly take on such a force. Not when it could be avoided.

"Not this time. I want to make a statement. I need them to know I'm not the same person they encountered before," Alrion said.

Lara looked at him and sighed. He had certainly awakened to his power following his near-death confrontation with Branthor. But she wasn't sure this new Alrion was necessarily better equipped. Not yet. "So just because you defeated a wizard you think you're the king of wizards now?"

"Not yet. I still need you to watch my back," he said as he pushed off and starting jogging down the other side of the hill. "It's not as bad as you said," Alrion shouted as he descended.

Lara could see him working himself up. How much did he really want this, and how much was he just playing the part?

"Time to announce ourselves," Alrion said gleefully. He created a giant ball of flame and kept it right in front of him.

Lara staggered back for safety. "You better know what you're doing," she said, shielding her face with her arm. But instead of just throwing it, Alrion gave it a great push. The giant sphere of flame tumbled down the hill towards the seething mass of Blighters. Within seconds there were cries of concern and surprise.

The Blighters started to move away, but there were huge clumps that had nowhere to go and were pummelled by the rolling flame. The smelled of charred Blighter smelt even worse than Lara had expected.

"You better keep them contained if you want this to work!" she shouted over the carnage.

Alrion nodded and brought up a tall wall of fire from the left, boxing in the Blighters. The ones nearest the wall couldn't stop in time and were caught by the flame. Alrion launched another ball of fire into the air, and had it hover over the middle of the pack.

"You're just showing off now," Lara said. Now the flames were further away, she could stand beside him.

"Not really, I'm just letting loose. It feels good." Alrion concentrated and the ball of fire split into many smaller parts, showering fire over the Blighters. "That should be enough to scatter them," he said.

The Blighters were running in all directions, the scene was total chaos. But there was a change, and they began to reform.

"There's something organising them. Leaders?" Lara said.

"There must be. I'll have to take them out," Alrion said.

Lara could see the determination on his face. She had to dissuade him from taking this too far. "You know I would like nothing more, but is it really worth it? It's one thing raining fire on them from here, but that's a huge pack. You would have to go amongst them to identify and eliminate their leaders. It's too risky," she said.

"Don't be so shy, we'll be fine." Alrion's face lit up with what Lara could only define as intense hatred. It seemed at odds with his light banter.

"If you insist," Lara said. There would be no way to turn him away now. The two of them descended the hill and Alrion raised another wall of fire.

"Is there any limit to how much of that you can do?" she said. It did seem like a ridiculous amount of magic.

"Yes, but I haven't found it yet. Don't worry there's a fair bit left in reserve."

"In that case, you better box them in on three sides. We can funnel them into a smaller space to make it easier."

"Done," Alrion said with a smile, raising the third wall of fire. Lara watched him work, and noticed a steady stream of sweat beading around his hairline. The fire was too far away, was the sweat from something else?

She watched the Blighters react, and the more they were confined and the fewer the number, the more controlled they appeared to be. Many streamed forward away from the fire, but most stayed within the walls of fire, just far enough away to be safe.

"I don't like this. It's as if they're inviting you in," Lara said.

"I wouldn't want to keep them waiting." Alrion threw out a wave of fire to burn those that had advanced.

Lara dashed ahead and dealt killing blows to those still standing.

They waited for a moment, to see what was next.

"No more are coming over. We can still walk away," Lara said.

"This is interesting, I haven't seen this level of control yet."

"Let's save that for the post-battle discussion. Keep your wits about you. This could be a trap." Lara knew to trust her instincts, and something within that swirling dust bowl was making her unusually uncomfortable.

"If it's a trap I will destroy it." Alrion clenched his fist as if to demonstrate.

"Less talking, more doing." Lara didn't want this to drag on too long. Alrion already looked weakened, despite his previous comments. The wizard nodded and started walking towards the smaller, but still significant mass of Blighters.

"Call out any you think are leaders. Better yet, take them out," he said.

"I'll do what I can," Lara said, scanning them. She had a few potential targets picked out, but wanted to watch their behaviour first. To give themselves an opening Alrion sent out a force wave that knocked over the first few rows of Blighters. He followed it with streams of fire that dispersed those standing behind.

"There." Lara pointed at a heavyset man with dark features surrounded by Blighters. Alrion sent a spear of fire over. A Blighter tried to block it, but it pierced through and burned its target.

"Nice one," Lara said. There was a chance that this would work. Provided that Alrion kept his head and stuck to the plan. The Blighters rearranged themselves, and all those Lara considered to be leaders moved further back, surrounding themselves with Blighters.

"They're on to our plan and have protected themselves. At least we can confirm who the leaders are," she said.

"Then let's finish this quickly. Follow closely behind me." Alrion ran forward, throwing out waves of force to clear the path in front of him.

Lara kept pace, throwing daggers at key targets as they went. The leaders amongst the Blighters appeared alarmed, as they had nowhere to escape to. Then, they all closed their eyes and looked downward. Alrion continued forward, but Lara felt that something was off and she slowed down. Looking around she could see the Blighters rearranging again. They were making space. "They're up to something. I don't like this. Pull back," she said.

"It won't matter soon enough." Alrion paused briefly to concentrate and created a ring of fire above the leaders.

"They're going to surround us. Be quick before it's too late!" Lara shouted.

"This is over," Alrion said. The ring of fire descended swiftly, capturing all the leaders. Then the ring slowly constricted, pushing the trapped leaders into the middle and catching them in the fire.

"All done," Alrion said. "Now they're broken."

"I'm not so sure about that." Lara could see that the Blighters weren't fleeing. They cried out in anguish and lost control. She didn't hesitate. She threw daggers and followed up to cut down those that had managed to get closer. Alrion just stood and stared.

"Snap out of it!" Lara shouted.

Alrion blasted two back. They knocked over the Blighters behind them and he ignited the whole group at once.

"I'll make a path out." Alrion threw out a wave of fire that swept along the ground in continuous motion. "This way!" he shouted over the roar and followed his wave of flame.

Lara cut down a Blighter and turned to run alongside. They trailed behind the wave of fire, pushing aside any Blighters that managed to come close. The fire died out and they continued running, leaving chaos and confusion in their wake.

Lara took the lead and headed for a neighbouring hill, hoping to drop down the other side and out of sight. Alrion was looking back, trying to gauge if they were being followed.

"Eyes in front!" Lara shouted. There was a group of five Blighters blocking their path. Alrion turned quickly and threw out another ball of fire. But it was weak and slow, only catching one of them. He stopped in his tracks, surprised.

Lara bounded ahead, aiming straight for the leader. The Blighters swarmed to attack her at once. She grabbed one and bounced off its shoulder, flipping over the Blighter and into a tight roll on the ground. She rose and dispatched the leader from behind. The Blighters had ignored her however, and were now after Alrion. His hand was covered in flame, and he used it to attack one and push it into the rest. While they were off balance, Lara swooped in and put them all down with accurate strikes from her twin daggers.

Alrion took a few steps away from the fight, and staggered. He dropped to his knees and took in some deep breaths.

"We barely made it. And you look half-dead. More than you bargained for huh?" Lara could feel the dryness in her throat and her limbs crying out. She could only imagine what Alrion was feeling.

"You could say that. I've never pushed that hard." Alrion was bent over, drawing shallow breaths.

"Was it worth it?"

"We're still alive, and well, they're defeated and broken," Alrion said, looking over at the survivors. They had finally broken rank and were fleeing in groups of ones and twos.

"True, we got the result. Bit too close for my liking. And not worth it."

"Would any fight in the open be to your liking?"

"Probably not, you know I prefer to operate in the shadows. But a little planning to stack the odds in our favour never hurts. You should remember that."

"The odds are already stacked in our favour, but I'll consider your idea of planning," Alrion said, throwing her a smile. Despite her reservations, she couldn't help but get caught up in his smile. But she had to make sure he understood the seriousness of what had just happened.

"Is that the first time you have run out of power?"

"Yes."

"Something to keep in mind. Especially if we keep getting into these kinds of situations."

"Yeah, I know, I'm on it." Alrion put his hand on her shoulder. She wasn't sure if that was supposed to be reassuring, but it was.

"Good, let's leave this mess behind us." She waited for him to take his hand back then stretched.

"You have to admit you were impressed though," Alrion said, giving Lara a cheeky grin.

"Yes, I was impressed. But no more ridiculous stunts. I'd rather we didn't die."

"I'll try," Alrion said and started to walk away. Lara jogged after him and they cut downhill and across the plain they were on to get back to the main road. Alrion started to see buildings rising in the distance.

"Is that it?"

"Yes, that's Brangtur." Just the sight of it, brought back the strong scents of sweat, steel and hides for her.

"Have you been here before?"

"Not for a long time. But I'm sure it is the same. Did your father say where to meet him?"

"No, but he's a blacksmith. It should be easy," Alrion said.

Lara laughed and smacked Alrion on the back.

"What's so funny?" he said.

"This is the city of blacksmiths. It will be like finding a needle in a haystack."

"We'll figure something out," Alrion said.

She could see the embarrassment on his face and decided not to take the joke too far. After a few moments, she changed the topic.

"I have another question. You know how you showed me that notebook a few weeks ago?" Lara said.

"The one with the strange message in it?"

"Yes, that one. Now that you've had a chance to think about it, do you have an idea of who left that message? It has to be a wizard, right?"

"It has to be, I can't think of another way. Nobody else has had proper access to it. And I even tried writing in it. I couldn't leave a reply message."

"So, who do you think it is?"

"I have a theory, but it's a bit crazy."

"Let me hear it. Can't be crazier than what we just did." Lara wanted him to open up a bit, to see if this had anything to do with his reckless behaviour.

"What if my mentor Falric survived? Maybe he's trying to contact me from afar. He knows about the notebook, he saw it before."

"That does sound possible, since he's a wizard, knows about it and wants to help you. But aren't you sure he died?" Lara could see a possible connection to Alrion's new attitude. He was still obsessed about Falric's death. And by his own admission he had been unable to do anything. Was he trying to overcompensate?

"I was sure, but who knows. He was a master of magic. Anyway, like I said it was a crazy theory. It seems better than the alternative."

The alternative that he actually died and you need to deal with that, she thought.

"Which is?" Lara said.

"That some wizard I have never met is following my progress. That just creeps me out," Alrion said.

Lara didn't reply, looking out into the distance. That did seem like the scarier alternative. "Take a look now," she said.

They could see the city better now, giant stone walls topped with immense bronze domes. The walls seemed to be decorated with intricate metalwork with huge metal doors hanging off the main gate.

"Wow," Alrion said, taking it all in.

"I forgot how big it all is. Makes sense for a city of blacksmiths no?"

"Definitely. Although I'm surprised the whole walls aren't made of metal." Alrion had a thoughtful look on his face.

"Good point, we'll have to find out why. Maybe they ran out?" Lara said.

Alrion laughed. "I could imagine my father designing such a city. Although I doubt he would have gone for the entirely metal design. He always harps on about harmony between different materials."

"He's been to Brangtur before, right?"

"I'm sure of it. He's such a passionate blacksmith that this seems like the perfect place for him. Why did he ever leave?"

"You'll have to ask him," Lara said. But she knew that finding a blacksmith in Brangtur would be difficult. For now, there was no need to burden Alrion with those details. She looked over at him and saw the bravado of the fight wearing off. It was being replaced by the look of a boy eager to see his father.

"What is it?" Alrion said, turning back to her.

He must have noticed her staring. "Oh nothing, just taking in the scenery. Let's get a move on," Lara said, picking up the pace.

BRANGTUR

The giant gates towered over them as they walked into the city. Streams of people were travelling in both directions. Alrion could smell the smoke and steel being worked. It was strange, smelling it outside of the workshop.

"It feels like a blacksmith workshop, and we are outdoors," he said.

"Not surprised that you get that impression. There's a lot of workshops here. They can make some seriously massive things."

"Do you know where the main workshops are?"

"I think they are this way. I'm sure you can follow the sounds and smells though," Lara said.

"You're probably right," Alrion said. They continued along the dusty path and turned right down a major road.

"The people seem busy, but happy," Alrion said as he took in the surroundings.

"I agree. I guess it's a safe and prosperous city," Lara said.

"Prosperous? What have you stolen from here?" Alrion was instantly suspicious.

"A good thief never tells. Besides, I don't steal from everywhere," Lara said, giving him an innocent smile.

"I'm not convinced. It's alright, you don't have to spill all your secrets just yet," Alrion said.

Lara was right about the sound of the metalworking though. He could hear the hammering getting louder as they progressed.

The houses were all simply made, in the same style as the city gates. Basic stone shapes, with ornamental metal trimmings. Alrion spotted the odd shop on the way, selling a variety of tools and household items.

"No weapons," he said with a surprised look. It seemed to him like an oversight in a city of blacksmiths.

"Weapons are a smaller market here. Tightly controlled."

"Makes sense, there are so many blacksmiths you could turn over a vast number," Alrion said.

Lara could see him thinking through the problem. He was more like his father than he would admit. "Yes, but I don't think that's all there is to it. I get the sense that they prefer not to make them."

"My father definitely prefers not to. He doesn't want to be known as making tools of war, or being responsible for that. He has always been happy making simple things to help people in their day to day. I didn't think others shared that view." Alrion paused and took a closer look at their surroundings. "I think we've started to stumble across the workshops. Keep an eye out for my father. You remember what he looks like right?"

"Of course. I don't forget a face," Lara said. They slowed their pace, and scanned the faces of the working blacksmiths. They were all shapes and sizes, but the common features being the sweating brows and the arms the width of tree trunks.

"No sign yet," Alrion said.

"I think we are running out of workshops," Lara said, pointing ahead. There was another gate coming up. The doors were open, but there was a sign above the top. It was a sword and shield embossed into metal.

"Looks like the weapons section. Let's take a look," Alrion said.

Lara nodded and followed closely. Stepping through the gate felt like a totally different place. There were still workshops, but there was an air of seriousness and reservation. The blacksmiths Alrion could see had an extra determination and responsibility about them.

"Who are they?" Alrion said, pointing to a stranger. He was a tall man in a red coat wandering through the area.

"No idea, but he looks like an inspector to me," Lara said.

"You're probably right," Alrion said.

"Alrion!" Vincent shouted. He put down his hammer and rushed over, grabbing Alrion in his arms. "You made it. I was so worried."

"Yeah we did. Glad I found you here," Alrion said, relieved and happy to see his father again. He even forgot Lara was there and felt safe and at home once again. Then he noticed her watching them and stiffened up. Vincent released his son and stepped back.

"Where's Falric? And who is this lovely young woman?" he said.

"This is Lara, she's helping out. It's a long story." Alrion choked on his words and stared at the floor.

"Nice to meet you Lara. And Falric?"

"He...is gone. Killed by the enemy wizard that was chasing us," Alrion said in almost a whisper. It was so hard to say the words out loud again. The sense of loss came back completely.

"No... I can't believe it. Let's walk somewhere private so you can fill me in." Vincent guided them in silence down a side street and they emerged in a tiny park. Just a small patch of grass, a single leafy tree, and a large wooden bench seat. "Let's sit here. Please tell everything," Vincent said.

Alrion took a deep breath and launched into a long discussion of everything that had happened since they parted. Vincent did not interrupt once, he just sat quietly and absorbed the information. "So that brings us here," Alrion said, gesturing at his surroundings.

"The enemy wizard was Branthor, and he may still be alive?" Vincent said.

"Yes, we don't know for sure. And there's one other thing. It's about Falric," Alrion said, reaching for his bag. He pulled out the magic notebook.

"Look at this," Alrion said.

Vincent reached out and opened the book. He read the note.

"Who wrote that?" he asked.

"I don't know. It must be a wizard, I couldn't find any other way of writing in it. But the only wizard that it could be is Falric. Nobody else other than Branthor knows about my quest, or about this notebook. Maybe wizards are tougher than we thought?" Alrion was holding on to the hope. He desperately wanted his father to buy into the theory.

"Possibly. Losing Falric is unbelievable, and a huge loss. It's worth considering that he might be out there somewhere. Let's put that aside for a moment. Against all odds, you reached the Pool of Knowledge and you found me. What's next?"

"I'm not sure. The knowledge from the Pool comes in drips here and there, in dreams or integrated into my day to day activities. I can't draw on it like a reference book. But I did have a dream, and my grandfather was in it."

"Really?" Vincent sat up straight and his eyes lit up.

"Yes. I don't think it was a message or anything like that. But I think it was a way of showing me what I needed to do next."

"What was it?"

"I was shown a room, which was guarded by four strangely dressed bald men. They had flowing robes and a special sigil on their clothing."

"Sounds like monks, the way you described them. There are a few different orders of monks throughout the world, we would need to locate the exact ones." Vincent started pacing.

"That's a start. I am sure if I saw the sigil again I would recognise it."

"I will ask around, maybe someone here knows something about them. But before that, I have something to show you," Vincent said and took off. Alrion and Lara jumped up to follow closely behind.

Vincent didn't say anything, he just moved with passion and speed. Alrion struggled to keep up.

What is my father up to? he thought.

"Your father is so energised by something. This is exciting," Lara said.

"He's a blacksmith, it can't be that exciting," Alrion said.

Lara laughed. As they rounded the corner they saw Vincent enter a workshop.

"See. Just blacksmith stuff," Alrion said.

"Just get in there and we will find out," Lara said. The two of them entered the workshop and were assaulted with an array of smells, tinged with the smell of sweat.

"I don't know how you can work in here." Lara was covering her nose and looking around.

"I try not to. There he is," Alrion said, pointing to the far corner. Vincent was standing next to a forge and had something on the anvil. As Alrion walked through the workshop he saw a variety of weapons being forged.

"Look at this!" Vincent said as they approached.

Alrion looked down and saw a blade sitting on the anvil. It required a bit more working to be complete, but it was stunning. The metal had a soft white glow to it, and the surface was perfect. "This looks pretty amazing. I thought you didn't make weapons?"

"It has been a while, but the guys here have been helping me. But that's not the best bit, touch the blade. It's not hot right now," Vincent said. Alrion reached out and dragged his fingers across the metal.

"What is that? It feels like it is vibrating," Alrion said.

"Runesteel. It can cut through anything, and never dulls. I thought the art of making it was long lost, but it seems not. Pretty amazing, isn't it?"

"Don't you need magic to make this?"

"Yes, but you don't need the wizard to make it on the spot. If you had some previously enhanced metal lying around then it wouldn't be so hard, would it?" Vincent said. He was grinning from ear to ear.

"What's this for?" Lara said, speaking up for the first time.

"Did Alrion tell you about how we had a nasty encounter with a Shade?" Vincent said.

"In passing," Lara said.

"Well, it was a rather inconvenient place to encounter one, on the deck of a ship. And as you may be aware, even though we had a wizard with us, Shades are highly magic resistant. It kept me up at night, knowing that potentially the Shade was still out there somewhere."

"This will help?"

"Yes. Their skins are incredibly hard to pierce, but magically enhanced weapons do work. All we had last time was a dagger, and I'm not confident that we finished the job. But with this, and its twin, I think we will be better equipped." Vincent made a thrusting motion with the blade.

"Twin?" Alrion said.

"I'm making two. One for you, and one for me. You need to learn how to defend yourself without magic." Vincent put the blade back down.

"Maybe you can make me one of these? A bit smaller though, I prefer a dagger," Lara said, illustrating the preferred length with her hands.

"I hadn't expected to, but since you're with us you need to be able to defend yourself. It may take a while. I'll have to finish the others first, and source some more Runesteel. But leave it with me."

"Great, I think that would be incredibly handy." Lara reached out and felt the blade herself.

"It will be. So Alrion, what do you think?"

"It looks impressive, I just hope I can learn to use it effectively. I thought you hated making weapons?" he said. Vincent looked away for a moment before answering.

"In principle, yes I do. But there are times when it is necessary. I am happy to do so when I know that what I create will stay in good hands and be of use to my family. I still wouldn't make weapons for anyone I didn't trust."

"You trust me already?" Lara said, a teasing tone to her voice.

"If Alrion trusts you, then I trust you. Until you give me a reason not to." Vincent gave Lara a questioning look, but she held his gaze.

"Is the metal heavier or lighter than usual?" Alrion said, changing the topic.

"The Runesteel? It's lighter, one of the many benefits. Feel for yourself." Alrion picked up the blade and felt it. It was much lighter than he was used to working with. He handed it to Lara and she pretended to struggle with the weight, dropping to her knees. Vincent laughed and she handed it back.

Alrion tried not to laugh, but he did show a grin. "Alright you sold me. When will it be ready?" he said.

"A day or two perhaps, but we will see how I go. I'm not in a rush right now, and you don't seem to have a destination just yet."

"That's true, we need to find out where the monks are from." Alrion had no idea where to even start with that.

"I'm sure a few days to rest before heading out again will be of help. In fact, why don't I shout you both to a meal and free drinks to welcome you to Brangtur?"

"What's the catch? We never went out at home, and you always cautioned me on drinking anything remotely alcoholic," Alrion said.

"No catch, let's just have a moment to relax. We're reunited again. And we need to honour our fallen friend."

"That's true. I haven't done enough." Alrion looked away, as if trying to locate the humble grave he had constructed for Falric.

"We've all been through a lot, and I fear this is only the beginning. Let's take a moment," Vincent said.

"Don't look a gift horse in the mouth Alrion," Lara said.

"Alright you convinced me. Let's go," Alrion said.

"Right behind you. Lara, would you mind staying back a second so I can ask you something?" Vincent said.

"Sure. Meet you out front," Lara shouted to Alrion.

Vincent watched Alrion leave then stepped closer to Lara.

"I appreciate the help you have given my son. However, I need to understand how you so quickly got caught up in this."

"I noticed the three of you back at Carford, and I knew there was something unusual going on. So, I lifted a ring from Alrion, and noticed that it was magical. I tracked you all since then, curious about what you were up to. Every adventure you had further confirmed to me that you were doing something monumental!"

"You followed us the entire way?" Vincent said. He couldn't disguise the surprise in his voice.

"Of course, it was easy. All I had to was keep hidden, you burnt a huge trail across the country."

"We did encounter a few situations."

"Exactly, so I kept track of you."

"What changed? What made you a helper instead of a watcher?" Vincent regarded her closely, interested in her answer.

"I noticed that Alrion was in trouble. So, I offered to help," Lara said. Vincent walked closer, until he was inches away from Lara's face.

"I know that you are caught up in this, and you want to keep going. And I don't need to know all your reasons. But I do know that you didn't just decide to help out. What happened?" Vincent said, in a low and steady voice that didn't accept excuses. She appeared shaken by the change in his tone and approach.

Hopefully with a direct approach I can surprise her into telling me the truth, Vincent thought.

"He doesn't know. This mysterious wizard found me. He had tracked me using the ring that I stole from Alrion. He forced me to give it back, and to keep following."

"Who was it?"

"I don't know, he somehow hidden his face so that it is always in the shadows."

"How did he force you to help Alrion?"

"He had a way of getting into my mind. He didn't force me, but it was like he knew what to say. I can't explain it," Lara said. Vincent could see the truth on her face, her confusion and worry. She wasn't faking it.

"I see. Alrion knows nothing of this?"

"No."

"That's fine, better that way. I believe your story, but this other wizard concerns me. It is troubling that the wizard only appeared around the time of Falric's death."

"I couldn't say if it was before or after his death. I only met up with Alrion afterward."

"Hey, you two, come see this," Alrion shouted.

"Keep this from Alrion, let's go." Vincent directed Lara to leave and followed her out. Alrion was standing just outside the door. Once he saw them he pointed to a man across the street. He was sitting on a bench reading a book.

"Who is that?" Lara said.

"I have no idea, but can you see that strange scarf he has wrapped around himself?"

"That's a monk's scarf," Vincent said.

"And from here it looks exactly like what the monks wore in my dream," Alrion said.

"He doesn't look like a monk to me, but let's go see what he has to say for himself," Lara said. Before Alrion or Vincent could reply she started walking off.

3

___

TRACKING THE SCARF

Lara stopped right in front of the man, looking him over without pretending to hide what she was doing. The man didn't react, his head focused on his book.

"Excuse me," Lara said. He didn't immediately react, but after a moment placed a small ribbon in the book and closed it. He looked up at her.

"Yes, can I help you?" he said. A puzzled look crossed his face when Vincent and Alrion also joined Lara.

"My name is Lara. And you are?"

"Brett," the man said. He looked them all over, a confused expression on his face.

"That scarf is quite impressive. Where did you get it?" Lara said.

"Oh this? It's nice, isn't it? Unfortunately, it is not for sale."

"That's fine, I just would love to know where you got it?" Lara said in her sweetest voice. Alrion had to stifle a laugh and she quickly jerked her head around to silence him with a blistering look.

"I'm afraid you really can't get one, so I don't see how that would help."

"Please, humour me. I absolutely must know." Lara thought back to all the women she knew who were fashion obsessed, and tried to channel that.

"Very well, if it means you will leave me to my book?" Brett said, his increasing annoyance clear in his voice.

"Of course."

"Last night I was enjoying a quiet drink in my favoured inn. It's called The Amber Anvil. I was just about to leave for the night, when a strange man burst in. He was clad in what looked like rags, his hair was strangely cut, and he had a wild look about him. But he had on this amazing scarf which had somehow survived whatever he had been through."

"So, a strange man came in wearing it. How did you get it?" Lara said. Alrion and Vincent stayed quiet, eager to hear what Brett had to say.

"Other than acknowledging his strange manner and dress, I returned to my book and my drink. A few minutes later I could smell something strange. I turned to notice that the man was hovering behind me. When I questioned him about what he wanted, he didn't say anything. He just stared at my drink."

"That is very odd." Lara said.

"It is indeed. He finally spoke, and said that he was in dire need of a drink, and asked if I could buy him a bottle to tide him over. I of course declined, which made him quite act quite erratic. I suspected that he was already drunk, and was perhaps fearing the prospect of sobering up." Lara was getting impatient with the way this guy was dragging out the story.

"You traded him for the scarf?" Lara said. For a man annoyed about being interrupted, he sure was taking his time with the story. Maybe he was punishing them.

"Please let me finish. At first, he challenged me to a drinking contest, with me supplying the bottle. I politely declined once again. But he was determined. So that's when he offered me the trade."

"You bought him a bottle and he gave you the scarf?"

"Not at first. He seemed quite reluctant to hand it over. But I was adamant that it was the only thing he had of value. He did finally relent, and I think he buried himself in the bottle even faster to forget about what he had lost."

"Great story, thanks for sharing. Where is this inn exactly?" Alrion said.

"It's on the other end of town. In the Vine district." Brett gestured off into the distance.

"Thank you, Brett, I apologise for taking you away from your book," Lara said.

"Well I did find it entertaining to share that particular story. Good luck with your search. I doubt that man has another scarf though."

"Don't you worry, I'll find out where I can get myself one," Lara said, winking at Brett. Brett immediately re-opened his book, and resumed where he was reading. Lara stepped away and Alrion and Vincent followed.

"Do you think that man he described is one of the monks?" Alrion said.

"Definitely. But clearly something has happened, it sounds like he has been through demanding times. You said that the monks in your dream were bald? From the way Brett described his hair it could have regrown in a strange way," Vincent said.

"I agree. If we find this monk we can find out where he is from. This is a huge break," Lara said. Luck was definitely with them. Finding Vincent and now the lead they needed. But things weren't always so smooth in her experience. She was waiting for the catch.

"Good. I needed one of those. Do you know where that inn is?" Alrion said.

"I don't know that one in particular, but all the inns are together. Follow me." Vincent took off with a confident stride through the district, leading them back to the area where they had entered the city.

"Has it changed much? The city?" Alrion asked his father as they walked.

"Not that much, I am a little surprised. The people are changing, and there are newer areas that are more developed. But the core is the same. I think this is what happens when you build things to last."

"I can definitely imagine this place never changing. It feels like it has always been this way." Lara noticed that the pace of the people seemed as slow as she remembered, even though it was now much more crowded. It seemed like the city had its own special pace that everyone could feel and maintain.

"So, are you a bit of a drinker yourself?" Lara said, looking at Vincent.

"In my younger days, perhaps. But not now. I think it's the kind of thing most men grow out of."

"What about him?" Lara said pointing at Alrion.

"I can't say, I haven't seen him in action. But I've heard a few stories," Vincent said, chuckling to himself.

"Honestly, I don't really get into it that much. But I've had a few experiences, like everyone has. What about you?" Alrion said.

"Nope, don't touch the stuff. Hate the taste. I can't understand how you could drink that." Lara shuddered at the memory.

"Neither can we," Vincent said, laughing out loud. Alrion kept looking around as they walked, taking in the changes in scenery.

He really hasn't been anywhere at all, Lara thought, observing him.

They had entered what looked like a market district. There were lots of stalls in the street, as well as a huge variety of shops. As expected the wares were mostly things made by blacksmiths.

"I still don't see any weapons," Alrion said.

"Yes, there are special outlets that deal in weapons. Either that or you commission them directly from the blacksmith," Vincent said.

"The swords that you are making, would they sell for a lot?"

"Priceless."

"You can't say that. Give me a number." Lara knew that when it came to priceless artefacts, there was always a number.

"Let's just say, that people would offer me enough money to buy a house here and never work another day in my life, spending my evenings in the inn and my days doing whatever I pleased," Vincent said.

Lara whistled with admiration. "That's quite a lot. It may not be enough for my tastes though. A start, perhaps," she said.

"Don't get any ideas," Vincent said, looking directly at Lara.

She laughed. "A girl can dream."

"I think we're in the right area now," Alrion said. They had crossed into another district with a wider street and lots of large inns. Each sign was bigger than the last, trying to grab the attention of passers-by. "What was the name again? The Amber Anvil?" he said.

"That's right. Haven't heard of it, but we shouldn't have too much trouble," Vincent said.

They continued at a slow pace examining the signs as they went.

"The Sloshed Shield, The Hammered Hammer. Wow these aren't very imaginative." Lara had never really thought about the names before, but now they really stood out.

"That's a fair call. But they're effective. Blacksmiths are a folk that like things to be straightforward," Vincent said.

"Surely the owners of these places could try a bit harder though?"

"Maybe, but I'm sure it works well," Vincent said. Alrion stopped abruptly.

"Is that it?" Alrion pointed at a smaller building on the corner of a block. It had a vaulted ceiling and a lot more wooden features than the surrounding buildings. It looked a lot more like a traditional inn.

"That's definitely it," Lara said.

"I'll be interested to see this monk," Vincent said.

The three of them headed directly for the inn. Judging from the exterior and the look of Brett, Alrion guessed this place had targeted a higher class of clientele. No wonder the dishevelled monk had seemed so out of place.

Lara's nose wrinkled at the familiar wave of beer smell as she stepped inside. The decor was well-maintained wood, with attractive lamps used to brighten the otherwise poorly lit interior. Since it was daytime the place was relatively empty.

"Let's head straight to the bartender," she said. She took the lead and didn't wait for Alrion and Vincent.

"Excuse me good man, I was hoping you could help me out," Lara said. The portly man with thinning hair looked up at her with a puzzled expression.

"That's not how people usually order a drink. What can I get you?"

"Some information. We are looking for a strange man you had in last night. Odd hairstyle, dressed in rags but had a beautifully crafted scarf with him," Lara said.

"Oh him? He's been around these last few weeks. Does the rounds, going from inn to inn. He bothers the customers, trying to get free drinks. However, he's been getting less and less luck. Last night he had to trade that fancy scarf of his, and you could tell he was upset."

"If he's such a nuisance why tolerate him?" Alrion said.

"Oh, one of my friends tried. He runs The Plastered Plate and wanted to teach the stranger a lesson. Had one of his bouncers try and run the stranger out. But this monk, he knew how to fight. Even while drunk he made short work of the bouncer and didn't even spill his drink."

"Wow, that's not something you see every day," Alrion said.

"Yeah, he's a nuisance but less trouble than he would be if we interfered with him. So, we just try and let him run free. He will probably get bored of this area and move on, so we're just waiting him out." The bartender shrugged and resumed cleaning a glass. Lara's stomach churned when he spat on the glass to shift a particularly stubborn speck.

"Does he come in here at a particular time?" Vincent said.

"Nah, I don't see him every day. He spreads himself evenly over all the inns here. Since he was here last night, I wouldn't expect to see him back right away. If you're looking for him specifically, it won't be hard but you'll need to do the rounds," the barkeeper said.

"Thanks so much for your help, much appreciated," Lara said.

"If you can get him to leave you'll be forever in my debt," the barkeeper said, his frustration quite obvious.

"We'll see what we can do," Lara said with a wink and turned to leave. All three of them left the inn, and reconvened outside.

"Looks like we need to make ourselves acquainted with the local night life," Lara said.

"Not me, I need to get back to the workshop so I can finish off these swords. Let me know how you go," Vincent said.

"If you insist. Have fun," Lara said.

"Where should we meet you?" Alrion said.

"Back at the workshop. I'll work until you come get me, then I'll take you back to where I am staying."

"Alright, we'll see you there."

"Good luck," Vincent said, and waved as he left.

"Now the real fun begins," Lara said.

"I'm not sure I can handle any more drinking related blacksmith puns," Alrion said.

"Nonsense, you'll love it. We just need to forge ahead." Lara saw Alrion's face break out into a smile.

"Fine, I'll give you that. Let's go," he said. The grin was still firmly planted on him.

~

Ten inns later, Alrion eased himself down onto a wooden bench on the street.

"Is there anywhere we haven't tried?" he said, weariness in his voice.

"You just have no staying power. There's probably a few left. But the good news is that none of them have seen him tonight, so we're almost there." Lara knew this monk would be out there, it was just a matter of elimination.

"I sure hope so, they are all beginning to be a blur."

"Just a few more, then we can regroup and figure out what to do next."

"You're right, I just need a minute," Alrion yawned, stretched out on the seat, and relaxed.

"Are you ready yet?" Lara said after exactly one minute.

"Yeah, bring it on," Alrion said. "Let's try this place."

"The Lucky Lance? Maybe it'll be lucky for us too," Lara said.

There was a good chance that this was the place they would find the link to Alrion's dream. The strange, wild, drunken monk.

Lara stepped into an explosion of light and sound. There were musicians playing a loud catchy tune, on a variety of stringed instruments. People were dancing between tables, and there was double the number of lamps as any other place they had visited.

"Quite a spirited place," she said, dodging some slightly drunk dancers.

"Knowing our luck, he will be hidden in the crowd here," Alrion said.

Lara took the lead and slowly navigated through the packed crowds, avoiding wayward dance moves and swaying drunks. "What do you think about him?" she said, pointing to the corner of the room. There was a man sitting by himself, nursing a glass of beer. His hair looked like it had been roughly cut by a child, and his clothes were so worn and dirty that you could no longer tell what the original colour was.

"Has to be him, but we would never have known he was a monk without the connection to the scarf," Alrion said.

"True, it was a lucky break. Maybe our luck will continue, let's see what he has to say for himself."

"I'm all ears," Alrion said. They changed direction, winding their way through the people and tables until they were standing right in front of the monk. It appeared as if he hadn't seen them, but he spoke up before they could address him. "What do you want? Go away," he said.

"My name is Lara and this is Alrion. What's your name?"

"Why should I tell you?"

"We're looking for a monk, and you fit the description."

"I used to be a monk, so you're half right."

"Then we need your help." Lara decided she would appeal to his charitable side first. He was, after all, originally a monk.

"And I need another drink, something better than this swill," the monk said, swirling around the dark liquid in his glass.

"We only have a few questions, maybe we can arrange some sort of trade," Lara said. The monk stopped staring into his glass and looked up.

"A trade? Hmm no, that won't do. A contest. Now's that a better way to do things," he said.

"A contest?" Alrion said.

"Yes, bring back a bottle of their best stuff. If you can best me in a drinking contest then I'll spill my life story."

"I don't..." Alrion said, but Lara put a hand on his arm.

"You're on," Lara said and immediately walked over towards the bar.

4

AN UNUSUAL CHALLENGE

Alrion looked uncomfortable. Lara could understand why. Clearly the monk was a seasoned drinker, and would be hard to match, let alone overcome in a drinking contest. She half ran the final stretch back to make sure she missed nothing.

"Are you sure that's necessary. I'm sure there are other ways we can figure this out," Alrion said.

"No, it's all I want right now. You can't convince me any other way," the monk said. He held his glass with both hands, and carefully sipped it, a disgusted look briefly passing over his face.

"One bottle of their finest liquor," Lara said, placing a brown bottle down on the table, with two short glasses. The third glass she kept hidden in her tunic. The monk reached out for the bottle immediately, and Lara quickly withdrew it.

"I just want to test it," the monk said. Lara uncapped the bottle, and waved it near his face so he could get a whiff of its contents.

"Is that acceptable?" she said. Alrion could smell the alcohol quite well from where he was standing.

"Yes, that is acceptable. You, are my opponent," the monk said, pointing at Alrion.

"I'll go for it, but he might win you know?" Alrion whispered to Lara.

"Don't worry, I'll cheat," Lara whispered back. Alrion nodded slowly.

"What are the rules then?" Alrion said.

"Very simple. I pour both glasses, we drink at the same time. If I am unable to pour the next round, you win. If you are unable to drink the next round, I win."

"Is this bottle even enough for you to lose?" Alrion said.

"Yes, it's strong enough. And we won't waste time. A quick game is a good game." The monk rearranged himself on the seat, and looked like he was ready.

"You're going to have to do the first few on your own," Lara whispered to Alrion as the monk poured the first round of drinks.

"I suppose since we are drinking together I should share my name. I'm Certan, nice to meet you both." He did a mini bow then picked up one of the glasses. "Cheers," Certan said, and held out his glass. Alrion raised his, and they clinked. Before Alrion could react Certan had thrown down his drink and placed the empty glass back down on the table. "Quickly lad, we don't have all day," Certan said.

Alrion raised the glass to his lips and drank it swiftly. Lara watched him choke it down, and struggle to prevent it coming up again. He used his palm to hit his chest a few times. "That's strong stuff," Alrion said, his voice hoarse and croaky.

"Only the best. That'll put some extra hair on your chest," Certan said.

"Really? That's horrible."

"I never really thought about it that way. Good thing it doesn't then eh?" Certan said, pouring another round. "Ready?"

Alrion looked apprehensive, but he reached for the glass.

"Just hang in there, we can't afford to lose this. I can assist soon," Lara whispered to Alrion. He nodded.

"Bottoms up," Certan shouted as he chugged his drink, almost as fast as the first time. Alrion handled the cup more carefully the second time. The reaction on his face was almost as bad as the first time.

"Trying to minimise the burn? Good idea, but it won't work," Certan said.

He's not going to last long at this rate. I have to intervene.

"Next time, you two should coordinate your drinking. It's fairer," she said.

"I agree. You have to match me," Certan said to Alrion.

"Sure." Alrion didn't look sure at all, but Lara had a plan for that.

Certan raised his glass and Alrion did the same, so they were touching. "Now!" Certan shouted. In unison, they tipped back their glasses.

Before Alrion could drink his, Lara quickly swapped the glass for her spare so that Alrion drank an empty one. He slammed it back down convincingly at the same time as Certan, while Lara tipped the contents of the full glass onto the sawdust covered floor behind her back ready to switch again on the next round.

"Now that's a nice burn," Alrion said.

"That's the spirit." Certan hadn't seemed to notice any foul play.

Lara gave Alrion a reassuring look while Certan was busy refilling the glasses.

"Round four!" he said.

Alrion readied himself, and as before prepared to actually drink. But as before, Lara swiftly swapped the glass out and Alrion continued his pretence. "Ooh I think it's starting to hit me," Alrion said.

"You just don't have my stamina. It takes a lot of training," Certan said, laughing.

"I think I've been training the wrong things then," Alrion said with a chuckle. A few more rounds progressed the same way, each time Certan slowing down just a little bit more.

The swap is getting easier and easier. We can win this.

"I must admit, you are doing better than I expected," Certan said.

"I am a bit younger, I have that advantage," Alrion said.

"He's just playing it down because he doesn't want to admit his history of drinking. Shame on you Alrion. You can never tell, can you?" Lara said to Certan.

"True, the young ones always find their way to the drink. Well nice chat, let's keep going. Round ten!" Certan said.

Alrion and Lara continued their deception.

"How long is this going to take?" Lara wondered.

"Round fourteen!" Certan said, but before he could lift his glass to pour again he slumped over in his seat.

"I think that makes you the winner Alrion," Lara said.

"I think it does. What's my prize?"

"You get to carry this drunk across the entire city," Lara said, pointing at Certan. There was no way he could walk. And the way he was staring into space, it seemed unlikely that he would be able to answer any questions.

"Come with us, we'll take you somewhere more comfortable to talk," Alrion said. Certan nodded his head and waved, but didn't utter anything other than some vague drool ridden nonsense.

"I think that's a yes. Let's go," Lara said. Alrion leaned in and dragged Certan to his feet. Alrion put one arm around him, and made some odd movements with Certan's body jerking around.

"Need a hand there?" Lara said pointing to Certan.

"No, I'm fine. Just fine tuning some magical assistance," Alrion said.

"You may want to make some more adjustments," Lara said, pointing.

The way that Certan was propped up on the other side looked completely unnatural.

"Oh yes, you're right I'll have some unwanted attention soon," Alrion said.

Lara rolled her eyes and came around to the other side to help. She assumed the right position as if she were helping. Alrion seemed to understand her plan, and Lara didn't have to hold any of the monk's weight.

They emerged from the inn into the cool air and Certan cheered.

"At least he's happy," Alrion said.

"You two are good folk," Certan said or at least that was what the slurring noise sounded like.

"Thanks for that. Are you curious where we are headed?" Lara said.

"Nope, doesn't matter as long as it is warm and I'll have something to drink." Certan threw back an imaginary shot.

"It's warm, and you'll have plenty of water," Alrion said.

"You did win, fair and square," Certan said. However, the way he emphasised the words fair and square suggested that he wasn't entirely convinced.

"You made the rules, not us," Lara said.

"Yes, I did. But I didn't say you could break them!"

"Don't be a sore loser," Lara said.

"Ho hum," Certan said, staring off into space. Lara looked up and they were still only halfway through the entertainment district.

"This is going to take a while," she said.

"I hope he actually has some useful information for us to make this whole effort worthwhile," Alrion said.

Lara could see from his face how uncomfortable he was. She almost felt bad for not helping to hold Certan's weight. But Alrion had magic, he could handle it.

They received more strange and judgemental looks in the market district.

"I feel like everyone is watching us, but at the same time isn't looking," Alrion said.

"Yeah, they are noticing us but are too polite to stare. I don't think this is a particularly new sight at all. So, they see us, try not to look then dismiss us."

"If that's the case, we should carry drunk people around more often," Alrion said.

Lara laughed a little. "It's a bit of a drag though," she said and Alrion joined her in laughing. Certan started laughing too, which was infectious.

"Does he even know why we are laughing?" Alrion said.

"I don't think he even cares," Lara said.

They continued this strange routine, with Certan becoming less and less coherent and Alrion looking more and more strained. But they finally made their way through to the working district and the entrance to the workshop where Vincent was toiling away.

"Hello there, I see you have a guest," Vincent said.

"They beat me fair and square," Certan said, piping up out of nowhere. Again, he emphasised the words fair and square.

"Good to see you are so gracious in defeat. Let's get him back to my quarters. I'll take over here," Vincent said, walking over and talking the load off Lara. Alrion shifted his stance and looked relieved.

"This is definitely the monk we need to talk to," Alrion said.

"He's not like any monk I've ever met," Vincent said.

"Most monks would not accompany you in this fashion," Certan said.

"Why is that?" Alrion said.

"They would have dismissed your pathetic attempts at cheating and stormed off. But me, I'm much more generous." Certan gestured with his arms wide, no doubt trying to show the extent of his generosity.

"I think most monks wouldn't engage in drinking contests. Not that I hold that against you," Lara said.

"You got me!" Certan said, mumbling the words. Vincent laughed, shaking his head. They hauled the man the rest of the way in silence.

"This is it," Vincent said.

They were standing in front of a small square building. It was the same style as the rest, rough but well cut stone, with a range of metal adornments on the doors, windows, and trims.

"This is your place?" Lara said.

"It's not mine exactly, but working blacksmiths that are qualified are given quarters to inhabit. These are for our use," Vincent said.

Lara opened the door, and Vincent and Alrion shuffled inside, trying not to knock Certan against any walls or doorways. The interior was sparsely decorated, but there was an old couch in a living room so they carefully set Certan down there.

"I appreciate the assistance," Certan said, in a drunken drawl.

"Let me whip up something to help," Vincent said, disappearing into another room.

"I don't blame you for what you did. Clearly this man here cannot match me in drinking. And I went along with it, because that was some good stuff. Thanks for playing along," Certan said slowly and carefully. Lara was about to reply when he slid to the side and started snoring.

"Well I guess you weren't fast enough with your switching," Alrion said.

"I guess not. But you know, I think the fact that he noticed even after drinking that much means that he's very skilled. Under that strange behaviour and clothing, he's the real deal," Lara said.

"I hope so, I need a good lead. I'd prefer it if my dream had contained some sort of map and directions, but it did not. I've not had any noteworthy dreams since."

"He's asleep already? Let him doze for a while. We can get more out of him when he sobers up," Vincent was holding a glass with a dark liquid in it.

"What's that?" Alrion asked.

"A special concoction to help sober him up and wake him up. But I'll save it for the morning. Let's all get some rest."

"Sounds good to me," Alrion said.

Vincent showed them to the additional areas he had prepared, with a separate mattress to sleep on. Lara watched Alrion fall asleep almost instantly, and she made herself comfortable.

Lara had the strange feeling that she was being watched, and she sat up instantly. It was the break of dawn, with a dim light filtering into the room. She could see a shape sitting in front of her, legs crossed. As her eyes adjusted she could see it was Certan, sipping the drink that Vincent had prepared the night before.

"This is good stuff, I'll have to get the recipe. As for last night, I must applaud your ingenuity and quick reflexes. You would have completely fooled anyone else." Certan held up his glass in a mock toast.

"Thanks for letting me get away with it."

"Are you ready for a story?" Certan said. There was a fire and intensity to his eyes that Lara had not noticed before.

"Glad to finally meet you. I think we're all ready for that story, and it better be a good one."

5

THE FALLEN MONK

Alrion awoke to the sound of voices. He rose quickly and investigated. Lara and Certan were sitting opposite each other.

"I see you are awake and enjoying my father's vile drink. Story time?" he asked.

"Yes," Certan said before taking another sip.

"I'll go get my father," Alrion wandered through the small dwelling into the main bedroom. His father was fast asleep. Alrion shook him gently.

"Yes?" Vincent said, drawing the word out.

"He's awake and sober. I figured you would want to hear what he has to say."

"Of course," Vincent said, scrambling out of bed.

"Plus, you'll be pleased to know that he likes your strange drink."

"He likes it? Everyone hates it. That's half the point of it," Vincent said.

Alrion left his father to wake himself up and returned to Certan. Lara and Certan had rearranged their seating to accommodate more people comfortably. "My father will be here in a moment, but you can begin. So, your name is Certan. What else should we know?"

"Yes, that is my name. As you guessed I was part of a highly secretive and skilled order of monks. They call themselves the Unbroken Wall."

"I've never heard of them," Vincent said as he entered the room. He found a few pillows to sit down on, and made himself comfortable.

"That's the idea. They are based out of a temple hidden in the middle of the desert. Hard to find, and away from any trade routes. You have to know the way there or else you'll die wandering."

"Lucky we have you then," Lara said.

"Do not get ahead of yourself, let me continue. This order of monks is incredibly old, and there are four masters at any one time. The eldest of the masters is hundreds of years old," Certan said.

"How is that possible?" Alrion said.

"By the nature of their study and skill. Their speciality is the study and application of the will. With it, many things can be altered, many so-called rules broken. They are able to push the boundaries of time and space, and the limits of the human body."

"As strange as that sounds, it is starting to make sense to me," Alrion said.

"I've never heard someone respond like that, very interesting." Certan tilted his head slightly and studied Alrion as if he was a puzzle to solve.

"What's an example of what they can do?" Lara said.

"They can break steel or stone with any part of their body. They can avoid attacks that no other can even detect. They can move with speed and strength that is impossible. They can even move things with their mind," Certan said.

"Sign me up," Lara said.

"They do take women, but it requires dedication and years of training. I doubt you have the determination to do it," Certan said.

"I liked him more when he was drunk," Lara said.

"They sound like a formidable force, and well-trained and disciplined. What happened to you?" Vincent said. Certan visibly stiffened, taken aback by the comment.

"I don't mean to offend, I'm sorry," Vincent said quickly.

"No, I am not offended by your question, it is quite valid. I was thinking on my failure, and my situation. I will explain." Certan stood up and paced around the room a little, looking out into the distance. Then he resumed his seated position. "Unlike many of the monks, I was not inducted as a child. I was a teenager, living out on the fringes of the desert. It was a small town, kept alive by the travellers who needed to cross the desert and could afford to pay for our overpriced supplies. We were not greedy, but the number of travellers was so low, we had to extract as much as we could from them to survive."

"You learned to live with very little?" Vincent said.

"Yes, it was a simple life. Looking back, you don't realise how special it is. Happiness without wealth feels hard at the time, but is infinitely easier. There is a lightness to it. As long as you can find a way to keep going, there are no particularly hard burdens. Your life and daily responsibilities consume your mind, keeping you safe."

"Sounds like good preparation for joining an order of monks," Alrion said.

"It was, in a fashion. But as a teenager, I acted as most do. I rebelled against the conditions we lived in. I found some like-minded friends and we started to roam further and further from our home. We found new people to trade with, stumbled across things left by desperate travellers and felt like we had additional freedom and wealth. We shared only amongst ourselves and became wealthy, in comparison to those around us."

"So, what happened?" Lara said.

"We became greedy. We heard that a caravan had lost a wheel and a huge amount of valuables were abandoned in the desert. We were the only ones with the strength, knowledge, and resources to salvage it. Even though it was further than we had ever roamed before, we didn't even think twice. The lure of the prize was too great."

"What was so alluring about it?"

"It would have been enough for us to leave and build a life somewhere else. When you are young, the urge to wander is so strong. You will do anything to follow it. But as you can guess, things did not go so well. We found the caravan. Of course, it was further than we had planned for, and laden with even more goods that we expected. We argued about what to do. One of us wanted to drag it closer, and bring about another group to collect it all. One wanted to try to fix the caravan and ride it home. I wanted us to take a few valuables and go home, just enough to get us on our way."

"Who won?" Vincent said.

"Not me. My friends decided to take our supplies, and set off to find a way to fix the caravan. My theory is that they thought I would wait until they returned and be forced to help them. But I was impatient and took off in another direction, hoping to go home. Unfortunately, it was the wrong direction and I got lost in the middle of the desert. Alone, hungry and parched. I collapsed, and considered myself done for."

"How did you get out of that?" Alrion said, captivated by the story. He needed to hear more.

"One of the monks found me. They took me in, and offered me a chance to join them. I had nothing more to do, my friends had abandoned me and it was a chance to join something incredible. I really enjoyed my time there." Certan's tone of voice changed and he started to look downwards.

"But something happened?" Vincent said.

"Yes, it was one of the final trials. They have a room there, it is called the Room of Desire. And it is filled with all the things that a young man desires, but does not need. Gold, wine, beer, treasures, you name it. As part of the trial they take you in there, and show you that it exists. They make you sample the wine, select a piece of gold and a treasure. Then they lead you out, not locking the door or saying anything else."

"Did you know it was a trial?" Alrion said.

"They didn't explain it as such, but I suspected something was up. However, once that wine passed my lips, I was obsessed. I couldn't stop thinking about it. The thoughts drove me mad. So, one night, I snuck back into the room and helped myself. The flood gates were open, and I didn't care who knew." Certan closed his eyes, a pained look crossing his features. It looked like he was reliving the moment.

"Presumably you were caught?" Lara said.

"Yes, immediately. It's like they knew. They weren't mean about it, they just said that everyone responds differently to the trial, and that I could not stay. I packed my things and left. Luckily, I knew how to navigate the desert by that point, so I could safely rejoin society."

"What did you do?" Alrion said.

"I wandered from here to there. I took odd jobs as a mercenary, labourer, whatever was available. When I wasn't working, I availed myself of local entertainments. Establishments like the one where you found me. It's a strange spiral down that I found myself in. I started to avoid the paying jobs, to deny myself access to the coin that would immediately go back into more drinks. But that just led to other behaviour, like trading away the scarf which was my last tie to the monks."

"Are you happy with your current lifestyle?" Vincent said.

"No, I'm not. But I don't see a way out. I am trapped in a downwards spiral that only ends in one way." Certan didn't shy away from it.

"Help us. This is your chance to turn things around. Please, I need to ask you a very important question," Alrion said.

Certan did not respond. After a long pause, he opened his eyes. "I don't think I have another chance, but I am a man of my word and will help you. What do you need to know?"

"I had a dream, and in it I saw four monks, dressed in garments with the same symbol that was on your scarf. They were sitting outside a doorway, to a pure white room. I need to go there, and undertake whatever trial that is. Does that make any sense?" Alrion said. Certan closed his eyes again. He looked asleep. After a few minutes, he opened his eyes once more and addressed Alrion.

"I know of what you speak. I have meditated to recall as much detail as possible. The room you speak of is called the Vault of Silence. It is the final trial a monk undergoes. Very few make it that far, and very few succeed. Yet we are all told about it, early on in our training. I am not sure why, but that's no matter now. It is all about the mastery of the will. If you can pass that trial, you have achieved the pinnacle of monkhood," Certan said.

"I have to pass that trial. What else can you tell me about it?"

"Unfortunately, I don't know the specific details. I just know that the four elder monks administer the test. It requires you to enter the room. I've only heard of one monk taking the test in all the time I have been there."

"What happened?" Lara said.

"We never saw him again. I guess he failed? I can't say for sure."

"That's reassuring," Alrion said.

"I am just telling you what I know. Without being aware of your background, I think you will find it very challenging. You do not have the proper training to succeed." Certan's face was emotionless.

Alrion could tell the monk was not trying to belittle him. Even still, he couldn't accept that statement. "I have to pass, so I will find a way," Alrion said.

"I can see the fire within your eyes. You have the passion, and the embers of a strong will. Perhaps that will be enough." Certan stood up and paced around the room. "I will draw you a map, so you can find your way through the desert. Then our business is concluded."

"That would be very helpful," Vincent said.

"Why not come with us? You can show us the way yourself, and you can resume your training," Alrion said.

"No, I cannot go back. It's not possible."

"Did they even say that? Or are you just being stubborn and embarrassed?" Alrion said. Certan stopped his pacing. Alrion could see that he was getting through to the monk.

"I am not sure. I will think on it. That is the best answer I can give you right now," he said.

"Thanks," Alrion said. It was a start, he could work on it. After hearing the story, he couldn't imagine undertaking the journey without Certan.

"You know, it'll be fun. We can all go, it will be an adventure," Lara said.

"Not on my watch," a voice said from the doorway. They all turned to look at their visitor. It was a woman dressed in leather travelling clothes, with tall boots and a short jacket thrown over her shoulders.

"Celes?" Vincent said, shock in his voice.

"You thought I would just wait at home after hearing what you were up to? Lucky I did turn up. You look like you are about to let my son run off with this young delinquent and this fallen monk," Celes said. Certan looked away, embarrassment on his face.

"Delinquent? I am no such thing," Lara said. Alrion could see her face flare up in anger.

"Mum, what is going on?" Alrion had never seen this side of her. She was always strong and loving and fair. But here she seemed different. He had never seen her dressed like this before. There was now an edge to her strength, and a confidence in her stance that suggested a whole other part to her story that he never knew about. He didn't know whether to be relieved or scared.

AN UNEXPECTED REUNION

Celes strode around the room, looking them all up and down.

"I see no need to change my initial assessment. Are things so dire?"

"Honey, calm down. There's a lot to discuss," Vincent said.

"You bet there is. You told me you were taking him to study at the Academy. Then I get a letter saying that you're on this huge quest and you'll write again from Brangtur? Not good enough."

"Sorry, we couldn't exactly turn around," Vincent said.

"So, where's that troublemaking wizard anyway? I want to give Falric a piece of my mind. I warned him quite clearly." Celes had a look in her eye that caused even Alrion to shrink back.

"He's no longer with us," Vincent said.

Celes stopped, and her mood changed completely. She stopped pacing around and her expression visibly softened. "I'm sorry, I had no idea. What kind of mess is this?" she said.

"Take a seat, we will talk you through it," Vincent said.

Certan rose and started to leave the room.

"Stay and listen, please. You're a part of this now," Alrion said. Certan hesitated, then returned.

"What I will say, must not leave this room," Vincent started to tell the story, and let Alrion take over in the parts where they were separated.

Celes showed no reaction until the story was finished. "I am sorry for my outburst," she said. Immediately she rose and walked over to Alrion, giving him a huge hug. He returned it, happy to have his mother back. His eyes teared up a bit, and he turned away to hide them. Celes returned to where she was sitting.

"Don't worry about any of that, I am happy to accept the blame. I should have explained more," Vincent said.

"What now?" Alrion said.

"I can't stop what is already in motion. But I can influence what happens next. I'll even support this quest you are on. But before we can leave, you two need to pass a test." Celes pointed at Certan and Lara.

"What kind of test?" Lara said.

"For you, it's simple. You will accompany Alrion and me on a little recovery mission. Vincent knows what it is," Celes said, looking at Vincent and smiling. Vincent laughed after a moment of recognition but didn't say anything. Celes turned to Certan next.

"For you, it's even easier. Go retrieve your scarf and return to us dressed as a person who has pride in his appearance. That will signify to me that are you ready," Celes said.

"I haven't even agreed to go anywhere, why would I undertake your test?" Certan said.

"Because you have nothing to lose, and everything to gain. I only just met you, but I can tell that a life of wandering is not fulfilling. You have made a mistake, now go rectify it," Celes said. Certan looked at her with a strange expression, like he was trying to puzzle out the meaning of her words. He looked away, deep in thought.

"I accept," he said and left the room without looking back.

"Wow, that was quick," Alrion said.

"He would have agreed eventually, I just sped up the process," Celes said.

"That's one problem solved. Maybe you can now explain our part of the test?" Lara said.

"It is better to show you. Let's go." Celes left the room and waited for them at the front door. Alrion gave his father a confused look, but followed along. Lara was quicker to move, and sidled up to Celes. Alrion couldn't make out what they were saying. But it looked like the two women were challenging each other.

"I feel like I don't know who mum is," Alrion said.

"Don't worry, she's the same. It's just a side of her that she hasn't needed for a long time. You'll be fine," Vincent said.

Alrion was not completely satisfied with the answer, but rushed to join Lara and his mother at the front door.

"We are off to the Market District," Celes said, and opened the door. She walked out onto the street with confidence, as if she knew the place well.

"How did you find us?" Lara said.

"Easy. Vincent and I stayed here many years ago, before we had Alrion." For a brief moment Celes let a smile dart across her face. But a serious gaze soon replaced it.

"Oh, that's interesting. You have a history here."

"We do, which will be explained soon," Celes said. A strong silence hung over them as they walked. Alrion looked at his mother with a confused expression. The strong, nurturing figure he had always known didn't quite fit with the person he was observing. There was a piece missing, which was driving him crazy.

I hope this makes sense soon.

He could see Lara trying to puzzle it out as well, with furtive sidelong glances.

The Market District was teeming with people, much more so than the night before. The stalls were packed full of interesting trinkets, and the cries of sellers competing for attention made it quite noisy. There were even food vendors set up, peddling fruit or cooked meat on sticks. They wove their way through the crowd and bustle and headed to a far corner of the district. As they progressed the crowds thinned out, until there were only a few passing people.

"Where are we going?" Alrion said.

"Wilhelm's Fine Wares," Celes said. Sure enough, they stopped in front of a large building that looked like it was a mansion. Anywhere else he would have assumed that a person of immense importance resided there.

"Does someone live here?"

"Yes, the owner lives here and also operates the front as a gallery and showroom." Celes walked up to the burly guard outside the front door and held up her hands. The guard patted her down and ushered her through.

"What's this?" Alrion said.

"Weapon and tool checks," the guard said. His voice was as rough as his face.

"They want to make sure we aren't going to steal anything," Celes said.

"Sure, nothing to hide here." Alrion raised his arms and had the same check done. Lara stepped up next.

The guard checked her the same way, then stopped suddenly. "What's this?" he said.

"Sorry, I forgot about those. I wasn't expecting to come here," Lara said innocently. She retrieved a stack of daggers from the small of her back.

"I'll hold them until you are done shopping," the guard said with a healthy measure of sarcasm.

"Thanks." Lara joined the others inside the building.

Alrion was shocked at the room on display. There were polished marble floors and cabinets full of jewels, treasures, and fine cloths. One table had rings, another amulets and earrings. In the middle of the whole collection was a stone pedestal. On it was a red velvet cushion with a clear dome over it. Inside was most incredible jewel Alrion had ever seen. "What is that?" he whispered to Celes.

"That's the Pure Diamond. It is the biggest diamond in the world, and said to have been created with magic. There's even talk that it glows blue when encountering those tainted with the Blight."

"Wow, that's incredible," Alrion turned to look at Lara to see her reaction. Her eyes were darting around the room, taking it all in.

"A girl after my own heart," Celes said softly. Alrion walked closer to take a closer look. He was immediately stopped by a thin man dressed all in black. Alrion hadn't even seen him.

"Excuse me," Alrion said.

"No closer. You cannot approach the diamond without prior approval," the man said. Alrion examined the man's face. It was hard and emotionless, with piercing blue eyes.

"Sure, I just thought it looked incredible," Alrion said. The man nodded and waved him away. Alrion diverted his attention to inspecting the table of rings. However, he also watched his mother and Lara wander through the room. It looked like they were just browsing, but he sensed a different intent and purpose from them. It was so methodical.

Thick as thieves, Alrion thought. Then he had a sudden epiphany. There was a reason his mother seemed so different and was instantly so critical of Lara. Maybe his mother used to be a thief too. He wanted to blurt it out, then realised that it wasn't wise given their current situation. But the more he thought about it, the more he was convinced.

"I can see that look on your face, save it for later," Celes said to him. Alrion nodded and found some more jewellery to examine. He didn't know much about it, but everything looked expensive and well-made. He could tell the craftsmanship was incredible.

"Thanks for your time," Celes said to nobody in particular and headed for the door. Lara was close behind her, and Alrion rushed to join them. They left the premises, Lara collected her daggers with a smile and a wink and the three of them walked off in silence. After they were almost out of the Market District, Celes led them into a quiet alley and stopped.

"I can tell you have questions," Celes said.

"More like statements. You want us to steal that jewel. And you're also a thief. And maybe you tried to steal it when you were here before," Alrion said quickly.

"That's actually quite correct. When I met your father, I was a thief. This jewel was my target. And we failed to steal it, and had to leave the city."

"We? He was in on it?"

"Of course. Who do you think crafted the keys for me?" Celes said with a sly smile. Alrion couldn't believe it. His father had always been so straight and by the letter of the law.

"Seems like a lot of security," Lara said.

"I didn't notice much. One guard out front and a man inside?" Alrion said.

"There's many more hidden around the place. And magical traps I'm guessing," Celes said.

"So, what's the plan?" Alrion said.

"I'm still working through it. But we will go tonight."

"Sounds good to me. This will be a real thrill. I'm excited," Lara said. Celes gave her a questioning look but didn't say anything.

"I'm going to investigate the area a little more, but we will draw too much attention as a group. You two go back to the house," Celes said.

"Sure, let's go," Alrion said to Lara.

"You don't want any help?" Lara said.

"No, I've got this. I need to see how much things have changed," Celes said.

"Understood, we'll see you later," Lara said. The two of them walked out of the laneway, leaving Celes alone.

"I can't believe it, she's a thief. I never knew," Alrion said once they were a safe distance away.

"I must admit, I had my suspicions when she showed up," Lara said.

"How could you tell?"

"The way she was dressed initially. Normal looking clothing, but it is light, protective, and quiet. She had lots of pockets for stashing tools, and she was very particular about assessing the situation."

"What's so unusual about being careful?"

"It was the type of careful. When you're ... retrieving something, you don't want any surprises. You must be able to predict everything that will happen, and plan ahead. You also have to be very adaptable and change things on the fly as required."

"So how many so-called retrieval jobs have you done?"

"More than I care to remember. But only a few really memorable ones."

"Have you ever been caught?"

"Once or twice when I was starting out. But I didn't know what I was doing, and it was small stakes. That doesn't happen later on. Not if you're careful and learn from your mistakes."

"So, what does happen?"

"You have an escape plan, and you abandon the job. If you get away, you can retry another day. You never stick around, that's suicide."

"I'll remember that," Alrion said.

"Yeah, if things go wrong on the job, you need to cut and run. It's not worth it."

"Got it. Have you had a job like they did with this one? Where you had to abandon?"

"Yes. Just the one."

"What happened?"

"I don't really want to talk about it. Another time." Lara avoided eye contact and started focusing on something in the distance. Alrion took her cue and stopped asking questions.

Once they arrived back at the house, Alrion looked for his father but couldn't find him.

"He'll be working on those swords," Lara said.

"Good point. So how do I prepare for one of these jobs?" Alrion said.

"In a day? No chance you'll be prepared. But I'll teach you one thing.

"What's that?"

"How to walk quietly." Lara walked across the room soundlessly, doing a pirouette at the other end.

"Now you're just showing off," Alrion said, impressed but laughing.

"Why not? Don't worry you'll be dancing along in silence in no time." Lara stepped back to Alrion then started demonstrating her footwork.

"Take a normal step," she said. Alrion did as instructed, his boot making a resounding thud.

"I think you overdid it, but that's fine. Now what you need to do is imagine that you are spreading out your entire weight over the entire surface of your foot. And gently rolling your weight as you step." Lara demonstrated in slow motion.

Alrion tried it, and stepped very quietly. He looked up at her in shock.

"If you go slow enough it's easy. The trick is doing it at pace."

Lara darted into the next room and even though Alrion was watching and listening closely he could barely hear her footsteps.

Shouldn't be too hard.

He started walking softly as Lara had demonstrated, and quickly sped up. For a moment, he was swift and silent, and feeling like a gliding shadow. However, he started to lose his balance and came to a sudden stop with a loud stamping of his feet.

"That's going to get us into trouble. What's the saying? You need learn to walk before you can run?" Lara said. Her eyes sparkled with amusement and she laughed heartily at Alrion.

"Hey, I'm a wizard, I don't have to obey the normal rules," Alrion said, joining her in the laughter.

"Just practice a bit more so we can rely on you tonight," Lara said.

"Of course. I was just thinking though, maybe there's a way I can do it with magic." Alrion ran to get his spell book and look through it.

Lara watched him go and just shook her head gently.

7

A TEST

Certan left the house in a hurry. Partly because he had a purpose, partly because he had to get out of there. His crazy wild ride had crashed and burned in style.

I can't believe what I have gotten myself into, he thought. Less than a day ago, he was living his practically unconscious life of oblivion. He had hit rock bottom, giving away the last precious memento of his time with the monks. The fact that he regarded the monks as another people also saddened him.

"This is your second chance," a voice inside him said. It was right. For some time, he didn't believe that he deserved it. But these people thought so, and they needed his help. So, he had to earn their trust.

Certan started to head to the Entertainment District, but then quickly changed his mind. Even if he could find the man who now had his scarf, he had nothing to bargain with. And he certainly looked like a mess. Certan glanced at a nearby puddle and saw his reflection. He had tried to ignore it, but he forced himself to look properly. He had been living hard, and it had taken its toll.

"Enough is enough," he said. He changed course and headed for the Blacksmith district. With any luck, he could pick up some work as a labourer or assistant. The Blacksmith District was alive with action, the clanging could be easily heard as he approached.

"It's a numbers game," Certan said to himself. As he entered he wandered up to the first workshop.

"We don't have any handouts, move on," a bearded man said as Certan approached.

"I'm just looking for an honest day's work," Certan said.

"Keep looking," the man said and turned his back.

"Thanks," Certan said, not even sarcastically. If he wanted to succeed he needed to return to the self that he was with the monks. In control and humble, throwing his ego to the winds. He continued to the next workshop. This time he at least managed to make eye contact with someone and speak first.

"Hello, I am looking for some work. Do you need a strong pair of hands?" Certan said.

"I'm sorry, we're fine right now. I appreciate the offer though. My brother works in the last workshop. Right before the restricted weapon section, why don't you give him a try?" the blacksmith said.

"I will do, thanks for the tip." Certan bowed and continued walking.

He ignored the rest of the workshops, and continued to the next set of gates. The workshop he was after was quite obvious, it was humongous and was the only one right next to the gates. Before he could approach though, he saw a commotion up ahead.

"Stop! Thief!" a male voiced shouted. Certan could see one of the local guards chasing after a young man. The youth was carrying a bag full of something and brandishing a sword. Without thinking twice, Certan moved into the youth's path to intercept him. The youth swung his sword, hoping to scare Certan away. But Certan didn't flinch, he dodged the attack and grabbed the young man's arm and nimbly threw him to the ground. The young thief was quick, and darted back to his feet, but Certan was standing in front of him.

"Move it or I'll cut you down," the youth said.

"You cannot. Accept that you have been caught," Certan said. The youth lashed out at Certan's legs with the sword. Certan saw the attack just in time to dodge, and kicked the sword so hard it clattered against a nearby building. The guard in pursuit finally caught up to them, panting with the exertion.

"Thanks for your help, citizen. We aren't equipped for foot chases and he had a head start."

"Happy to help out since I was here anyway," Certan said. The guard looked him over, a confused expression on his face.

"Are you some kind of monk? Or just homeless?"

"Probably both are accurate. I have been wandering for a time. I'm looking for some work now though."

"I have something for you. My friend runs security for a place in the Market District. They are always looking for more help, and you're quite capable. Here take this," the guard said, handing Certan a coin.

"I cannot accept this," Certan said.

"Just take it, I get a commission for anyone I send over anyway. Get yourself cleaned up and some better clothes. They will provide you everything else you need. Report to the Wondrous Wall Inn and tell them that Sean sent you for a job," Sean said.

"Thank you for your help, I really appreciate it."

"Don't mention it, you've helped me out and I get paid if they hire you so it's a win for me either way. What's your name by the way?"

"Certan."

"Well Certan, you take care of yourself. See you around."

"Thanks, Sean." Certan bowed and turned back the way he had come.

This is the break I needed. The money I earn from this job can buy back my scarf and I'll be back on the path. The right path, Certan thought. Things had turned the corner.

～

Lara heard a noise and walked over to investigate. She saw Vincent arriving back at the house. He looked exhausted after a long day.

"What's all this?" he said.

"I'm trying to teach Alrion how not to be a lumbering beast," Lara said.

"That may take a while," Vincent said.

"I would agree, but you might be surprised," Alrion seemed to be taking the gentle ribbing in good spirits.

"I must admit, he's at least trying," Lara said.

"Good to hear. Where's your mother?" Vincent said.

"She's doing some investigating," Alrion said.

"Casing the place for guards, traps and entry points more specifically," Lara said.

"She must be pretty serious about this heist. I wonder why, after all this time," Vincent said.

"Is it really true that the two of you tried to steal this jewel back in the day?" Alrion said.

"It's all true. It's the main reason why we left Brangtur. It was only a matter of time before they figured out who it was. We were so close. I didn't realise she was still thinking about it, all these years later. But that's a story for another time," Vincent said.

"How are the swords going?" Alrion said.

"Very well. I should be able to finish them tomorrow, if everything goes to plan. I'm pretty excited. They have surpassed all my expectations."

"And my dagger?" Lara said.

"I think I can get there, but only if I can finish the others first."

"Just don't forget. You know he's going to need someone watching his back," Lara said pointing at Alrion.

"Oh, I know, don't you worry. Let me prepare something to eat, you two keep training." Vincent left them and entered the kitchen. Lara could hear a lot of banging pots and pans around. He eventually emerged with dinner, as promised. It smelled better than it looked.

After they all finished up a simple meal of meat, bread, and potatoes Celes entered the house.

"I've done as much as I can do. We are definitely going in tonight," she said.

"Hungry? We saved you some," Vincent said, pointing to a plate of food.

"Starving. You haven't cooked for me for a while," Celes said with delight.

"Trying to win my way back into the good books," Vincent said, giving her a cheeky grin. Celes gave him a wry smile.

"Keep trying, but good start," she said.

"And we've been busy too. I've taught Alrion how to not barge around like a drunken bull." Lara gave Alrion an approving look and he smiled back.

"Good, that will come in handy. This is going to be a tough one. But we are in luck. They seem to be understaffed. A lot fewer guards than my previous attempt. Maybe there's a lot less interest in the diamond," Celes said.

"So, we can actually pull this off?" Alrion said.

"Of course, one way or another. Where's the monk?" she said looking around.

"Not sure, I haven't seen him today," Alrion said.

"He will return, when he's ready," Vincent said.

"He'd better do it soon. Since we are taking this jewel, we need to be leaving town as soon as possible," Celes said.

"I'm sure he will be here," Alrion said.

"If you say so. Now, everyone make your final preparations. We should leave as soon as possible. It's going to be a long night," Celes said. Alrion adjusted his clothing to have a cloak with a hood covering his face. Lara did the same, but also had to select which tools she would be taking, expertly stashing them away.

"Don't wait up," Celes said to Vincent, giving him a quick kiss.

"You know I will. Take care," he said to all of them. Alrion and Lara said their farewells and followed Celes out into the cold night air.

"Shouldn't we be discussing the plan?" Alrion said.

"No, we are keeping this simple. Do as I say exactly and every-thing will go smoothly," Celes said.

"She's right," Lara said.

"Alright, I can do that." Alrion let Lara and his mother take the lead, and fell in behind them. Celes directed them back to the Market District.

"How do you feel?" Nervous?" Lara said.

"No. Well, maybe a little. But just because I have no experience as a thief. My magic is a little..."

"Over the top?"

"That's fair. Which will be quite helpful if we get caught."

"Which we won't. Right Celes?"

"Right. Just so long as you follow my instructions." Celes didn't bother turning to face them, her eyes were locked into gazing into the distance.

Lara was excited. She hadn't been on a heist for a long time, especially one with another thief. It had been a long string of solo efforts. She realised how much she had missed it. The joint excitement of sharing the risk and reward with others.

I'll have to convince Alrion to do more of these, she thought. That would be fun.

"Keep up," Celes said, increasing her speed. Lara understood the approach. It would take them a long time to enter the building quietly and unseen, so the sooner they reached their destination the better.

She spent some time studying Celes as they went. There was an ease to the way she moved, which obviously came from a lot of experience. But Lara sensed something else. A nervous energy too.

This has to be huge for her. She's going back for this diamond, so many years later. And with her son in tow too. I better do well in this trial.

"We're here," Celes said and stopped. They were in a dark alley in the middle of the Market District. Alrion and Lara paused and looked around.

"There," Celes said pointing to a grate for drainage. Alrion knelt down and lifted it, carefully dragged it away.

"I hate this part of stealing stuff," Lara said as she peered into the hole.

"It's the best way in, and nobody wants to guard it," Celes said.

"Is this ladies first?" Alrion said.

"No, this is the exception," Celes said and Alrion prepared to climb down. Lara went next. They were in a completely dark tunnel.

"Seems deserted. Is it safe to light our path?" Alrion said.

"Yes," Celes said. Alrion lit the way with a small flame dancing above his palm. As the flickering light bounced around the tunnel they could see what it really was.

"This doesn't look like any ordinary tunnel." Lara subconsciously checked her tools.

"No, this is actually a secret exit. It's the escape tunnel for the mansion we are entering."

"Won't they be expecting that?" Alrion said.

"No, there's only one key. Or so Wilhelm thinks." Celes pulled a tiny intricate key from her pocket.

"How did you get that?" Lara said.

"Vincent made it for me many years ago. But I never used it."

"And you kept it all this time?" Alrion said.

"It was a keepsake from the old days. But now, it's an opportunity. Let's keep moving," Celes said. Alrion walked ahead, lighting the way. The tunnel was old, and grimy. As they walked it became less damp and smelled different. The pungent odour was replaced by something different. Alrion moved his hand slightly as they walked, to better illuminate the area. Lara used that opportunity to study the walls, but didn't see anything of note. The tunnel just kept going and going. Finally, she saw something different in the distance.

"I think we're coming up to something," Lara said. As they approached she could see it more clearly. A massive iron door. Incredibly thick with lots of reinforcement. The lock was a large square protrusion with a tiny keyhole.

"Just as I would expect," Celes said.

"There's no breaking through that. Lucky there's a keyhole on the outside," Lara said.

"Turns out that while Wilhelm's definitely paranoid, he's not an idiot. Here goes," Celes said, walking forward and inserting the key into the lock. She turned the key slowly, a bead of sweat appearing on her brow.

It seems to be moving, Lara thought, observing Celes. Then she heard a loud click.

8

DIAMONDS ARE FOREVER

Celes stepped back and pushed the door hard. At first it didn't give, but then began to give way. It creaked like it had never been opened, and revealed a store room of sorts.

"It looks like we are in. Extinguish the light please," Celes said. Alrion let the flame disappear and waited for additional instructions.

"Where to?" Lara said.

"Alrion, stay in this room and guard our exit. Lara and I will retrieve the diamond and meet you back here," Celes said.

"Sure, take care," Alrion said. Celes went ahead, noting the state of the room as they passed through. Just crates and other storage, and it didn't look used recently.

"We won't keep you waiting too long," Lara said and she followed Celes through the room.

Celes kept up a quick pace, but maintained her stealthy movement. She had never been in this part of the mansion, so she was using her intuition to guide her. Once they left the storeroom she paused and felt for the direction of the wind. There was a slight draft coming from the right, so she decided to start there. Lara stayed close behind and didn't say anything.

What a relief she's a professional. This will make things simpler, Celes thought. At the end of the corridor they came to a stone staircase.

"Half a flight of stairs at a time, wait for my signal before following," Celes whispered. Lara nodded, her eyes clear and focused. Celes lightly dashed up the stairs, pausing at the turn and scanning ahead. When it was clear she signalled Lara, and continued. They continued this ritual a few times until Celes noticed that they were emerging into a habited area.

Kitchen. Another area she wasn't particularly familiar with, but she knew it was located near the rear of the mansion. She crept carefully to the nearest corridor and peered through. Again, she had the choice of left or right.

"Left," she whispered to Lara. It was a pure gut decision, but she didn't have time for any other. The corridor was well-lit, so Celes moved with caution. She expected quite a few guards but wasn't sure where they would be posted. It seemed unlikely to have them congregated around the kitchen, but she wouldn't put it past Wilhelm. He was incredibly protective and could easily have randomly reallocated patrols.

Celes passed a doorway and stopped. She stepped back and looked again. She recognised it.

"This way," she said to Lara. The two of them entered the room. It was a connecting room, filled with coats and boots.

"Utility room for the guards. We're going to come across some soon," Celes whispered.

"I'm ready," Lara said.

"No kills."

"Of course."

"Good, now keep close." Celes crept through the room, noting the changes that had happened. But the ugly painting of Wilhelm's father preparing for a hunt was still there. She would never forget it.

Celes finally spotted a guard. He was tall and thin, lounging against the wall. She almost didn't spot him, his dark black clothing blending into the shadows. Celes tapped Lara and pointed at the guard then at a doorway behind him. Lara understood and stood at the ready. Celes crept into the hallway and dashed past where the guard was posted. If her memory was right, she would be able to weave through another room and take him by surprise.

The first room had an open door, so she snuck in. It was a dining room.

Was this here before? It had been a long time, but she didn't recognise it. But she pressed on anyway. She stepped around chairs left out, and cursed at one that she almost tripped over. But she kept her composure and could see the silhouette of the guard from the light of a faraway torch. She retrieved a dagger from her belt, and readied it. Her heart beat faster and faster. Her instincts were still good, but it had been a long time.

Gradually she crept forward, readying her weapon. She wouldn't need to inflict any damage, just take the guard by surprise then tie him up in the dining room. That would be enough. She practised the manoeuvre in her mind then reached out to put the dagger up against his throat.

But the guard seemed to anticipate her movement. He moved towards her and grabbed the dagger before she could alter her stance. She grabbed another and tried again, but he saw that coming and held her other hand. There they stood, face to face, hands interlocked.

"The monk?" Celes said in disbelief. What was he doing there?

"Celes?" Certan said. He was in shock. He didn't even notice Lara behind him, kicking his legs out from under him.

"Wait!" Celes whispered with force, before Lara could land a knockout blow. Lara paused, confused. Celes pointed to the dining room and dragged Certan over with her.

"What's going on?" Lara said.

"This is the monk."

"Certan?" Lara said.

"Yes. I got a job, I didn't expect this. It was part of my plan to start on a new path."

"Yes, yes very good. Just stay here and come with us when we leave. How many other guards are there?" Celes said.

"At least five. But I'm new so that won't tell me anything. That's why I'm here, away from the valuables," he said.

"Fine. Just act normal and don't leave this spot," Celes said.

"As you wish," Certan said, and walked back to where he was previously posted.

"There's always something," Celes whispered to Lara.

"Always," Lara whispered back. Celes pointed to a far doorway and made her way over. Lara followed close behind.

Celes noticed two other guards as they wound through the main floor but decided to avoid them. Running into Certan had been a sign, she had decided. And they didn't have time to disable all the guards. If only they could avoid detection on their way in, they could manage anything on the way out.

The entry to the main hall was visible, but Celes paused before rushing over. She didn't want to trip over any traps or security. Her quick look around during the day had only spotted guards, not anything special. But she knew how tricky Wilhelm was, there was bound to be something.

"Stay close," she whispered to Lara and began her approach. Creeping softly along and sticking to the shadows, she made good progress. She could see a guard walking around the main hall, and timed herself so that she would arrive at the entry while he was on the other end of the room. She entered the main hall and swiftly ducked down to hide behind a table. Lara joined her immediately.

"So far so good, but I've got a feeling there's going to be some traps. Tread carefully," Celes said.

"Got it," Lara said. Celes snuck over to the end of the table and peered around the corner. The guard was just passing and wouldn't see her. She darted out and took cover behind another table, leaving space for Lara to join her. Before making another move she scanned the room again. She could not see any other guards.

That's odd, I was sure he would keep more here, Celes thought. But she didn't share that with Lara, there was no need to worry her unnecessarily. Satisfied that there were no obvious threats, Celes waited for the guard and used his patrol route to move closer. They repeated this two more times to be almost within reach of the Pure Diamond.

"I'll get the diamond, if something happens you leave and take Certan and Alrion with you," Celes said.

"Are you sure?"

"Yes, I can handle this. And if for some reason I can't, for me it's only a delay. You cannot afford a delay."

"If you insist," Lara said.

"Good. Here goes," Celes said and made her move. She crouch ran with steps as light as a feather, ducking under the rope and appearing right next to the Pure Diamond. She remained low to the ground though, in case she had to hide quickly. Celes slowly rose and examined the glass housing.

Doesn't appear to be any traps. That is a concern, but I can't back out now.

With her left hand, she gently lifted the glass housing, and with her right she reached for the diamond. She grabbed it without incident and replaced the glass housing. *Done.*

"Once a thief, always a thief." A man's voice rang out from the gallery above. Lamps were quickly lit around the room, illuminating it within seconds.

Celes stood, not trying to hide herself. "Stay down," she whispered to Lara and deliberately dropped the diamond.

"Don't think you can try anything. And that's just a dummy. Well, a beautiful dummy. Good enough to fool you and everyone else." Wilhelm showed off another diamond in his hand, then tucked it back into his coat. He started to descend from the gallery. He was flanked by at least twenty guards.

"What game are you playing?" Celes said, acting confident. She wasn't sure how she had been tricked so easily.

"I never forget a face. Especially one that got away. I did never find out your real name though. Which is a shame. But I guess you can tell me now, Shadow Fox," Wilhelm said. Lara drew in a startled breath.

"So, you're still obsessed after all these years," Celes said.

"I could say the same to you."

"What tipped you off?" Celes said. She was pretty sure she knew, but wanted to give him a moment to gloat. That may provide her an opportunity.

"I saw you here today. You were discreet and fast, but I remembered you. Even after all these years. And I knew that you would be impatient, so I just had to wait. I'm not even sure how you made it in, but it doesn't matter. All I had to do was wait for you to take the bait. And here you are." Wilhelm was standing right in front of her now. He looked about the same. He was a gnarly old man before, and he still was now. He just looked like he had shrunk a little and walked with more difficulty.

"For now." She would find an opening, some way or other.

"Oh, you aren't getting away this time. No, all exits are sealed and you are surrounded. There's no way to get out," Wilhelm said.

Celes looked around, sizing up the guards. They didn't look that tough, and only a few had crossbows. There was always a chance. But before she could put a plan into action, she saw some movement out of the corner of her eye.

Lara darted from nowhere and had a knife to Wilhelm's throat. "We'll be leaving thanks. Call off your dogs," Lara said.

Wilhelm was visibly shaken, but recovered quickly. "Why would I do that?"

"Because I could kill you if I sneezed, and it's awfully dusty in here," Lara said.

"I guess that is a risk, but if anything happens to me, you're as good as dead. I'm your only hope."

"You're right about that. But you're going to help me whether you like it or not." Lara threw a glass vial on the ground with her free hand and it shattered instantly. Smoke started to spew from the ground and Lara shoved Wilhelm into it.

"Get them!" he shouted, choking on the smoke.

"Follow me," Celes said, heading for the nearest exit from the hall. She kept low, trying to break line of sight. The diversion with the smoke worked well, splitting up the guards nicely. There were two posted at each door, but they didn't see Celes coming. By the time they noticed, the first guard was already on the floor and the second was taken down by Lara as he tried to attack Celes.

"Just run!" Celes shouted once they were through the door. They retraced their steps, not worrying about being silent anymore. Speed was of the essence. They initially had no problems, the guards rushing around not aware of their presence or too slow to react. But there were three guards waiting where they had left Certan.

"Doesn't look good," Celes said. However, she noticed another guard walking up to them. He glided between them, quickly knocking all three down.

"Nice!" Lara said. Certan waved at them, and disappeared into the nearby dining room. Celes and Lara rushed to join him.

"I'm not sure where your exit is, but we should have a relatively clear run," he said. True to his word, they didn't see anyone else.

Alrion was waiting for them at the exit.

"What's going on? I heard a commotion," Alrion said.

"Complications. Don't worry, let's just head out," Celes said.

"Certan?" Alrion said as he noticed the monk.

"Plenty of time for explanations later," he said.

"Sure, well nothing happened here let's go." Alrion led the way out into the tunnel.

"Can you see that light in the distance?" Alrion said.

"Yes, what do you think it is?" Celes said.

"Not sure, but there's no way that is coming in from the street." Alrion created a miniature ball of fire and threw it along the tunnel.

Celes watched its progress, and heard a cry of pain.

"We're not alone," Lara said.

"Slow down, let's not rush in," Celes said. The group slowed their advance, and continued at a more measured pace. As they closed the distance, it became obvious what the light was. There was a force of twenty armed guards standing in formation at the end of the tunnel and blocking the exit.

"Those are city guards," Celes said.

"Waiting for us," Alrion said.

"That Wilhelm, he was well-prepared," Celes said.

"Not prepared enough. Otherwise they would have known that such a small force is not going to cut it. It's a shame I couldn't use your stealth lessons Lara, but this will be more fun. Leave it to me," Alrion said with a smile.

Who is this young man, and what did he do with my son? Celes thought. At least she had an opportunity to see for herself just what he could do.

9

SETTING OUT

Alrion took two steps forward. He had an idea he wanted to try. Clearing his throat, he weaved a wave of force in front of him, but instead of sending it out he let it hover and vibrate. Then he spoke into it.

"Leave now and you will not be harmed," Alrion said. His voice sounded lower than in pitch than normal and boomed around the tunnel.

"How did you do that?" Lara said.

"I just had an idea, and it worked," Alrion whispered back at her. The soldiers looked a little rattled, but had not moved.

"As you wish!" Alrion shouted, then let the spell dissipate. It had worked surprisingly well. He wasn't sure if he had melded ideas he already had, or drawn upon some knowledge hidden in his mind. But it didn't matter.

Alrion started walking forward with purpose, preparing his next move. He could see the soldiers take a defensive stance. Alrion drew upon his spark and ignited flames above his hands. Then he combined them with a wave of force. Rolling spirals of flame tumbled along the ground, arcing up before they hit the soldiers. They dove to the ground, narrowly avoiding the flames. Alrion kept walking. He threw another wave of force, this time adding no fire. The dust swirled around as it travelled along the ground, but this one didn't suddenly jump up. It stayed low and knocked around all the soldiers who had ducked the previous attack.

"They have a wizard!" one of the soldiers said.

Another replied "We're sitting ducks in here."

Alrion noticed that they had retreated a few metres. A bit further and he would have access to the ladder. He drew upon his spark one more time, concentrating on the ground in front of the soldiers. A low wall of flame rose up, stopping at chest height. The front row of soldiers scrambled back. Alrion advanced, and moved the wall of fire forward as well. The soldiers continued to retreat.

"Just a little bit further." Alrion pushed the wall forward, the soldiers bunching up as they ran out of the tunnel.

"That should do," Alrion said, maintaining the wall of fire in its current location.

"And that will work. Nice work!" Lara said, noticing that the path to the tunnel stairs was now clear.

"Let's be quick, I can't do this all day and I don't want them to try anything," Alrion said.

"Agreed. Time to leave," Celes said. Alrion continued his steady pace while he concentrated on the spell. The rest ran ahead, climbing out of the tunnel.

"You won't get away with this. We know who you are!" one of the soldiers shouted. But Alrion didn't take any notice. Once the rest were out he climbed out himself.

"Is the spell still active?" Celes said.

"Yes, what's our next move?" Alrion said.

"Just hold it long enough for us to block this exit. That will buy us enough time," she said. Lara noticed a nearby box full of scrapped metal items.

"Help me with this," she said to Certan. The two of them dragged the box over the top of the tunnel exit.

"That should do," Celes said. Alrion let the spell go and they ran from the alley as quickly as possible. Once they re-joined the market streets Celes slowed and the rest matched her pace.

"Quickly and quietly, let's get back to the house," she said. Alrion looked back, but couldn't see any pursuers. He was happy at what he had done. The spells had taken more Spark that he had expected, but it all worked out fine. And he didn't need to let on just how much power he had expended. Each step away helped him relax a bit more, but he couldn't calm down until they reached the safety of the house.

Celes was inside first, with Certan ushering the others in ahead of himself. They found Vincent standing inside, arms crossed.

"How'd you go?" he said. He didn't seem impressed, as if he knew something had gone wrong.

"We had a small hiccup. Wilhelm was waiting for us. But we escaped, due to some ingenuity from Lara and some pyrotechnics from Alrion," Celes said.

"Sounds like a disaster," Vincent said.

"Well, a partial disaster. But we all made it out, and Lara and Certan passed the test," Celes said.

"I may have gotten a job and cleaned up, but I have not retrieved my scarf," Certan said.

"That is not an issue. You can get another, if the monks find you worthy," Vincent said.

"This is true, I agree with your plan. I will join you," Certan said, bowing to Vincent.

"It wasn't a total loss," Lara said, retrieving something from her jacket. It was a massive, pristine diamond.

"Is that the replica?" Celes said.

"No, it's the real deal. I swapped them in the confusion. Wilhelm won't realise until it is too late," Lara said.

"Give me that," Celes said, snatching it from Lara's hands. She looked it over carefully.

"You really did it. I underestimated you," Celes said. Alrion could see the begrudging look of admiration on his mother's face.

"Mission accomplished then," Lara said with a laugh. "Although on a more serious note it was my honour to accompany the fabled Shadow Fox."

"Thankfully we kept my record intact." Celes handed the diamond to Vincent. "Incorporate this into Alrion's sword. He will need it the most,"

"Good idea, I could lodge it into the pommel without too much effort. And it won't draw attention that way, people will just think it is an ornament," Vincent said, turning it over.

"Does that stone really work? Will it react to the Blight?" Alrion said.

"I'm sure you will have a chance to test it soon enough," Vincent said, putting the stone away.

"Those soldiers said they knew who you were," Lara said to Celes.

"They know my alias, not who I am. As long as we leave soon, there won't be a problem," Celes said.

"They will eventually track us here if we stay. But I agree we should be safe to sleep here tonight," Vincent said.

"Then let's make our preparations. Do they have rules against using the forges at night?" Celes said.

"No, I'll get to work," Vincent said with a sigh. He walked over to the door and disappeared into the night.

"The rest of you, get some rest. We leave tomorrow," Celes said.

"You're coming too?" Alrion said.

"Of course, I'm wanted remember?" Celes said. Alrion just shook his head.

"Who is she?" he wondered to himself.

The next morning Alrion awoke to find everyone else ready and waiting.

"Sorry, were you all waiting for me?" Alrion said.

"Yes, but don't feel bad. A wizard needs rest to replenish his energy," Vincent said.

"How would you know that?"

"I may not be one, but I was the son of one. Now go ready yourself, we need to leave as soon as possible," Vincent said. Alrion gathered his things, and did a final check of the house. He noticed something sitting on a table near the front door and walked closer. "That's for you," Vincent said, pride in his voice.

Alrion saw that it was a sword in a leather scabbard with an ornate leather strap. The diamond was expertly attached to the pommel of the sword, and looked like it was always meant to be there. Alrion slowly drew the sword out, the pale metal gently shining in the sunlight. He touched the edge and instantly recoiled his finger. "That's sharp," Alrion said.

"What did you expect?" Vincent said, chuckling. Alrion shook his hand, feeling foolish.

"It looks great. How did you finish it in time?" he said, returning the sword.

"Finish them in time." Vincent turned to show Alrion the sword strapped to his back. "I have a matching one, although with no giant diamond. I was a lot closer to completing them than I was letting on. I had originally wanted to take more time with the finishing. But I'm happy with the result," he said.

"What about me?" Lara said, sticking her empty hands out in front of her.

"I didn't forget. Lucky for you there was some leftover metal. Use it wisely." Vincent tossed over a dagger within a plain leather scabbard.

Lara pulled the dagger out and examined the edge. "Looks really sharp. Is this the real deal?"

"Of course. You'll be able to take down a Shade with that," Vincent said.

"Good, that makes a girl feel more comfortable."

"Glad I could help."

"I just have to say, this is a crazy gift," Lara said.

"I know. Forget about that and just use it well. You've proved yourself."

"If we're all ready, we need to leave immediately." Celes tapped her foot impatiently.

"After you," Vincent said and Celes stepped through the front door without hesitation. The rest followed close behind. Alrion paused to look back at the house. It already had a lot of memories for him, let alone his parents. He decided to return here one day, when things were simpler.

They walked with purpose towards the main gates.

"Can't we pass through the city and exit from the other end?" Alrion said.

"Yes, but it's a smaller gate and it will be closely watched by the guards. This one may be as well, but we have a better chance of slipping through," Vincent said.

"I hadn't thought of that." Alrion felt a little silly for even asking.

"I was thinking we head straight to Vainbly," Celes said.

"Excellent idea," Vincent said.

"Is it close?" Alrion said.

"Yes, we can get there on foot within a few hours, then plan our next move. Hopefully there's also horses available to speed up our journey."

"It's a long walk, I wouldn't recommend it," Certan said. Alrion gave him a smile. As they approached the main gates, Alrion could see that the guard had been doubled. People were being stopped too and interrogated.

"Follow my lead." Celes quickly grabbed Lara and shoved her a few steps ahead. "Stop! Thief!" she shouted, pointing at Lara.

The young thief was initially stunned, then quickly cottoned on. She took off, swiftly weaving into the crowd. The ruse worked, the patrolling guards quickly set off after Lara.

"Don't worry they won't catch her," Celes said to Alrion. After a quick look around, she started walking forward once more. Alrion tried to keep an eye out for Lara, to see how she fared. His mother was completely right.

The guards were hampered by their armour and the crowds. Lara was nimble and crafty, changing direction and weaving through gaps in the crowd that were impossible for them to follow. But she didn't speed too far ahead, always pausing just enough for the guards to feel as if they were gaining.

"She's something else," Alrion said under his breath.

"Take care of that one," Vincent said, slapping his son on the shoulder. Alrion didn't realise his father had heard his comment, and decided to focus on Lara's progress rather than continue that potentially awkward conversation.

Lara laughed as she ran, it was good fun. She hadn't been chased like this in a while, in an open street during the middle of the day. As she glanced back she could see her group advancing carefully through the crowd, not garnering a second glance from any of the guards.

Too easy. She looked ahead, to plan out her escape from the city. She spotted a group of guards blocking the path. They must have heard the commotion and formed a mini blockade.

"No time to think, just react," Lara told herself. She spied one of the city banners hanging from the gates and instantly decided to go for it. Adjusting her direction, she instead headed for the walls of the gates. There were studs in the wall that were quite large, so she grabbed the first one within reach and started clambering up. The guards started to catch up as she ascended, and she could hear their shouts from below. Lara paused long enough to look back down and smirk at them, and decided that she was out of harm's way. Now she just had to exit.

After a quick tug of the banner, she observed its strength and how it hung. It wasn't ideal, but she had no time.

"Here we go," she whispered, steadying herself then leaping forward. She grabbed the cloth banner, using it to slow her descent. The force of her fall caused the banner to start detaching from the wall, and this gave her a nice arc through the air. Just before the banner was about to fall completely she let go, and toppled straight into one of the guards.

Before they could react, she scrambled to her feet and darted away and into the crowd of onlookers beyond the city walls. The guard line crumbled and they took off after her, two of them staying behind and watching the pursuit.

Now that she was beyond the walls, Lara increased her speed. There was less reason to keep them close, as her party would also be out soon. She needed to finish this chase, so she could disappear and rejoin the gang.

One guard was particularly swift, and Lara noticed that he had ditched some of his armour to run faster. She wasn't worried about being caught, but if he was fit he could keep within range for a long distance, which would be a problem. So, she slowed a little and dropped a few glass balls onto the ground. The guard didn't notice, and when he stepped on one completely lost his balance and toppled over.

Lara laughed and increased her speed. She had to disappear quickly to make the most of the opening.

10
———

IN THE SHADE OF A BLAZE

Streams of travellers looked on in amusement as Lara ducked and weaved through them. She stayed low and fast, looking for a way to escape from the road and into cover. There was a small bunch of trees to her left but she ignored them. It was too obvious. She needed something a bit better.

A partially-covered wagon caught her eye and Lara headed straight for it. It was being pulled by a horse with a weary man urging the plodding horse onwards. Lara stayed low to avoid the man's line of sight and quietly vaulted into the wagon, ducking under the cloth covering. An overpowering smell of animal hides assaulted her nose, but it was worth it.

She heard the rhythmic clank of the guard's remaining armour as he ran past, he didn't even pause for a moment.

"Gotcha!" Lara whispered, a big smile on her face. As he ran in the wrong direction she was slowly being taken back to the rest of the group. She waited a few minutes for safety, then peeked out of the wagon. There was no sign of the pursuing guard. Lara leapt out of the wagon and joined the stream of travellers, trying to blend in. She spotted Alrion in the distance, and slowly worked her way through to join him.

"Nice moves," Alrion said.

"They never had a chance." Lara flashed Alrion her biggest smile.

"We can take this path, it diverts around the city and passes through a few farming communities," Vincent said, and the rest followed his lead.

"You did well. Nice improvisation too," Celes said to Lara once they were off the main road.

"Thanks, although you didn't give me much warning."

"You didn't need it, and the stunned look on your face was perfect!"

"I think you enjoyed that way too much," Lara said and Celes could not contain her laughter.

"It was certainly entertaining, but we've lost time. Let's push on. No breaks until we reach Vainbly," Vincent said.

Nobody said another word.

Lara kept an eye on the countryside, interested in the new environment. She had never travelled this way before. She mostly kept to the bigger cities, and the ways to get in and out unseen. They passed through several small farming communities. Each one was a small cluster of farms and houses, with vast tracts between them. But the road persisted.

"This road seems out of place in such a quiet and rural place," Alrion said.

"They still need to access the cities, and sell their goods. In fact, my first commission as a blacksmith was for farms just like these," Vincent said.

"Really? What was it?"

"Horseshoes. Quite tricky actually. But it brings back fond memories."

"It must have been a fun time," Alrion said. Vincent didn't comment further and Alrion returned to gazing at the landscape. Lara did the same.

Vainbly came up sooner than she expected. In between some snacks, the rolling countryside looked so similar that she was almost entranced by the trip. The town was rather unassuming, with a small river running out in front. They crossed a petite stone bridge to enter the town.

"There should be a decent inn here, although it's been a while I have no idea if it's still open," Vincent said.

"What was it called again? The Frisky Farmer?" Celes said.

"Something like that."

"Looks like it's still here," Lara said, pointing to a distant building. Right in the centre of the town was a large structure with a peaked roof and large wooden doors. A simple sign hung above the entrance.

"Let's get inside and have a decent meal," Vincent said.

Lara glanced around as they walked through Vainbly. It looked like a fairly quiet town, without much going on. But she could see the evidence of trade from Brangtur. There was a bustle and clinking of coins that betrayed the simple setting.

The smell of ale smacked them in the face as they entered the inn. The hall was full of patrons, each with a beer or two.

"Looks like the whole town is here," Lara said.

"Are you alright?" she said to Certan. He nodded without replying, but he was visibly affected. Once she had mentioned it the others seemed to cotton on as well.

"I'm sorry, you just sobered up and the first place we took you was an inn. Do you want us to go somewhere else?" Alrion said.

"Thank you for your concern. It's more of a physical reaction right now, which I can manage. Despite the unpleasantness, I'm finding value in it as a type of penance." Certan looked uncomfortable but resolute.

"Wow that's harsh," Lara said.

"I'll enquire about rooms, try and find a table," Vincent said.

Lara disappeared into the crowd, reappearing at a far corner of the hall and waving.

Celes spotted the wave and directed the rest over. They managed to squeeze onto a tiny table, knocking elbows. "It'll be a brawl just trying to eat anything," Celes said.

"If this lot can handle it, we should be able to," Lara said gesturing at the crowd. They were predominantly men and of large builds.

"Must all be labourers from the area," Alrion said.

"Or travellers? I'd say this is the first stop out of Brangtur for many, depending on your destination. Do you think they will look for us here?" Certan said.

"They may do, but I doubt the guard has the resources to venture outside the city. As long as we don't hang around longer than a night I don't see any danger," Celes said.

"There'll be danger, regardless," Certan said looking around the room. He seemed quite distracted. A slim woman deftly weaved through the tables and dropped down an armful of ales. To her credit very little sloshed out and onto the table.

"We didn't order these," Celes said.

"The man up there did. This is the only drink we have available. Food is on its way, but there's a delay in the kitchen," the dark-haired woman said. Before there could be any further questioning she disappeared into the crowd. Celes looked over and saw Vincent waving at her in the distance.

"Fine," she muttered and pulled one of the ales closer. Alrion followed suit, and Certan who found a spot on the ceiling to examine in detail instead.

"Don't worry, I'm with you," Lara said, pushing aside the ale.

"We have rooms for the night, and dinner as well. Lucky that we found a table, this is the busiest time of the day. It should be much quieter in the evening," Vincent said, squeezing in next to his wife. She passed over his ale and he drank deep.

"Sounds good to me. What do you we in the meantime?" Alrion said.

"We need to source some horses. Any volunteers?"

"I'll do it," Lara said.

"Great. Celes and I will scout around the town, and make sure there's no unwanted attention from Brangtur. Alrion, did you want to come with us?" Vincent said.

"No, I think I'll do some training. I have a few things to look into as well," he said. Lara saw the excited glimmer in his eye.

He's up to something, I wonder what.

"How about you hang around here too Certan, although our rooms may be more comfortable," Vincent said.

"I will remain to assist Alrion." Certan paused just long enough to give direct eye contact to Vincent then turned his attention elsewhere.

After a brief meal of meat and potatoes, the group went their separate ways. Alrion and Certan walked upstairs to find the rooms. Certan settled into a corner and meditated, while Alrion retrieved his spell book.

He leafed through the pages quickly, hoping to not find his recently discovered spell for amplifying his voice. His excitement grew as he reached the end of the book and didn't find it. He combed through once more, paying special attention to the pages that might contain a mention of it. But there was not a single reference to be found.

According to what Falric said, I should be able to read the spells that I am capable of using. And if I used it, and it's not in the book, that means either I created it or I just know it now.

It seemed unlikely that he had created such an obvious spell. Which meant he had probably absorbed it from the Pool of Knowledge. He was buzzing with excitement.

"I wonder what else I can do," Alrion whispered. He leafed through the spell book again, but this time with a different purpose. Instead of a specific spell, he wanted information on how to increase his strength and capacity.

"The knowledge I have gained must work in a similar way to the books. The more capable I am, the more spells I can unlock for my use. I just need to keep pushing my strength and try new spells," Alrion said quietly to himself. It was important to find a focus for himself. His current goal was so far away, some strange test in a distant land. On the way, he had to improve his skill. His encounter with Branthor was a lucky escape. Next time he didn't want to rely on luck. He looked over at Certan, but the monk didn't react.

He must be busy, I'll push on, Alrion thought.

After an afternoon consulting the book, Alrion didn't have many more answers. But he had consolidated some of his learning, and was excited about his new focus. His plan now meant finding opportunities to use his magic as much as possible.

"You're still up here?" Lara said as she entered the room. Alrion put away the book.

"Yes, is it late?"

"Yes, the sun has already set. We are about to have dinner. Come down," Lara said. Alrion was confused, he hadn't noticed it getting dark. He looked again, and saw that he had cast a light spell and hovered a sphere of light above his shoulder. Unlike his previous attempts, this one didn't emit any heat. Just light. He waved it away and rushed off to join Lara.

"Certan, come down when you're ready, you need to eat some at some stage," Alrion shouted.

"You're just in time," Vincent said as Alrion arrived downstairs.

"Of..." Alrion began to say, but was cut off by a loud groan. He spun quickly and noticed the main doors of the inn slowly bending over. Suddenly they splintered into large chunks, and a massive shape occupied the doorway. Alrion knew what it was instantly. He looked over at his father.

"Yes, I know what it is. Lara, can you fetch the swords?" Vincent said calmly, without taking his eyes off the creature.

"Is that a Shade?" Lara said.

"Yes," Vincent said.

"On my way." Lara turned and sprinted off.

"My body is my weapon. I will engage the creature while you wait for yours," Certan said, rising gracefully from his seat. There was an intensity to the look in his eyes.

The Shade stepped forward, and grabbed a nearby patron who hadn't had time to flee. The rest had retreated to the bar and hidden behind it. The poor man screamed in terror. But Certan did not hesitate. He dashed ahead, engaging the Shade head on. The Shade threw the limp body it was holding at Certan, who adjusted his stance to duck underneath. He didn't just dodge though, he caught the body and carefully set it down on the ground behind him. The Shade was enraged, lashing out at Certan. He blocked the attack with his arms, and slid under to continue his approach. The Shade moved to strike him again, but Certan was too fast. He landed a strong blow to the creature's side, knocking it back.

"It's tough," Certan said.

"Incredibly tough. It's why we need these," Vincent said.

Lara had returned with the two blades. The diamond on the end of Alrion's sword glowed furiously.

"I'd say it works," Alrion said, accepting the sword from Lara and looking it over. Then he set it aside. Before his father could say anything, Alrion launched into an attack. Last time he had been on the sidelines, but this time he could prove how much he had grown since then. He led with a wave of force, which rocked the Shade slightly.

"Be careful, it looks like the same one. It remembers our last fight," Vincent shouted. Alrion heard, but did not respond. He was completely focused.

Fire didn't do much, but maybe it was the intensity. I'll overload it.

He drew on his spark and started building for a fire based attack. But this time, rather than just let it loose, he tried compacting it. He launched a miniature ball of flame. It was so hot that it started to ignite the air that it passed through. The Shade didn't even try to block the attack, which hit right in the middle of the chest.

"Damn I missed," Alrion whispered. Before he could initiate another attack, he saw that his previous one was behaving strangely. Rather than just exploding on the surface of the Shade's skin, it was still continuing.

"It's burning right through," Vincent said.

The Shade seemed to notice too, trying to shake off the ball of intense heat that was slowly passing through its body. But once it realised that the attack was not fatal, it stopped and focused its attention back on Alrion.

I have to get the upper hand, so we can finish it.

His force attacks had been quite powerful, but hadn't done that much to the creature. He decided that he could overcome that with sheer quantity. He concentrated and drew up several strands of force.

Alrion unleashed them in a barrage, trying to hit the same target area with each strike. He could see the attacks landing, each one having a minimal effect on the Shade. But it did seem like something was happening. Lara noticed the attack, and pulled out her new dagger.

"This will do the trick," she said and hurled the dagger at the Shade. Despite the movement of the Shade and the multiple attacks from Alrion, the dagger flew true and pierced the Shade in the chest, right where the heart was. The monster staggered back, not expecting the attack and furiously grasping for the dagger. However, Certan was faster, darting in amongst the confusion and striking the dagger with his open palm, forcing it in up to the hilt.

The Shade stumbled back and fell against the bar. As it came to rest, it's skin started to change undoing its transformation. The black surface was crumbling away, revealing pale skin underneath. Alrion looked on in wonder.

Lara retrieved her dagger, wiped it quickly and stashed it away.

"Never forget that this was once a person, even if they are beyond help now," Vincent said, walking closer and sheathing his sword.

"I don't want to alarm anyone, but I think we have a bigger problem here," Celes said pointing at the bar. Alrion's concentrated flame ball had passed through the body of the Shade and was about to hit the kegs behind the bar.

11

ALTERNATE PATHS

"Everyone out!" Vincent shouted, pointing at the door, and making his way there. The group scrambled out as fast as possible.

"I can probably stop it," Alrion said.

"No time, and too risky," Vincent said, grabbing Alrion's arm. A whoosh sound and a forceful shockwave buffeted them and as they looked back at the inn, they could see it was being consumed with flames.

I wonder, Alrion thought. He watched the flames with interest. If he could create flames, and issue them from himself, maybe he could bring them back.

"Let's try this," Alrion whispered. He reached out with his hand, trying a reverse of his previous spell. It was a twist on the fireballs. Instead, he was drawing the flame back to him, trying to build it into another ball. He visualised the ball of flame hovering above his hand, and containing all the flames and fire that had overtaken the inn. He could feel the heat and the power concentrated in a single spot.

Alrion opened his eyes and looked. The spell had worked.

"What are you planning to do with that?" Vincent said, looking over at Alrion. There was a curious concern in his features.

"Extinguish it," Alrion said, but what he really wanted to try, was to integrate the flames and the power. What if the Spark was more than just a concept? Maybe it was more literal than that. He tried feeding the flames into himself, trying to absorb their essence. He could feel himself heating up and the fireball shrinking.

"Stop it, that's not safe. Dump it," Vincent shouted. Alrion couldn't understand the concern, then looked at where Vincent was pointing. His arm was glowing bright red and looked wrong. Alrion panicked and looked around, finding a patch of dirt next to the inn. He funnelled all the flames into it without any finesse. The ball of flame streamed over and collected within the dirt, extinguishing but not without displacing quite a bit of dirt. Alrion sank down to his knees.

"What were you thinking?" Vincent said. Alrion looked around and the whole group were looking at him with concern.

"That's my line. Do you have an answer?" Celes said.

"I was just trying something out. I saved the inn, didn't I?" Alrion said.

"This isn't a game, you shouldn't take risks like that," Celes said.

"Your mother is right. The situation was contained, you didn't need to do more," Vincent said.

"Yes I did. I have to grow and learn an incredible amount in a short time, and there's nobody around to teach me. So, I will take every opportunity to do that," Alrion said.

Vincent sighed and walked into the inn. Celes followed after him. Lara walked over to Alrion.

"See I'm right, you should listen to me more and not take as many risks," she said, hoping to get a smile from Alrion. When she didn't she tried a different angle. "They're just worried, don't take it to heart."

"I know, but there's this incredible pressure on me and I have to do it. I can't let everyone down." Alrion felt older, like the weight of the world was on his shoulders.

"You have help, so don't forget that," Certan said.

"Yeah, look at the monk. He did the killing blow on that Shade. Now that's a team effort," Lara said.

"Well, you're right about that. Let's take a closer look at it," Alrion said.

Lara helped him up and they walked over to look at the body of the former Shade. "At least it works. But look here, mine isn't the only wound in the heart," Lara said.

"We encountered a Shade earlier, and it took a dagger in the heart and was knocked overboard. This must be the same one. I wonder how it tracked us here," Alrion said.

"Overboard?"

"Yes, we fought it on the ferry," Alrion said.

"Wow." Lara wiped the dagger she had pulled out earlier on her clothing and hid it once more.

Certan was kneeling over the body. "I haven't seen one of these up close. It looks like the body has completely reverted to a normal state. What a strange process," he said.

"I don't understand it myself, but this is what happens to people who have an advanced taint from the Blight," Alrion said.

"We've worn out our welcome," Vincent said, tossing a bag at Alrion.

"Time to leave, we will camp outside the town. At least we have horses now," Celes said joining them.

"It looks like the same Shade that attacked us on the ferry," Alrion said to his father as they walked over to the stables.

"I know, I recognised it instantly."

"How?" Alrion couldn't contain his surprise. Since when was his father an expert on Shades?

"I've seen a few in my day, they tend to closely resemble the person they originally were. It's there plain as day if you look closely."

"I'll remember for next time."

"I'd like to say there won't be a next time, but that would be a lie. We need to divert from the main path. I'm not sure what tipped them off, but they tracked us too easily. I'll think it over tonight," Vincent said.

They entered the stables, and only the horses greeted them.

"Where is everyone?" Lara said.

"Evacuated. They don't feel safe now. I can't blame them," Vincent said.

"I know the feeling," Lara said. The group saddled up and rode out of town. Alrion could sense eyes watching them, and hoped it was just scared townsfolk and not more creatures of the Blight.

After a short ride, they took a minor dirt track and left the main road.

"Can you give me a light?" Vincent asked and Alrion paused for a moment. After a minute a small orb of light danced above Vincent's shoulder.

"Thanks," Vincent said, and continued riding.

"I wouldn't have tried that if he hadn't asked, good to know," Alrion said to himself. The group rode in silence until they came to a small clearing.

"We will set up camp here. Alrion, help me with the horses," Vincent said.

Alrion nodded and helped guide the horses to a nearby spot and tie them up. He was about to head back, when he noticed his father's eyes looking directly at him.

"What happened back there?" Vincent said.

"What do you mean?"

"Is something happening with you. I've never seen you act so recklessly. Your mother is worried." Vincent looked worried too, although he didn't mention it.

"I almost died when I fought Branthor. It was only through luck and sheer determination that I caught him off-guard. But I can't let that happen again. There's too much at stake. And..."

"And?"

"There seems to be stuff spilling over from when I drank from the Pool. Knowledge of spells, intuition on how to combine things. I can't discern what is something that should work, and what is some crazy idea of mine. Or even things that should work but I can't do yet," Alrion said.

Vincent looked at him thoughtfully. "I hadn't thought of that, I guess I need to find out more about how this all works. You're right though, you don't have the luxury of time to slowly learn all you need. Just make sure you rely on the rest of us to help. It's not a criticism of you, it's just a safety net."

"Alright, I agree. I'll let everyone help and try not to do too many crazy things." Alrion wasn't sure how long that would last.

"Good, I feel better now."

"I thought it was mum that was the worrier?" Alrion knew his father had been worried too.

"It is," Vincent said and walked back to the camp.

Vincent and Certan took turns taking watch, but the night passed without incident. The next morning, they snacked on some bread and Vincent addressed the group.

"I've been doing some thinking, and I have a plan for how we move forward."

"We're all ears," Lara said.

"We need to split up. I'm confident that you and Certan can support Alrion. Celes and I will go a different route."

"Why?" Alrion said.

"We know we are being tracked, so it's better to split up and divert their attention. Celes and I can go back to the main road and continue on to Plynth. It's a massive town, and we can do some digging into who and what are following. With any luck, we will draw them in," Vincent said, tossing a lump of hard bread into the dying embers of the fire.

"So where do we go?" Alrion said.

"There is another path, and a longer route. You can follow it and stay off the beaten track. It will cost you time, but it will be safer and you will have the necessary seclusion to work on your spells," Vincent said.

"We'll be crossing the river?" Certan said.

"Yes, exactly."

"It's a well-known detour, but the best plan given the circumstances. Where will we meet you?" Certan said.

"You can find us at Plynth. By the time you arrive, we would ideally have taken care of our pursuers. Then we will set off together for the desert. If we miss there, we can agree to meet at the desert entry. We will find you," Vincent said.

"That would work," Certan said.

"There's a single desert entry? Won't that be obvious?"

"There are many, but only one that will take us where we need to go. And it is not well-known. I have discussed this with your father," Certan said.

"If you say so. When do we part ways?" Alrion said.

"As soon as we pack up," Vincent said.

Alrion nodded, a bit surprised even though he understood the reasoning. They packed up in silence, Alrion double checking he had everything with particular care. Once he was prepared he walked over to the horses. Vincent was standing there talking to Celes. "Well, you two make sure you take care of yourselves," Alrion said as he approached.

"Will do boss," Vincent said, winking.

"You'll do well," Celes said, giving Alrion a hug.

"Isn't this fun? All of us on an adventure together," she said, gesturing at the group.

"It would be more fun without a Shade crashing the party," Vincent said.

"He doesn't mean that," Celes said, speaking behind her hand, and pretending to whisper.

"How will we find you in Plynth?" Alrion said.

"Don't worry, we will find you," Celes said.

"Alright, I guess this is it then. See you soon," Alrion said, giving them a wave. He mounted his horse and rode back towards the camp. As he turned he saw his parents mounting up and preparing to ride in the opposite direction. Impulsively he drew on his Spark and prepared a spell. He shot a flash of fire through the air, arcing high over the trees and vanishing into the distance in the direction that Vincent and Celes would be heading.

~

"We've got our marching orders," Vincent said to Celes with a chuckle, and the two of them started to ride away.

"Are we doing the right thing?" Celes said.

"Of course. He needs room to grow, and we can help from afar." Vincent needed to be strong, to make sure his wife didn't worry.

"As long as you're convinced. It's hard for me to let go."

"I know," Vincent said, giving Celes a kiss.

"Let's get moving, the faster we get there, the more we can do," Vincent said.

"I'll race you," Celes said, spurring her horse on and laughing.

Alrion saw his parents disappear into the distance and turned back to face Lara and Certan.

"Should we head out?" Certan said.

"Definitely. Are you familiar with the route?" Alrion said.

"Yes, I have travelled through here before. We should hurry to try and cross the bridge as soon as possible. Once we cross over the river, it will be harder to track us."

"Let's go then," Alrion said, letting Certan take the lead. Lara rode alongside him, but looking straight ahead. Alrion thought about his companions. With Certan's skill, strength and familiarity of the territory and Lara's instincts and adaptability he had nothing to worry about. Together they had taken down the Shade that had eluded them with Falric's aid.

"Why am I so worried then?" Alrion asked himself as they rode. He couldn't shake the feeling that they were not out of the woods yet.

12

THE QUIET ROAD

The way back was quick and simple, and Alrion didn't spot a single person. They were able to move onto the secondary path without fear of being watched.

"So now this is uncharted territory," Alrion said, half to himself.

"For you, perhaps. But we are far from safe. This is still a well-travelled alternate route. Many do not continue the way we are going, so the further we travel the safer it will be. But I again suggest we make haste," Certan said.

"Agreed. While we're riding though I had a question," Alrion said.

"Yes, please ask." Certan slowed so that they were closer together.

"It's for both of you. Until recently I had never encountered the Blight. Blighters and Shades are new to me. But what about you? I feel like I've been quite sheltered," Alrion said.

"You have been, but don't feel dismayed. It's a good problem to have. I am lucky in that my exposure has been quite limited. The areas where I have lived, and especially with the monks, have been unpopular places for creatures of the Blight. There are few people, or much food or water," Certan said.

"Do they still function like a person?" Alrion said.

"In terms of having to eat and drink, yes. But their minds are warped. They also seem to have some sort of communal connection. You don't see them attempting speech much, yet they seem to be able to coordinate."

"What about you Lara?" Alrion said.

"My whole life, they have been present. I hate them with a passion. But I've enjoyed the relative safety of Avaria these last few years. I think they've only recently infiltrated this place in any numbers, and I'm sorry to say that's largely because of you." Lara pointed directly at Alrion.

"Sorry," Alrion said.

"Don't be sorry, they fear what can destroy them."

"Exactly. You have the knowledge now, deep within you. You must unlock it and set things right," Certan said.

"You make it sound so easy," Alrion said, trying to lighten the mood. He did get a laugh from them both. He kept an eye on the scenery as they went by, and it looked like another relatively deserted area. Alrion looked for signs of people passing through, and didn't see any. The path seemed undisturbed and they didn't see anyone in either direction.

"I thought you said that this was a well-known route, albeit longer and more secluded," Alrion said to Certan.

"It is."

"Then why is it so quiet? There's no sign of any activity," Alrion said.

"That's a good point. I admit I haven't travelled through here recently. Perhaps things have changed. Are you familiar Lara?"

"No, I haven't been this way," Lara said. Alrion spotted a clearing coming up off the right of the path and diverted his horse.

"Come here for a moment," Alrion said. The others followed, Lara giving Certan a confused look. Certan didn't have an explanation. "Shouldn't there be signs of people camping here?" Alrion said.

"It's not that far from Brangtur, maybe it's not a popular spot," Lara said.

"Not that far? Anyway, since we are here I need a break. And I want to try something." Alrion dismounted and tied up his horse to a tree. Certan and Lara followed. "So, we lucked out a bit last time, but then I did almost burn down an inn. If we encounter another Shade, what's the plan?" Alrion said.

"My attacks seem mostly ineffective, I think their skin is too protected," Certan said.

"Do you have attacks that penetrate? I think that underneath, they are still vulnerable. And their heart seems to be the weak spot," Alrion said.

"I do have something, but it requires focus and attention. Hard to use in the middle of a fight," Certan said.

"But what if we bought you time?" Lara said.

"Possibly, I need to be in close proximity too." Certan had a thoughtful expression on his face.

"That's fine. I don't currently have an effective way of defeating them with my magic, I can only assist. Lara and I have the right weapons to pierce the Shade's skin, but the amount of force required is quite substantial and it's not always reliable. So maybe we can try your attack next?" Alrion said.

"It's worth a try. What are you proposing?"

"See that tree over there? It looks pretty sturdy. Let's try a coordinated attack. Lara and I will provide an initial attack to distract and wear it down, and you can come in with the big finish."

"Sure. I'll signal when I am ready." Certan sat on the ground, legs crossed and began to meditate.

"Do what you do, pretend it's a Shade," Alrion said to Lara.

"After you," Lara said. Alrion stepped to the side and began to prepare a barrage of spells. His best success was the force based waves, and he decided to try a variation of that. We wove a pattern of intertwined waves, all hitting the similar zone but at various times and from different directions and angles. He kept the intensity a little lower, just in case the tree wasn't as sturdy as it looked.

Once Lara could see the tree begin to be hammered by invisible force, she started running in an arc towards it. She opened with an array of tiny daggers hurled with precision. Thud, thud, thud, thud, they impacted with the tree in a neat line. Alrion adjusted his spells to avoid the areas where the daggers were implanted. He glanced over at Certan and saw no change.

Lara darted back and began another run, approaching from another direction. She produced more daggers and they hit one by one neatly underneath the first row. Alrion watched her through the last one and tried to catch it with a wave of force and push it even harder. The dagger wobbled slightly but stayed on track, only this time disappearing completely into the tree trunk.

"Ready," Certan said. Lara tossed a small vial at the tree and it smashed against the trunk letting out a cloud of smoke. Certan stood and ran towards the tree, keeping his right hand above his hip. Once he reached the tree he raised his hand and held it just above the surface of the trunk. He unleashed all the internal force he had accumulated all at once.

Alrion heard the almost deafening blast and ceased his attacks. Certan remained in place, sinking to a crouched position. Lara stood down, returning to Alrion's side. Once the smoke cleared Lara gasped.

"Wow!" she whispered.

"That's quite effective," Alrion said. Only the stump of the tree could be seen. And what was remaining looked to have been cleanly sliced in an arc. There were tiny fragments of splintered wood floating through the air.

"Perhaps I overdid it, but we needed to be sure." Certan stood with difficult and walked over to join Alrion.

"I feel bad for that tree," Alrion said.

"It was a necessary act, so that more good can be done. The tree knows that," Certan said.

"If you say so. How long does it take you to recover from that?" Lara said.

"Completely? A day. I can be effective again within a few minutes, but any additional attacks will be less powerful."

"So just don't miss then," Lara said.

"Of course," Certan said.

"I'm happy with this. If for some reason the Shade survives that attack, we should be able to disable it or finish it off. I liked the smoke screen, nice touch," Alrion said.

"Well, he did say he had to be very close. That's a vulnerable place to be, so why not mask his approach as much as possible?" Lara said.

"I hope you have more of those, quite useful," Certan said.

"I do, I can make them. The ingredients are a little hard to get a hold of, but I have my sources." Lara tapped her nose and looked around innocently.

"I bet you do," Alrion said, laughing. They took a short meal break before heading out once more. As they rode, Alrion steered his horse over to join Certan.

"I was curious about the power you have. Where is it from?" Alrion said.

"It the power of the body. You all have it, but do not use it. It takes both physical and mental training to master it," Certan said.

"So, there's no reason I couldn't do that?" Alrion said.

"Theoretically, but I am not one of the four masters so I don't know all the secrets. I suspect however that your other power would make this task difficult, as you would need to essentially not use it at all."

"That makes sense. So, anybody could do that with the right training?"

"Or the right situation. Not as effectively or as controlled. There is a story shared with us, about a young mother whose son has been trapped under a fallen tree. There is nobody to help, and there are wolves circling in. What does she do?"

"Destroy the tree. Or prop it up with something else and get the boy out," Lara said.

"Impossible without the right tools or training. And there is no time for planning and execution. So, what she does is lift the tree and push it aside, then carry her son home. But how does she do it?"

"I don't know," Alrion said.

"Because her need is so strong, her body can perform the impossible. She does not know how it was done, and could not do it again when asked. But because it is her only choice, she can do it. So, it is with this. We train our bodies and acquire the knowledge of how they work, but we unlock the power with our minds. We use our wills," Certan said.

"You use your will to unlock the power in your body and direct it as you see fit?" Alrion said.

"Exactly. Only the four masters have ascended to the heights of control and passed the final test. It is known as the Vault of Silence."

"Vault of Silence, you mentioned it before. Is that what I described in my dream?"

"I believe so. If they allow you to undertake that test, then you can achieve the same mastery perhaps. But I do not know all the details. That is one reason it is known as such," Certan said.

"The silence part is also keeping the trial secret, huh?" Lara said.

"Exactly. I believe that the information shared about it is only to give the monks something to strive for."

"Sounds daunting," Alrion said.

"It should be. Much of what we do is masked in secrecy, and I am not sure how far down the path I was. But I don't think I was anywhere near ready for that trial." Certan had a downcast look again.

"And you just obliterated that tree with the instruction from your mind. That paints quite a picture," Alrion said. Those words hung in silence, and Alrion let his horse fall back in pace to be beside Lara.

"You'll be fine, don't forget you have us," she said.

"I won't. It's just such a huge mountain to climb. Anyway, that's a future problem. Let's just enjoy the ride," Alrion said.

The road started to incline upwards, slowly but surely. As they continued they started to see glimpses of the river. It was larger than Alrion expected, and seemed to move with speed.

"The bridge is up ahead," Certan said. As Alrion caught up he finally saw it. Built with wood, the bridge was not as impressive as Alrion expected. The main surface was a plain walkway. But it looked sturdy and was secured on each end by large columns and decorative elements. What really caught his attention however, was a single shape in the distance. It looked like a man, standing in the middle of the bridge.

"We have company," Lara said.

"Who is it?" Alrion said.

"I don't mean to alarm anyone, but I think it's a case of what, not who," Lara said.

"A Shade?"

"Likely," Certan said.

"See what your sword says," Lara said. Alrion pulled out his sword and examined the stone on the pommel. It was a light glow, but matched the colour exactly from when they last encountered a Shade.

"So, it is," Alrion said, tensing up without even realising. He dismounted and tied up his horse, signalling to the others to do the same.

13

AN OLD FRIEND

They approached the Shade carefully on foot, watching its movements.

"I don't like this. It's just waiting for us," Lara said.

"Something definitely seems different," Certan said.

"You're probably right, but we need to take the advantage. We are prepared, let's see if we can take it down before anything bad happens," Alrion said.

"Did you want to take the bridge out?" Lara said.

"No, I don't want to be looking over my shoulder for this thing. We finish it now." Alrion needed to do this right. He couldn't stand having another Shade hunting him down. For his peace of mind, he had to see it destroyed.

"Fine by me. I will wait on the edge of the bridge and begin my preparation. Be careful of the tight quarters." Certan knelt down before the bridge and started to meditate.

"It's still just standing there," Lara said.

"I know. But let's open the attack, we don't want Certan charging in without cover," Alrion said.

Lara nodded and pulled out a handful of daggers.

"Go!" Alrion whispered and started preparing his spells. As Lara threw her first salvo of daggers, Alrion hurled his force spells, focusing on the legs. He wanted to make the Shade unsteady on the bridge. Lara's daggers bounced harmlessly off the Shade, and it remained motionless. Alrion's spells also had no effect.

"My throwing daggers didn't work, I'll need some assistance," Lara said.

"Sure." Alrion couldn't understand why his other attacks had just failed to do anything, but he didn't have time to ponder it over. He instead changed his focus to supercharging the speed of Lara's daggers. They flew faster and harder directly at the Shade, who was still motionless.

Three daggers dug into the Shade's torso with the additional force provided by Alrion, but again the Shade didn't react.

"I don't like this," Lara said.

"I know. But Certan will be ready soon," Alrion said.

"Here we go again," Lara said, and prepared another round of daggers. Alrion prepared his spells and watched them fly, throwing twice as much force behind them. He was finding it easier to spot and catch the daggers with his force waves. The Shade made no attempt to dodge, and the daggers made a neat row just below the first three.

"Ready," Certan said, and Lara stepped forward to lob a crystal vial through the air. It smashed right before the Shade, throwing up a smokescreen. Certan rose swiftly and moved with incredible speed, as if he was flying along the ground. He disappeared into the smoke and Alrion heard the impact of Certan's attack.

"It connected!" Lara said.

"Definitely. I hope that did it." Alrion found the smoke screen a hindrance, unsure of what happened. He started to walk closer, and Lara joined him. As the smoke cleared they saw Certan kneeling before the Shade. It had been knocked back but otherwise appeared unharmed.

"What? That can't be," Lara said.

"I felt something strange happen. I can't describe it though," Alrion said. Suddenly the Shade reached out and grabbed Certan, drawing him close. Certan cried out in pain as the Shade spun him around and seemed to dig its fingers in.

"We. Meet. Again," Certan shouted, in harsh and disjointed words.

"What are you saying?" Alrion continued approaching his friend.

"You. Left. Me. For. Dead," Certan said.

Alrion stopped dead in his tracks.

"What is it?" Lara said.

"No. It can't be!" Alrion said.

"Yes! This. Is. What. Happens. When. You. Turn. A. Wizard. Further," Certan said.

"What is he talking about?" Lara said. Alrion looked closer at the face of the Shade, and saw the confirmation he was after.

"This Shade is Branthor. He's become something else. I don't know how, but he survived and he's morphed into some sort of monster. That's why none of our attacks worked on him," Alrion said.

"No!" Lara said, shocked.

"I. Did. Not. Expect. This. It. Is. New. But. I. Will. Conquer. This. Form," Certan said. The pauses in-between words had reduced, but it seemed hard for him to communicate.

"What do we do? We need to rescue Certan," Lara said.

"Let's see if we can just release him first, then together we can come up with something. I get the feeling that it's not completely in control, so we may have an opportunity," Alrion said.

"How do we do that?"

"Let's just grab him, I'll use my sword to sever the hand holding Certan back," Alrion said.

"Good, I'll come with you, I'll try and distract it," Lara said. The two of them carefully advanced, step by step. There was no further communication from the Shade via Certan.

"What do you want?" Alrion said.

"You. Know. You. Can. Still. Join. Me," Certan said.

"Why would he join a freak like you? You're an absolute monster. All you deserve is a sword through your heart!" Lara said to Branthor, lacing the words with as much spite and disdain as she could muster. Certan and Branthor pivoted to look at Lara. Branthor's face still seemed straight and emotionless, but Lara thought she could see the anger within it.

Alrion took the opportunity to draw his sword and empower his swing with additional speed and force. Before Branthor could react, Alrion sliced through the Shade's hand, freeing Certan. Lara reached out and grabbed Certan, dragging him away.

Branthor let out an unearthly scream, that seemed to come from the depths of the ground. Alrion helped Lara drag Certan back to safety. He looked back as they ran, and Branthor was motionless but still screaming.

Then there was silence. Lara and Certan collapsed just past the bridge, and Alrion stopped to look back. There was no movement. Then Branthor rose. He lashed out with his arms, the bridge starting to disintegrate around him. Branthor reached out but there was nothing to hold on to and he fell into the river.

Alrion leaned over, trying to see where Branthor had ended up, but there was no sign of the Shade. The river carried on, as if nothing had happened.

"Thank you for the rescue." Certan seemed to have recovered his senses.

"Are you alright?" Alrion said.

"I believe so. I felt like a puppet at the hands of a child." Certan had a distasteful look on his face. "He does not seem in full control of his new form."

"I can believe that. But he seems almost indestructible," Lara said.

"He might be. My spells had no effect. Whatever he is, he is more than a normal Shade. And what he just did then, I don't think that was a physical attack. I think he accessed some of his Spark," Alrion said.

"An almost invulnerable monster with magical powers, now that's a disaster!" Lara said.

"He may never regain control, we don't know," Certan said.

"Regardless, we need to be ready next time we encounter him. We can't always rely on him destroying a bridge and floating away," Alrion said.

"How do you think he found us?" Lara said.

"It has to be deduction. He sent the Shade to confront us at Vainbly, and came here himself. It is the main alternate route, isn't it?" Lara said.

"That would mean he either knows where we are headed, is coordinating his attacks or maybe even both," Alrion said.

"He drank from the Pool of Knowledge too, didn't he?" Lara said.

"Yes, even before I did."

"Then he may have all the same information. Maybe he also had the vision about the monks?"

"If he did, we are in grave danger. We must get there before he has a chance," Certan said.

"Was it absolutely critical that we cross the bridge?" Alrion said, looking out. The bridge was completely destroyed, with only remnants hanging from either side.

"It's ideal. Let's find a way down and see if there's another way to cross." Certan stood up by himself, and tested his legs.

"Everything ok there?" Lara said.

"Yes, I'll be fine. Need to stick to normal activity levels for the next day though," Certan said.

"I can't promise anything," Alrion said, trying to make a joke out of it. Certan looked at him and didn't react.

"Let's try over here," Lara said, pointing at a mostly overgrown track. She took the lead and the others followed.

"There's no way we can get the horses down there," Alrion said.

"We'll have to leave them. I'll just untie them so they can go forage," Lara said. As she darted off Alrion inspected the track from closer. It appeared to be an old path, that was overgrown and worn down by the elements and time.

"Looks like it hadn't been used in a long time," Certan said.

"No need with the bridge," Lara said, returning.

"I'll miss those horses, we made great time," Alrion said, looking back, trying to catch a glimpse of them.

"They will survive. To be honest, I am more comfortable on my own feet. Others will be along and find them soon enough," Certan said, starting on the path and stepping over a slippery stone. The group had to walk slowly and carefully, as the path was quite steep and the growth had to be continually pushed back just to make progress. Alrion almost tripped and lost his balance several times, but he held on and hoped that his friends didn't notice.

After an hour, they had managed to find their way down to the bank of the river.

"It looks quite swift, but I can't offer much wisdom here. I grew up in and around the desert," Certan said.

"I'll take this one, don't worry." Lara started to wade into the river, one step at a time. After a few steps, she wobbled then quickly regained her balance. Heading straight back she kicked her legs out to try and shake off some of the excess water.

"What do you think?" Alrion said.

"Too dangerous to cross safely, although we could manage it. But I had a better idea." Lara had a wicked smile which was slowly breaking out.

"Why does that make me nervous?" Alrion said.

"No reason. You're the one that takes all the foolish risks around here," Lara said looking around.

"She's right you know," Certan said.

"Fine. What is it?" Alrion said.

"Why fight the river, when we can use it to our advantage. Go with the flow as it were," Lara said.

"If you're thinking what I think you are, Certan is going to be more nervous than with the horses," Alrion said.

GOING WITH THE FLOW

Lara inspected some of the plants by the shore. She selected a few samples, and sliced the long tendrils with her dagger.

"This will work for a short-term solution," she said.

"We're going to a build a boat of some kind?" Alrion said.

"More like a raft. There's plenty of trees around, and you and Certan are handy at knocking them around."

"For now, he can do the knocking," Certan said. The monk didn't even look up when speaking, he was so focused on his recovery.

"I'm on it," Alrion said.

Lara watched him concentrate, a comical expression on his face. She suppressed a laugh, and watched carefully. After a pause, she heard a noise nearby and watched a branch fall to the ground. Alrion ran over and inspected the fallen limb, unbridled glee in his steps. Lara joined him and looked for herself. The cut was precise and perfect.

"You could be in for a new career as a carpenter," she said.

"I don't think my father would approve."

"I guess he would rather you be a blacksmith?"

"With the right care and focus, I could probably work the metal with spells instead. But I think the time for that has passed." Alrion broke eye contact with her.

"You never know," Lara said, trying to keep things light. Under her direction Alrion cut down the nearest trees, and cut the trunk and branches to her specifications. Lara prepared the ropes by binding together the strands from the plants.

Certan joined them at this point and lashed the logs together, under Lara's watchful eye. It took longer that she had expected, but Lara stepped back and saw what looked like a serviceable raft.

"Not my finest work, but it should float," she said.

"Are you sure?" Certan said.

"Of course, let's go test it." Lara identified an appropriate spot on the bank and pointed it out. The three of them pushed it into the water, and Lara waded in further. While Certan and Alrion steadied it, she climbed on.

"Watch this." Lara jumped up and down on the raft. It rocked a little, and took on some water, but kept its buoyancy.

"I'm satisfied, please don't do that again," Certan said. Alrion couldn't help laughing. He climbed on next and helped Certan onboard.

"Can you shove us off?" Lara said to Alrion. He held on tightly to the raft and leaned into it. The raft lurched away, almost flipping over. But Certan and Lara were able to scramble and balance it out, then the raft was caught in the river's flow.

"And now we wait," Lara said, sitting back, and looking very satisfied with herself. The countryside was going past at a reasonable rate.

"I must say I'm impressed. We seem to be going quite quickly. Is this a more direct route?" Alrion said.

"I believe so, what do you think Certan?" Lara said.

"Probably. The benefit is also that we will continue overnight. Perhaps we should take turns sleeping?" he said.

"Definitely. This isn't exactly the safest vessel," Lara said with a laugh.

"Have you given her a name, Captain?" Alrion said.

"Her?" Lara said.

"I thought all ships had female names."

"Only in the books. But for you, sure. Let's name her Lady Grace after her poise and elegance," Lara said. Alrion burst out laughing again. Even Certan cracked a smile.

"Is that an aspirational name?" Alrion said.

"No, she is exceptionally graceful already. Look at how she navigates these dark and stormy waters," Lara said with a straight face.

"Can't argue with that. And you even got Certan to smile. He's not been this jovial since we first met him."

"It was fuelled by alcohol then, as you know," Certan said.

"How do you feel now?" Lara said.

"Not quite myself yet. I feel as if life has been muted. Before I was in a haze of loud sounds, bright colours, and ridiculous antics. Now that they have been stripped away, things seem duller than they should. I know it's just perception, but it may take time to readjust."

"How long did you live like that?" Alrion said.

"It must have been a few years. I am amazed that I didn't completely lose my skills and conditioning. I can't explain it."

"And that all stemmed from one event?"

"Yes, sadly. It was like the flood gates opened and I was swept away. I relinquished control, so I could pretend I had no responsibility over my actions. But that is not true, I was just hiding away."

"Do you miss it?"

"The mind and the body still ache for it. I find myself thirsty despite having drunk lots of water. It might be a while before that passes. But it wasn't real. It was a long dream with no substance, and I don't want to lose myself like that again." Certan looked out over the river, not really focusing on anything in particular.

"We'll help you with that, and I'll continue trying to get you to crack a smile," Lara said.

"Sounds fine to me," Certan said.

"Good, good," Alrion said, watching the terrain fly past. They rode the river in silence for a time, each lost in their own thoughts. Certan broke the silence abruptly.

"I've been watching our progress, and I had a good idea," he said.

"What is it?" Alrion said.

"It would help to provide you with some training in times like this, so that you might be better prepared for your trial."

"What did you have in mind?"

"I must admit I know little of magic. But there is a certain visualisation and mental focus, right?"

"Yes. When I prepare a force spell, I am visualising what will happen, applying my will, then fuelling the spell with my internal force or Spark."

"Good. Then we can do an exercise to help you train your will." Certan peeled off a sliver of wood from their raft and tossed it onto the river. It landed on the water, but instead of bobbing along the surface, it rose up and floated just above the water.

"That's odd," Lara said. Whatever it was looked like magic to her.

"Yes, and it's not hovering in place. Somehow, it's still moving with the water just floating at a fixed height above. Are you doing that with your mind?" Alrion said.

"Yes. Now you try," Certan said. Alrion looked at the sliver of wood, then worked on peeling off another one. He tossed it off the raft, and it bobbed on the water as expected.

"Try harder," Certan said. Alrion went silent. Lara watched him with interest. The young wizard's eyes squinted increasingly. Eventually the tiny piece of wood lifted up and floated alongside Certan's piece and Alrion let out a loud breath.

"There!" Alrion said.

"It's not the same," Lara said. Alrion's sliver of wood seemed motionless, yet Certan's seemed to go with the flow of the river.

"You have achieved an appropriate result, but not mastered the process. Keep trying," Certan said. Alrion kept it up, and soon sweat dripped down his face. While he was still trying Certan spoke up again.

"Lara, why don't you try it," he said.

"Me?"

"Of course. It's using your mind, there's no magic involved. Alrion has an advantage in that he has been practising the visualisation more, but otherwise there's no difference," Certan said.

"Watch out, I'm going to beat you." Lara prepared a sliver of wood of her own and threw it next to the two others. It plopped into the water and floated along.

"Not like that you won't," Alrion said.

Lara scowled at him, and returned to her concentration. She knew how to focus herself, surely this piece of wood wouldn't mind falling in line. Little by little it began to rock from side to side, then floated slowly up to match Alrion's piece.

"See!" Lara said.

"Well done. I'm still winning though," Certan said. Neither Lara nor Alrion could seem to make their piece move the same way as Certan's.

The competition continued in the same fashion for a while without any change. Alrion and Lara seemed to be quite tired from the effort, but Certan was relaxed and confident.

"I think it's time to mix things up," he said. He leaned over and whispered something into Lara's ear.

"Really?" Lara said with interest, and refocused on her tiny wood shaving. She tried harder and harder, then just sat back. Her piece of wood was moving in concert with Certan's.

"Looks like I did it. How's things over there Alrion?" Lara said. Alrion's piece was the same, but looked stilted and forced in comparison to the other two.

"That's not fair, you told her the trick," Alrion said.

"No, I gave her a hint. But you need to discover it for yourself," Certan said. Alrion just huffed at them both and went back to his concentration. After some intense focus his piece of wood moved more, mimicking the flow of the water.

"Nice try, but you're faking it. It's unrealistic," Certan said. Alrion gritted his teeth and kept trying to work even harder. Finally, something snapped. He relaxed and sat back, losing the intense look on his face as if he had given up. But now his piece was in sync with the other two.

"I don't understand," Alrion said.

"Give it a minute," Certan said. Alrion look thoughtful.

I hope he gets it.

"Hang on. I'm not controlling the piece of wood, but I am maintaining the belief that it must float above the water," Alrion said.

"Exactly. Beliefs are powerful things. See the difference between forcefully propping up the wood shaving, and changing your belief to alter its behaviour?" Certan said.

"Wow. So how much can you do with this?" Alrion said.

"Everything. You are only limited by the strength of your will. Some things will be harder to alter than others, and knowledge of the way the world functions does make things easier," Certan said.

"So, anyone could do this. Why aren't they?" Lara said.

"Firstly, they don't believe it is possible. Very few would accidentally find a way to do this. Secondly, a strong will is required. The two of you have already gone through many trials, so you are better qualified to do it," Certan said.

"Incredible. I am starting to understand how you can do what you do," Alrion said.

"Excellent. This class is over. But let's see how long we can keep our tiny wood shavings floating," Certan said, grinning at them.

"You're on," Lara said.

"I'll win this, you just watch," Alrion said.

"You know, you're a pretty good teacher," Lara said to Certan. She was impressed at the ease with which he had gotten them to succeed.

"Thank you, I hadn't considered that."

"You're probably not as far behind in your monk training as you think," Alrion said.

"Perhaps, but it may be for nothing. They may not accept me back."

"If they're as wise as you say, they definitely will," Alrion said.

"Shush, I need to concentrate," Lara said. The competition wasn't over after all, and she had to win.

"Fair enough," Alrion said.

Hours later, Certan let his wood shaving gently drop to the surface of the water.

"You could have kept that up all day," Lara said, accusing Certan.

"Of course."

"Did you really think you would beat him?" Alrion said.

"Well, I beat you," Lara said. Alrion didn't reply.

"I think we may be nearing our destination," Certan said. In the distance they could see walls, indicating a city of some kind.

"I wonder if we will find my parents there," Alrion said.

"Of course." Lara scanned the distance, as if she were able to see them. She had a bad feeling, as though there were more troubles ahead. But she kept that to herself.

15

INVESTIGATION

Vincent urged the horse to go faster. Now they were on the open road, he wanted to travel as quickly as possible. Celes did the same, pulling even with him.

"This reminds me of the old days," she said, a glint of mischief in her eyes.

"It sure does. We were so carefree back then," Vincent said, his voice taking a heavier tone.

"Yes, well these are serious times I admit. But I know I'm ready for another adventure. Aren't you?"

"Yes and no. I've been dreading this."

"Because you knew that Alrion may be a wizard?"

"Yes, and I knew that it would not be an easy life, given what my father accomplished."

"He will rise to it, he already has. You've taught him well," Celes said, reaching out to place a hand on Vincent's shoulder.

"We both have. Now we just need to support him." Vincent placed his hand over his wife's.

"And we are. What do you expect us to find out there?" Celes said, taking her hand back.

"We have been tracked the whole way. The only explanation is that Branthor built a network of followers. Regardless of whether Branthor is alive or not, we still have to deal with that. I don't believe that Shade attack was random."

"I think you're right. Just as well you have the world's best thief with you," Celes said.

"World's best? I'd like to see the finalists for that prize lined up. That would be a sight," Vincent said.

"Yes, maybe even some contenders that we don't know about."

"I would hope so, the world has changed a lot in the last twenty years or so that we've been hidden away," Vincent said.

The extent of the changes was evident, even in the empty stretch of road they were riding down.

"So how do we pinpoint these followers? Any tricks we can use?" Celes said.

"I don't know of any ways to detect Tainted Ones, other than that diamond we gave to Alrion. I think we will need to be observant and do an investigation. Who would you start with?"

"Guards and officials," Celes said.

"Why?"

"If you want to track people and have access to information, that's the best way. I'd say if we can find Tainted Ones in official posts, they will be connected to Branthor."

"Sounds reasonable to me. I'll be the muscle, and you can be the brains," Vincent said.

"So, the usual," Celes said with a smirk. Vincent shook his head gently and laughed.

"The usual then," Vincent said.

The city gates of Plynth loomed large, yet appeared unchanged. The black metal gate was as imposing as ever, and the stone walls looked just as ancient as Vincent remembered.

"Are there more guard towers now?" Vincent said.

"I think so. Lots more guards too," Celes said, looking around.

"Seems like a lot more security overall," Vincent said.

"Definitely. Take a look at her," Celes said, directing Vincent to a guard. The woman was referring to a drawing and questioning a young couple trying to enter the city.

"They're looking for someone," Vincent said.

"Exactly. Why don't you hang back and I'll investigate?" Celes said. She threw her reins at Vincent and hopped off the horse. Within moments she had disappeared into the crowd.

"There she goes," Vincent said to himself. After a moment, he stopped trying to look for her, and shuffled off the main road with the two horses.

Celes felt a thrill from the intrigue and curiosity of the situation. She had to get a look at whoever they were after, and needed to do so without revealing herself in a crowded thoroughfare.

Good exercise as a refresher.

As she approached the guard, Celes tried to blend in with some other travellers. She continued walking, and leaned in to try and catch some of the conversation.

"You aren't listening to me. You are a young couple and look almost exactly like the ones I have here," the female guard said.

"It's a passing resemblance at best. What does that have to do this us?" the young man said. He was quite agitated and trying to contain himself but slowly failing.

"I can't let you in, it's too much of a risk. What I can do though is take you into a holding area, where you can be interviewed by someone else. If that passes, we will let you in," the guard said.

"Just do it, we need to enter the city and they will discover soon enough that we aren't who they are looking for," the young woman said to her companion.

"Fine, but I think this is ridiculous," the man said, trying to get the last word in. The female guard nodded.

"Yes, I appreciate your frustration. This way please," she said, leading them into a side passage off the main gate. As she rolled up the drawing Celes managed to get a quick glance at it. Then she reversed direction and made her way back to Vincent.

"So?" he said.

"Not good. They're holding that young couple for a further interview because of their likeness to a drawing."

"And the drawing looks like?"

"Alrion and Lara." She could see Vincent's expression drop.

"I had feared that."

"Yes, it's not subtle at all." Celes was worried by the brashness of their actions. How far had they infiltrated?

"Do you think that guard is in on it?"

"Probably not. But I would suggest that whoever comes to interview the couple will be," Celes said.

"Sounds logical. I guess we need to infiltrate that guard post then," Vincent said.

"Exactly, and you're going to help."

"Of course, and I'm sure you have a plan already." Vincent had a weariness to his voice.

"Yes, I do. Let's head over to the armourer that makes the guard uniforms. You can find that out, right?" Celes said.

"I'm sure I can. Let's get to it," Vincent said. Celes winked at Vincent then expertly leapt back into the saddle. "I don't know how you can still do that," he said, chuckling.

"I'm allowed to have a few secrets of my own," Celes said.

"Fair enough. I won't ask." Together they rode through the gates, avoiding any unwanted attention.

"At least they're not looking for us," Celes said.

"Yet."

"Yet?"

"After whatever you are going to pull off today, they most certainly are going to," Vincent said.

"Not necessarily," Celes said, her voice trailing off. But they both knew that there was little chance that their investigation would go unnoticed.

~

Vincent introduced himself to the first blacksmith that they encountered, and steered the conversation around to who did the guard uniforms.

"Oh, that's most likely John down the hill. Why?" the blacksmith said.

"Well I'm looking for work, and I'm over making household implements. I'd like to do something more interesting," Vincent said.

"After a few of those, I doubt you'd find it interesting. But fair enough. I could use an extra hand, let me know if you're interested. Or maybe see me after you get bored," the blacksmith said.

"Definitely. Thanks for the help." Vincent left the workshop and met Celes back on the street.

"You found it alright?" she said.

"Yes, it should be just down this hill. Man named John."

"See! I told you."

"You did indeed. What's the plan?"

"You just distract the blacksmith and I'll take care of the rest," Celes said.

"As you wish." Vincent was curious to see what she would do. The guard armour was not fully plated, but it would be heavy and noisy.

There was only one blacksmith at the bottom of the hill, and Vincent approached him directly.

"John, is it?" Vincent said.

"Yes, who is asking?"

"My name is Will. I'm interested in some blacksmithing work, and I heard that you work on the guard uniforms."

"That's right. Why are you interested in that?" John said. He was looking at Vincent with suspicion.

"I've been working in a small town so long, there's only so many knives, and horse shoes and other boring items that I can make. I thought the work you do might have a bit more sophistication to it," Vincent said.

"You're right about one thing, it is more sophisticated. But it's still boring. Just a different kind," John said.

"A change is as good as a journey, so they say," Vincent said.

"All the same, I don't think I can afford to bring on more help, not with what they pay for these," John said.

"Do you mind if I work with you for free then? I could learn some new skills, you could get some free labour and we can both profit before I move on," Vincent could see John's mind ticking over, considering the pros and cons.

"I could use the help. But you should understand that I have an exclusive contract for these, it will do you no good trying to set up shop here," John said.

"I wouldn't dream of it. I can see you are busy today, could I get a quick tour then we start proper tomorrow?" Vincent said.

"I will need to structure my day differently, so that works for me. Come this way." John waved at Vincent and disappeared further into the workshop.

~

Celes observed the conversation and smiled.

Thanks for the help my dear husband. Once the two men had disappeared she snuck into the workshop looking for a suitable uniform. She spotted one that looked like it had just been completed.

No, too obvious. She continued the search, locating a temporary store nearby.

"This will work," Celes said to herself. Not everything was there, but the main elements were. It wouldn't too difficult to complete the look herself. Once she had extracted the chest pieces and helmet, she paused to listen out. She could hear voices in the distance, but wasn't sure if they were coming closer.

"It's a noisy place, I'll just get going," she told herself. She found a bundle of leather and wrapped up the pieces within it, and left the shop as quickly as she could. Once she was out the door she slowed her pace to look less suspicious, then found a quiet alley nearby to rest.

After a few minutes, she heard footsteps and readied herself.

"It's just me," Vincent said as he turned the corner. He saw Celes ready to pounce. She visibly relaxed and stepped aside to show off her prize.

"Nice work. Clearly, I bought you enough time," Vincent said.

"It was a charming gesture, but you didn't need to."

"Are you going to try this on now?"

"Yes, if you'll assist," she said. Vincent looked out for passers-by, and helped Celes into the outfit.

"You'll need a white tunic to match," he said.

"I know, I spotted a stall not far from here. Would you mind?"

"No, I'll be right back," Vincent quickly left and returned shortly, showing Celes the clothing.

"Approved," she said, and they adjusted her outfit to allow her to put it on.

"How do I look?" Celes said.

"Like an unusually attractive guard," Vincent said.

"Right answer."

"Just try not and get it too dirty, you need to return it tonight," Vincent said.

"Why?"

"I'm going to work there for a few days."

"Whatever for?"

"I could learn a thing or two from John, and it gives us a reason to be here. I thought it would help us blend in." Celes had to admit that he made sense.

"That would be useful, I guess I'll have to be extra careful then," she said, winking at Vincent.

"What's the plan?" he said. She leaned in close and whispered to him for a full minute.

"I stand around and bail you out if you need help?" Vincent said.

"Exactly," she said and waved goodbye.

"Good luck," Vincent said, and watched her leave.

Celes walked down the street with confidence. She had to assume the role of the guard perfectly. The guards belonged here, and were respected and obeyed. So, she acted like she owned the place.

She strode into the guard block without even pausing. As another guard passed by Celes nodded her head, and the guard did the same.

"Now to find that interview room," Celes said to herself. The building was one long corridor, with many rooms off either side.

This must be built alongside the city walls. She noticed that one door in the distance had a guard posted outside. That was promising. Celes walked up to the door and addressed the guard.

"Is this the couple that are awaiting questioning?" she said.

"Yes. Are you the examiner?" the guard said.

"No, I'm here to relieve you as the examiner has been delayed," Celes said.

"Oh, that's unusual. Are you sure?"

"Yes, they aren't sure how long it will take and you're needed back on patrol," Celes said.

"Great, thanks for letting me know," the guard said and left the post.

This is too easy, Celes thought. She opened the door and stepped inside. The young couple were seated at a table, but the rest of the room was empty. They looked up at her expectantly.

"Sorry, I am not your examiner. Just checking in on you. One should be on the way soon," Celes said.

"Fine," the man said, and did not engage in any further questions. Celes stepped back outside and stood just as the previous guard had. Now it was time to wait.

After an hour or two, and many guards passing back and forth, she noticed someone different walking down the corridor. It was a male guard, but he was wearing a black cloak with white trim.

He looks different, I must keep an eye on him. The guard walked briskly, then stopped suddenly in front of the door.

"The couple awaiting questioning are inside?" the guard said. His speech was precise and calculated.

"Yes," Celes said, thinking it best to be as brief as possible.

"You are dismissed," the guard said, waving her away.

"Yes sir," she said, and turned to leave. After she had taken a few steps she heard the door open and close. She didn't have a good feeling about him, and the sound of the lock clanking shut was chilling to her ears.

Celes wasn't sure what to do. She had identified the examiner, but was fearful for the couple. It wasn't based on anything, but she just didn't feel right. So, she decided to circle around and find another way to access that room.

Turning around, Celes walked past the room and listened out. She didn't hear anything. Continuing on, she located the next door and entered it. It was another holding cell, but was empty. It looked identical to the one she had already seen.

"That's a start," Celes said to herself. She examined the room to look for any strange designs or flaws in the construction that would allow her to access or hear from the adjoining room. The stone was solid, and ceiling was well-constructed. But she did notice a smaller stone slightly out of place near the floor. She carefully lowered herself to the ground, and manipulated the stone with her hand. Very slowly it moved. With some persistence, she was able to remove it.

There was a gap behind the stone, and another stone on the other side for the adjoining room. She wouldn't be able to budge the other stone, but she hoped that it might be able to be moved. She reached into the hole, but couldn't touch the other stone. She used a dagger instead, levering it just enough to dislodge it. This created a passage for the air to travel between the rooms. Now she just had to try and listen in.

"I can see immediately that the two of you are not who we are looking for," a male voice said. Celes assumed that it was the examiner.

"Good. Can we go?" the young man said.

"Not quite yet. There seems to be a complication," the examiner said.

"What's going on? We have been completely cooperative through all this," the young woman said.

"You've been caught up in something by mistake. But unfortunately, that means that you need to be dealt with. Perhaps after I deal with the person listening in on this conversation," the examiner said. Celes heard footsteps approaching her.

16

DARK TIDINGS

Celes knew that somehow, she had been detected. She pushed up quickly and considered her options. She couldn't wait for him to find her, she had to be aggressive and take him off guard. She wouldn't have the element of surprise, but he might not expect her to be so bold.

She headed for the door immediately and looked out into the corridor. There was nobody.

"This is it," Celes told herself, and ran over to the holding cell next to her. She tried to minimise the noise, but she maintained her speed. The examiner seemed confident, she had to try and exploit that. As she reached the door she heard a scream from within. Celes burst through and assessed the situation.

The examiner was holding the young woman hostage with a knife to her throat.

"Well hello, lovely of you to join us," he said to Celes.

"This is against regulation, why are you doing this?" Celes said.

"What would you know of regulations, you're not a real guard," he said.

"Who are you really?" Celes countered.

"I'm the one asking the questions here, you're not really in a place to be making demands," the examiner said. He pointed to an empty chair.

"Take a seat," he said. Celes considered the request, then complied.

I need to keep him thinking he is in control. Then I can use an opening.

"You look somehow familiar, but I can't pick it," the examiner said.

"We've never met before, I wouldn't forget that face," Celes said. The examiner's features were not extraordinary, but he had a deep black scar on his forehead.

"You mean this? It's a souvenir from my encounter with some rather nasty Blighters. Such bothersome creatures, but useful with the right motivation and stimulation," he said.

"You're tainted then. You admit it?"

"Yes, there's no harm in doing that. None of you will leave this room alive," the examiner said. The young man started to yell in protest but an icy look from the examiner silenced him.

"What do I call you?" Celes said.

"You can call me Brine. Not that it matters really." He dismissed her with his eyes, looking elsewhere.

"Brine, interesting name. So, have you been tainted long?" Celes said.

"I said I was doing the interrogation here," Brine said, tightening his grip on the young woman. She whimpered as the knife edged closer.

"Ask away," Celes said. There was not yet an opening that was safe.

"Let's begin with your name. What is it?"

"Celes."

"Good, that wasn't hard, was it? Why were you spying on this couple?" Brine said. Celes decided that she would answer truthfully, it would help her later when the tables were turned and she was trying to get information from him.

"I noticed that they were stopped for looking like people I know. I wanted to see who was asking. Now my fears are confirmed."

"Oh, this is interesting. I want to hear more." Brine half turned to face her.

"I can't concentrate properly seeing that woman so distressed," Celes said, trying her luck.

"Naughty, naughty. Trying to convince me to let her go when you drop the juicy information? So amateur. But you know what, I'll let you have this one." Brine withdrew the knife from the young woman and shoved her into the corner violently. Her husband ran over and comforted her. "You two stay there for now, if you become a distraction I'll deal with you permanently." He turned his attention back to Celes. "So, can you talk now?"

"Yes, I can. I have a question though, what makes you so confident? You're just a man who is tainted. You don't have any special powers," she said.

"Maybe I do, maybe I don't. But I suggest you answer my questions and this will go smoother for everyone. You don't want to make me angry," Brine twirled the knife in his hand to ensure his words had the correct impact.

"I'd need to see the sketch again, but it looked like my son." Celes watched Brine's reaction carefully.

His eyes lit up in interest. "Take as close a look as you want," he said. He removed a rolled-up parchment from his cloak and threw it at her. Celes unrolled it and studied the picture. It was a very good sketch, of Alrion and Lara. Celes adjusted her seated position, and loosened one of the knives strapped to her foot.

"There's no doubt about it. That's my son. Why are you looking for him?" Celes said.

"Never you mind, the important thing is, where is he?" Brine said. He started to walk over, licking his lips. It was like he could taste the information, and he wanted more. Celes saw the opportunity and took it. She used her leg to fling the loosened knife at Brine's leg.

"What?" he cried at is it made impact, and Celes used the opportunity to jump up onto the table and vault off it, launching herself at Brine. He didn't notice in time, and all he could do was throw up his hands. They landed on the ground, Celes with a knife at Brine's throat, and Brine using all his strength to hold it at bay.

"I can do this all day, and time is not on your side," Brine said.

"Why is that?"

"I have reinforcements coming. Reinforcements of the Blighter variety."

"If you do that you'll blow your cover." Celes knew she had to dissuade him from doing that. If it were at all possible.

"Not if there's no witnesses. It'll be so tragic," Brine said.

Celes banged her right boot on the ground and a small blade popped out. She used that to kick Brine's left leg. He cried out in pain, and Celes used that moment to overpower him and flip him over. In seconds, he was face down on the floor with his arms pinned behind him.

"You can't possibly escape," Brine said.

"Watch me." Celes pushed harder and Brine stopped struggling. She quickly extracted a short rope and bound his hands.

"Are you alright? Run for it," Celes said to the young couple. They looked bewildered, but Celes's speech seemed to snap them out of it. The young man helped his wife up and they ran to the door.

"They're coming," Brine said, in a sing-song way.

"Get up," Celes said, kicking Brine in the small of the back and dragging him up. He complied and stood shakily.

"This leg injury is going to slow me down," he said.

"You'll live. We're leaving." Celes shoved him closer to the door but kept a knife pressed at his back.

"On the double," Brine said, mocking her. They entered the corridor and Celes could hear commotion from one end.

"I told you they're coming," Brine said.

"This way," Celes said, pushing her prisoner in the opposite direction. He began walking and Celes stayed close behind. She could hear the noises of conflict getting louder and louder.

"Would you mind if I had a rest?" Brine said. He was practically laughing, and was struggling to contain himself.

"Yes, keep moving." Celes really hoped that there was an exit at the end of the corridor, she hadn't scouted that far ahead.

"They're inside! To arms!" a male voice shouted. Celes didn't even turn around, she just pressed on and forced Brine to increase his pace. She could see the sweat forming on his dark locks, either walking with that injury or something else was causing his quite a bit of exertion. As they reached the door at the end of the corridor, Celes pushed Brine to the side and kicked the door open. The last rays of daylight peeked in, and Celes felt relief.

There was a small training area before them, and a path.

"Keep moving," Celes said, pushing Brine out the door. They shuffled slowly through the yard, Celes looking back to see if they had company. Nothing yet. As they reached the path, she could see that it led to a main street. "Almost there," she said. Just then she heard another scream, and watched a hapless guard be overwhelmed by Blighters. He fell to their attacks and they started to pour out from the compound. Celes pressed on even faster, Brine almost fell instantly due to the shove.

"Oh, who might you be?" Brine said. He stopped completely, looking at a man on the path. The man stepped forward and punched Brine in the face. He fell in a heap instantly.

"I wanted to do that for a while, but I don't have the strength to carry him," Celes said.

"Happy to assist. I think we better make a move." Vincent reached down and picked up Brine, slinging him over his shoulder.

"I don't know how you made it here but I don't care. Can you move with him?" Celes said.

"Fast enough. Do you think they can track us?" he said.

"No idea, let's just get some distance between us." Celes put her knife away and started to run.

Vincent did his best to keep up, and they pushed for the main street. The Blighters seemed distracted, and weren't sure where to go.

Celes and Vincent ducked off the main street and took any available lanes. After ten solid minutes, they slowed and took a breath.

"Any sign of them?" Vincent said.

"I don't think so." Celes glanced around, but the streets looked empty. She let some of the tension go.

"Good, let's take it a bit easier from here."

"Where will we go?"

"John gave me keys to a place we can stay. Let's start there," Vincent said.

"Great, take us away." Celes looked back once more, but couldn't see or hear any Blighters.

"They seemed to lose the trail when you knocked him out," Celes said.

"I doubt it's a coincidence. He's tainted, right?"

"Yes, he admitted it, even seemed proud of the fact."

"Crazy. Well let's get him back so we can ask him more. However, we need to be comfortable with the possibility that he can call more of them upon us." Vincent upped his speed and caught up with Celes.

They arrived at the tiny house within minutes. It was surrounded by what looked like an abandoned workshop.

"This it is. He runs a few jobs through here when he needs extra hands, and they stay here. It should work well," Vincent said.

"At least we will have some privacy," Celes said. They entered the house and Celes located a chair. Vincent plonked Brine down, then bound his feet to the chair.

"That should hold him, let's wake him up," Vincent said.

"Not just yet, let me find something." Celes rifled through her things and found a small vial. She showed it to Vincent.

"What is that?" he said.

"It's a serum that should keep him talking. Hopefully it still works. I used to use them all the time to ease key information out of people," Celes said.

"I thought you just got them drunk."

"This works better and, sometimes they work well together. Let's see what he has to say," Celes said. Vincent shook Brine a little until the man began to show signs of consciousness.

"Where am I?" Brine asked. Once his vision improved he saw Celes and Vincent standing in front of him.

"Right, I was knocked out. Nice punch there," Brine said, nodding at Vincent.

"We have some questions. Drink this." Celes shoved the vial into Brine's mouth and he swallowed it without question.

"You probably didn't need that, but it doesn't hurt. Does it?" Brine said.

"No, you won't feel anything," Celes said.

"Good. My mind feels very fuzzy though. What did you want to know anyway?"

"Why are you after this couple," Celes said, showing Brine the drawing he had tossed to her earlier. Vincent sneaked a peek at it too, and noticed the perfect likeness for Alrion and Lara.

"Just following orders. They're to be found," Brine said.

"Whose orders?" Vincent said.

"Wraith." Brine squirmed after he said it, as if he were trying to retract the words.

"Never heard of him," Vincent said.

"He's a new player, at least in this form." Brine seemed surprised that he had said that. "Looks like your vile concoction is working."

"Good. Why does Wraith want these two?" Celes said.

"He didn't say, but then again I never asked. I guess they are a problem for him?" Brine said.

"How do you communicate with him? Do you meet somewhere?" Vincent said.

"Oh, I met him once, not that I had to really. I think he wanted to impress us, so he made an appearance. No, we talk up here," Brine said, tapping his head.

"You can communicate via thoughts?" Vincent said, surprised.

"You don't know anything, do you? How do you think I called all those Blighters before? We're all linked. Everything you have told me about yourselves, I have passed on," Brine said, quite pleased with himself.

"To who?" Celes said.

"Everyone who is tapped in. All those who are tainted can access the channel. It's like a river of consciousness that we all share. The more powerful can broadcast their message and rise above other chatter," Brine said.

"I see," Vincent said, starting to pace around the room.

"Tell me more about Wraith. What does he look like?" Celes said.

"Like a Shade," Brine said.

"A Shade? He's a Shade?" Vincent said.

"Yes, believe it or not. He's a strange one. But he is mighty powerful so we listen, yes we do."

"Did he have a name before he was turned?" Vincent said.

"Yes," Brine said. He seemed to be holding back.

"What is it?" Celes said. Brine started to twitch, like something was affecting him. He started to have trouble breathing.

"What is it?" Vincent said, grabbing Brine by the coat.

"B...Branthor," Brine said, before collapsing down in the chair. Vincent stepped back, surprised at the response. He noticed that Brine didn't seem to be breathing, so leaned in close to examine him closer.

"He's dead. I don't believe it," Vincent said.

"How?" Celes felt panicked.

"Not sure, maybe it was this psychic link they seem to have. If that's the case, it means Branthor is on to us."

"It means he always has been."

"What about Alrion? Before that we must think. It's not safe here."

"I'll go on the lookout. If they try and enter tonight I'll find them."

"Good. Why don't you change out of the guard uniform before you go? I'll take care of that and figure out what to do with Brine," Vincent said.

Their day had taken a vastly darker turn.

17

DENIED ENTRY

Lara skilfully guided her companions in steering their makeshift raft towards a safe landing spot. There was a low embankment with a lot of mud, perfect for a solid dock.

"Lean more this side, paddle faster," she shouted. Alrion and Certan did their best, still somewhat confused by her angry and rapid instructions.

"Easy, easy, there," Lara said. The raft shuddered with a quick contact with the bank, but stopped completely.

"Not bad for her maiden voyage," Lara said.

"I'd go again," Alrion said.

"It was definitely a learning experience," Certan said. Lara wasn't sure if Certan was too keen on their little river excursion. But he had been a good sport. And they had made good time.

"Do you think we can reach the city gates before nightfall?" Alrion said.

"Plynth isn't that far, we should be able to. But I'm not an expert on this area, it depends on how close we landed," Lara said.

"Either way, I don't think such a thing as nightfall will be able to stop us," Certan said, looking at Lara.

"You're right, I can get us in anywhere, anytime. Provided we can find our way back onto the main path," she said, picking her way between trees and large shrubs. They were in a heavily wooded area, with no sign of any trails or paths.

After an hour of uncertain heading, they found what looked like a minor path.

"This has got to be it, let's follow it," Lara said.

"Fine by me, it's the only thing even slightly resembling a path around here," Alrion said. Certan didn't comment, just followed quietly.

"Everything alright back there?" Lara said.

"Of course, don't mind my quietness. I'm not usually that talkative anyway. It comes in fits and spurts," Certan said.

"You make talking sound like a disease," Alrion said.

"That's probably quite a good comparison. It is quite infectious, and some people are terrible carriers," Certan said. Lara laughed.

"I like your brand of humour Certan. It's a little strange, but always surprising," she said.

"I've never heard it described as such, so thank you," Certan said, performing a small bow.

"That may be the road we are looking for," Alrion said, pointing out a much wider track that was connected up ahead.

"Looks about right, let's follow it." Lara led the group there, keeping a little ahead to spot any potential dangers. When she was satisfied, she slowed down and waved the others on. They followed along and joined the main road. "Signs of life, we must be close now." Lara pointed at a few travellers in the distance.

"I have a good feeling," Alrion said.

Lara couldn't agree, something still felt off to her. It was probably just the encounter with Branthor, but her gut wouldn't let her relax.

The city gates loomed large in the distance, and Lara could see a crowd of people milling in front of them. Something was definitely off.

"Looks busy, but at least we made it in time," Alrion said.

"Something doesn't look right. I can't put my finger on it yet, but I don't think that's normal," Lara said. Alrion gave her a puzzled look but didn't question it.

As they approached they heard commotion and yelling.

"I told you something was up," Lara said. There were signs of a recent battle at the gates, with the guards bloodied and weary. They had formed a line blocking entry to the gates, and they were actively pushing people back.

"Let us in!" An older man was pleading with them.

"No entry, the gates are closed," the guard said. His tone suggested that he was sick of repeating it.

"Certan, why don't you go ask them what the problem is? Alrion will hang back and observe, and I'll tail you to see for myself," Lara said.

"Certainly," he said, and started to make this way through the crowd. He was insistent yet polite, and made consistent progress through the large throng of people. Certan stopped in front of a relatively energetic and talkative guard at the end of the formation

"Excuse me, can you please explain what all the commotion is about?" he said.

"I'm sorry but there's just been a Blighter attack. It occurred after we detained a suspicious couple, so for security reasons we are letting nobody else in. I am sorry, try again tomorrow," the guard said.

"Of course, safety is the primary concern. Although I do fear for my own safety being trapped outside. Should I be on the lookout for anyone in particular?" Certan said.

"I can't comment on specifics, but we have a drawing here," the guard said, removing a parchment, and handing it to Certan. He examined it carefully and returned it.

"And these two tried to gain entry?"

"Yes, well two people matching that description. If you spot them I advise you to keep your distance and come alert the guard of their location. They may still be at large."

"Good advice. Thank you for your assistance," Certan said, bowing.

"You're welcome, thank you for your understanding. Take care, I am sure the situation will be improved tomorrow," the guard said. Certan returned to the others as quickly as he could navigate through the impatient mob.

"Blighter attack is why they closed the gates and are keeping people out," Certan said as he joined his companions.

"That makes sense. Not good for us," Lara said.

"It gets worse. They detained a couple that look exactly like you two. They even showed me the drawing they are using for the comparison. Even if they open the gates tomorrow you can't enter. They're looking for you," Certan said.

"That, I did not expect. You contained your reaction well," Lara said.

"What! That's ridiculous. How many guards are there? Could we just storm in?" Alrion said.

"Calm down, it must be some sort of misunderstanding," Lara said.

"They think we are tainted or something. We've done nothing wrong. I can't believe it," Alrion said.

"It could be a coincidence that there was a Blighter attack, or it could be related. Either way, there's no way the two of you are passing through the gates anytime soon," Certan said.

"Maybe I can destroy part of the wall," Alrion said.

"A man with only a hammer sees everything as nails," Lara said.

"I think it would work. What do you suggest?" Alrion said.

"Certan or I should sneak in or climb the wall. We will find your parents and figure out what's going on. Then we can decide whether to pass through the city or go around it," Lara said.

"That is a good plan. I agree," Certan said.

"Sure, but it's not as fun as my idea. Magic makes everything better," Alrion threw a mock fireball at the walls.

"There'll be plenty of opportunity for that, I have no doubt. But let's start with a stealthy approach. Do you think you are best suited to infiltrate?" Certan said to Lara.

"Yes, leave this one with me. Let's find a place to camp, and once we are settled I'll come back. I'll have a better chance once the crowd disperse and the guard relaxes a little," Lara said.

"Let's go." Alrion made a start and the others followed close behind.

"What's the big rush?" Lara said to Alrion.

"It's just so frustrating. We're hitting problem after problem, it's like we are always one step behind. I'm working so hard on improving my magic, but it's not helping," Alrion said.

"There will come a time when we may need to rely on it. However, growing in strength and experience is more than just increasing your power. Most of us can achieve quite a bit without a touch of magic," Certan said.

"That makes sense. It's like there's something inside that I just need to unleash," Alrion said.

"Unfortunately, your mentor Falric is not here, I am sure he would know what to say. Maybe there's a way you can deal with that without blowing things up," Lara said.

"You're right. I'll consult my book and think it through, do some exercises. It will keep my occupied while we wait," Alrion said. They continued walking and found a nice clearing a little off the main tracks.

Certan and Alrion settled in and Lara prepared to leave. "Keep an eye on him and make sure he doesn't do anything stupid," Lara whispered to Certan.

"Of course, we'll be fine."

"Don't do anything I wouldn't do. Wish me luck," Lara said loud enough for Alrion to hear.

"Good luck," Certan said.

"Don't get caught," Alrion said.

"I'll do my best," Lara said with a wink, and dashed off into the cover of the nearby trees.

Lara took her time weaving back through the woods. She didn't want to return too quickly, and also wished to avoid being spotted by anyone. If the guard had showed the drawing to Certan, there could be others on the lookout for her and she didn't want to bring unwanted attention. Once she returned to the city gates, she noticed that the crowd had mostly dispersed. The gates were firmly closed, and there were two guards posted in a guard station above the walls.

I can't waltz in the front door, I'll need to find another way in. Without going too close, she started to skirt around the walls and see if there were any additional entrances.

As she progressed she didn't find any, but she did notice that there were no more guard towers.

"They don't expect to encounter anyone outside the main gate, I wonder if there's a way to climb the walls," Lara said to herself. Since it was quiet she approached the walls and looked at them closely. There were quite a few cracks, metallic supports, and other decorations on the wall to act as climbing aids. Of course, if she fell there was no safety net, but with the help of her dagger it would be possible.

"Only one way to find out. This better not end horribly," Lara whispered. She scrambled up the wall, using a large crack as her initial hand-hold. Next, she swung herself up to another crack, using her dagger to wedge in and hold her weight. It was a little unsteady, but worked.

Only a million manoeuvres left, Lara thought, staring up.

"Maybe I should have let Alrion blast a hole through here," she said as shuffled up to metal bar she could hang from. Her fingers started to slip, so she furiously kicked around to find a better foothold, and once she did, moved to another handhold. Sweat started to pour down her face.

Looking down, then regretting it, Lara realised that she was halfway up the wall.

May as well keep going. After some mental preparation, she began again. There was a relatively sizeable chunk of wall missing halfway up the remaining distance. If she could get there, then she would be able to rest a bit before completing the climb. Feeling a second wave of energy coming on, Lara pushed forward with confidence, spotting the best hand holds as quickly as she needed them.

With a concerted effort, she was poised to leap into the safe nook, but her feet slipped. Lashing out frantically with her dagger, she pierced the wall enough to slow her descent, find another handhold and propelling herself into the space.

"That was not very ladylike," she said, laughing quietly. Her adrenalin was pumping as she considered what could have happened. After taking a minute to calm down, she took more care approaching the last leg of the climb.

With great relief, she toppled over the top of the wall. Recognising it as a battlement, she quickly scanned both directions to see if there were any guards patrolling. She noticed a torch in the distance to her left, and started to crouch run in the opposite direction.

"Great another torch," she whispered. There was nowhere to run. She crept over to look at the way down inside the walls. There were a few houses and some trees nearby, but nothing to climb down easily.

That tree isn't so far away, she thought as she heard footsteps converging from both directions. Not wanting a confrontation, she leapt out into the darkness, aiming for a relatively thick tree branch. She landed on it, but couldn't maintain her balance, and stumbled further into the tree. Her hand couldn't seem to grasp any of the branches and she braced herself for a rough landing.

Suddenly she stopped. One arm had somehow snagged something, and she was hanging in mid-air. It was hard to see what was below her, but it looked like grass.

"Please don't break anything," she told herself as she let go of the branch.

18

A NEW LEAD

As she saw the ground approaching Lara put her arms out and tried to go into a roll. She had partial success, but didn't land straight and tumbled out of control thumping into another tree trunk. Everything was dead quiet.

I'm alive, but how noisy was that? she thought. The eerie calm continued, raising the tension. She heard voices conversing above her, but couldn't hear what they were saying.

"I hope those guards didn't notice," she wondered. When nothing happened, she slowly tested all her limbs. Everything seemed to work. Taking care, she stood up a bit shakily, but as she walked everything seemed to improve.

"Let's not do that again," Lara said to herself. She tried to appear like she belonged, as she stumbled around looking for a main road.

"It would help if it wasn't so damn dark," she whispered. But the darkness was also useful, since it kept her hidden. She crept past the nearest houses and found her way to some signs of life.

"Now, assuming Vincent and Celes are here, where would they be?" Lara mused. She decided to try and head to the most populated area of the city. That would be a good place to start. It just depended on whether the couple wanted to be found or not.

Lara didn't notice many people on the streets, which made sense if there had been a Blighter attack recently. That made her job a little easier, although she could stand out a little because of it. The buildings became bigger and bigger and Lara realised she had reached the main hub.

She had been here before, and as she stopped to look the place became more familiar. Her unorthodox entry and the dark had confused her a bit. Deciding to take a methodical approach, she walked over to the main gates to start her search. The buildings in the area were devoted to the guards, and it looked like they had borne the brunt of the Blighter attack.

What drove them here all of a sudden? Not a good sign. Moving on she came to a crossroads. To her left she could continue on to the trade and commercial district, or she could go right and enter the worker's area.

Vincent likes to associate with other blacksmiths, but I doubt he'll be able to stay there. I'll try the local inns, Lara thought. She headed left and followed the lights and signs of life.

The bleak, quiet streets she had encountered quickly melted away. It seemed like the people who weren't hiding indoors were out celebrating. As Lara walked past, she decided to try the quietest inn. There was no way that Vincent and Celes would be joining the celebrations.

After scouting a few locations Lara settled on 'The Jocular Javelin-Thrower'. The crowd wasn't bursting out onto the street, and the noise level seemed lower. She stepped in and looked around.

The clientele was a lot less jocular than whoever the inn was named after, with minimal conversation. Most were just nursing their drinks in silence. However, Lara did spot some friendly faces in the corner. She made a beeline for them.

"Bit of a depressing place, isn't it?" Lara said.

"Lara! Great to see you!" Vincent said, jumping out of his chair to envelop Lara in a big hug. "Where's Alrion?" he said, instantly suspicious.

"Camping outside with Certan. I had to climb the bloody wall to get in." Lara made a show of dusting off her clothes.

"Yes, I'm not surprised. It's been a bit of an adventure here. Take a seat, we have some information to share with you," Celes said.

"I'm sure you do, but you won't believe what happened to us," Lara said as she sat down. Vincent and Celes sat quietly, waiting to hear.

"We ran into Branthor. He's become a Shade!" Lara said. She looked at Vincent and Celes's reactions, and was confused.

"You don't seem surprised about that?" Lara said.

"The Shade part is interesting, but otherwise it confirms what we just heard. Branthor is calling himself Wraith and running quite a network of Tainted ones," Celes said.

"Figures, we have this absolutely crazy encounter and you have uncovered the same information."

"Tell us what happened," Vincent said.

"We went the alternate route, and nothing interesting happened. We saw this figure on the bridge, and it looked like a Shade. We attacked it with everything we had, and nothing seemed to really damage it."

"That's unusual. How did you get away?"

"It grabbed Certan and used him to talk to us. It seemed distracted, or unable to fully control its new form. But you know what worked on it? That sword you made. We managed to sever the hand holding Branthor, and it raged, destroying the bridge, and disappearing," Lara said.

"Good to know we have a weapon against it. We've had some similar excitement here, finding a Tainted One deep in Branthor's network. He summoned the Blighters to attack us. We think that perhaps as he was talking to us he was killed via his mental link," Vincent said.

"How is that even possible?" Lara said. She felt a chill go down her spine.

"I am not sure, but clearly there is a lot we don't know about how they operate. Let's get you some food and drink and talk this all through," Vincent said.

Lara relaxed a little, and settled back into the chair.

Hours later, they had shared all the details of their exploits.

"So where to from here," Celes said.

"I think we should continue our investigation, and let Alrion continue to the desert," Vincent said.

"So, we're the diversion?" Celes said.

"Yes. I don't like what happened here, but at least that army of Blighters was not directed at Alrion."

"It may help, keeping us a smaller group. We have Certan to guide us there," Lara said.

"Yes, he's all you need. Hopefully with this information you can dodge Wraith and his attackers more easily," Vincent said.

"Wraith?" Lara said.

"I don't think it is worth calling him Branthor anymore. He has become something else. May as well use his new name."

"Wraith it is. I guess I'll return to Alrion tonight and we can leave tomorrow, avoiding the city."

"That's best, they'll still be looking for you. Perhaps even more keenly since they have associated the Blighter attack with your presence," Celes said.

"More forest. Yay," Lara said.

"It'll be worth it. One more thing," Vincent said, leaning in closer.

"Yes?"

"Take care in the desert. It's a bleak place, so I hear. We may try and join you later if possible," Vincent said.

Lara said her goodbyes and left the inn. She felt re-energised by the familiar company, food, and the news. There wasn't much for her to go on, but she still felt like it was a success. She had found Alrion's parents, shared the situation and learnt some key information that may help them travel more safely.

Lara walked back the way she came, wondering if she should try and sneak out via the main gate or try her climbing trick again.

"I really don't want to scale that wall, once is enough," she said to herself, looking over at the looming structure. As she went to turn she almost walked into a man standing right in front of her.

"Sorry," she said, before looking more closely. He was tall and in a dark cloak, his face hidden.

"Not a problem, I did in fact step in front of you," the man said. He was in no hurry to move either.

"It's you! What's going on?" Lara said.

"Come this way so we can talk more," the man said. Lara followed along, puzzled at why this mysterious wizard was contacting her again.

"How are you?" he said.

"Fine. We've had a few adventures, but nothing we couldn't handle."

"Good. Things are going to become more difficult soon. You won't be able to hide your journey to the desert," the wizard said. Lara stopped in her tracks.

"How do you know about that?"

"It doesn't matter, let's just say I am invested in your journey. You're going to need help. Alrion needs more training," the wizard said. He stopped off the main path, under a tree.

"Give this to the monk, he will understand it," he said, handing Lara a slip of paper. She unfolded it and read the contents.

"What is this?" she said.

"Directions to a wizard who lives in the desert. You must make sure that Alrion meets him. He is called the Desert Wizard for good reason."

"He's going to wonder where I got this information," Lara said.

"You'll figure something out. What's important is that you find him and that he trains Alrion."

Lara thought that was a good plan. But she didn't trust this mysterious wizard. "I can do that. How is it that you can just tell me what to do?" she said.

"Because I am asking things you already want to do."

"That doesn't make any sense."

"It will, in time. I won't hold you up any longer, good luck," the wizard said.

"How will I contact you if I need help?"

"Alrion knows how."

"But he doesn't know about you?"

"He will discover the way. Don't worry that about that. Just don't lose that note, it's critical," the wizard said. He gave Lara a short wave and vanished.

"Gone again. How do I keep getting caught up in these things?" Lara wondered. She pocketed the note and thought about how to get out.

"Not climbing that wall again," she told herself and headed for the main gate.

She noticed that there was only a light presence guarding the gate.

Not trying to keep people from going out. It would be easy to sneak past, but the gate itself would be an issue. However, she did notice something peculiar. She crept closer, avoiding the guards, and sticking to the darkness. Once she reached the gate she took a closer look.

"This is useful," she whispered. There was a square cut into the side of the gate. It looked like it opened. She carefully pushed it, to see what it did. The square pushed forward, revealing a small opening in the door.

Probably used for accepting things through the door, or negotiating. I wonder if I could fit, Lara thought. There was only one way to find out. She glanced back and saw that the guards were continuing their patrol, not particularly paying attention to the gate.

"Here goes." Lara grasped onto the gate frame with both her hands and thrust her head through the square gap. With a little finessing, she was able to get her shoulders through then she fell out onto the other side. A quick movement as she landed helped soften the blow, and she stood up quickly. There were no signs of movement on the other side of the gate.

That was a lot easier. She dusted herself off and walked off into the night, slowly increasing her pace. The crowds had subsided, but she could see small fires in the distance, where some were camping overnight.

All they had to do was climb the wall, she thought with a laugh. Quickly weaving through the woods, she found Certan and Alrion seated comfortably leaning against some trees. Alrion had hung a magical light sphere from one of the hanging branches, which illuminated the area nicely.

"You look like you've had a bit of an adventure," Alrion said, looking up from the books he was reading.

"Don't get me started. Next time I consider climbing a city wall, just stop me please," Lara said.

"That's quite an impressive feat. How you did get down?" Certan said.

"With great difficulty and luck. I'll fill you in on all the details but there's two important things. First, there was a Blighter attack in the city. It was due to a Tainted One. He was looking for Alrion and me," Lara said.

"That's not a good sign. What's the other thing? Did you find my parents?" Alrion said.

"Yes, they told me all about the man they discovered. We think the Tainted share some sort of mental link and coordinate their movements that way," Lara said.

"That may explain a lot." Alrion looked deep in thought.

"We need to better understand our enemy," Certan said.

"We have news too," Alrion said.

"What's that?" Lara said with concern. Nothing should have happened while she was away.

"I found another message in this notebook. Take a look." Alrion handed it to Lara to review.

Find Ashra in the desert, he will advise you further.

"Who is Ashra?" Lara said. She had a sinking feeling in her stomach that she knew what the answer would be.

"I have heard that name before, he's a wizard. Hates visitors, which is why he lives in the desert," Certan said.

"Interesting. Do you know how to find him?" Lara said.

"No, he doesn't like to be found."

"It's a lead right, we will figure it out," Alrion said.

"I wasn't sure what to make of this, but I think it will help." Lara retrieved the slip of paper the mysterious wizard had given her and handed it to Alrion.

"Where did you get this?" Alrion said.

"Some raving drunk was going on about a wizard in the desert. I thought it would be a good lead, so I stole these directions," she said.

"This is awfully coincidental, you finding this and me seeing this message. What did that man look like?" Alrion was looking at Lara with a questioning gaze.

"Unremarkable. Maybe he got it from someone else? He had nothing else of interest to say or on him," Lara said. Alrion turned the paper over and handed it to Certan.

"I can follow these directions. It would make sense to head there before the temple. It's more or less on the way. Additional training sounds quite important to me," Certan said.

"Then I guess we see where they lead. But I don't like this. I feel like we're being led by the nose and I don't know by who," Alrion said.

"Wow, I thought you would be happy with this. It's another wizard. Isn't that good?" Lara said.

"Sorry, it's not your fault. Why don't you tell us more about what my parents said? There could be something in there that is crucial," Alrion said.

Lara was happy to do so. She didn't want him thinking too much on how she could have happened upon that information just as the mysterious message was left. At least now she knew for sure who was leaving the notes in Alrion's book. But she still didn't know his identity.

Next time, I'll find a way.

19

ENTER THE DESERT

The next morning Alrion rose early. He didn't sleep well and was anxious to get a move on.

"I just have to see if there's anything to this wizard. Or if it's a trap, I want it over with," Alrion said.

"We can rush to get started, but we mustn't rush the journey. The desert is a hard place to traverse. I know the way, but we must take care. If we are attacked while we are weakened it will be disastrous," Certan said.

"Are there many tainted in the desert?" Lara said.

"It depends where you go. Usually not, as it is not a good environment for them to survive. I saw more than I expected on this journey, so we should be prepared for anything," Certan said.

"We won't be able to go through the city, so we may lose some time. Does it matter which way we enter?" Lara said.

"It does, but all our current options are equivalent in utility and danger. This detour won't have much impact. But I do agree we should start now," Certan said. Alrion did a final check, and they left their makeshift camp site.

"Do we need to stock up on water?" Alrion said as they walked.

"No, provided we take a small amount with us. The wizard will have a source," Certan said.

"That's if we find him. You said he doesn't like visitors," Lara said.

"We will find a way, it's too important," Alrion said.

"Exactly. Besides, you have me. I can survive in the desert, and so you will too," Certan said. They spotted a small fast flowing river on their walk and stopped to fill a flask each. Certan paused, looking over his flask. He swapped it with another then filled it to the brim.

"What was that about?" Alrion said. Certan retrieved the flask he had hidden away.

"For a long time this flask here meant something different. It was my supply of alcohol and everything that went with that. But now it is something else, something better," he said.

"Are you using it?" Lara said.

"No. It's my penance, a reminder of my excesses." Certan's voice had a pang of regret.

"A reminder of how strong you are," Alrion said.

"Thank you, I will remember that." Certan put the flask away and started off once more.

They took a meandering route, avoiding the city, and using the best paths available. This took longer than they had initially wanted. Slowly Alrion saw the terrain transform. The colours of the grass and plants slowly changed, from a bright green to a washed out green and yellow. The grass become thinner and shorter and the trees were also reduced in height.

"You can see the availability of water decreasing," Certan said, pointing out the surroundings.

"I was just thinking the same thing," Alrion said.

"Are we close?" Lara said.

"Yes, we are, we have come further than I had expected. We will stop soon," Certan said.

"Stop?" I don't see the desert? How far is it?" Lara said.

"Not much further, it's a little deceptive. However, from here on it is best to travel at night. We need to rest soon, so we can make proper progress when it is cooler," Certan said.

"You're the expert," Alrion said, slapping Certan on the back.

"Trust me, it's better this way," Certan said. Alrion was trying to imagine the intensity of the heat, but struggled.

"I trust you. It's probably going to be one of those things that needs to be experienced to be explained," Alrion said.

"I can explain, but you won't know. Not really," Certan said.

"Night works for me," Lara said.

"We already knew that," Alrion said. Certan let out a small chuckle.

"Let's make camp up there, it looks relatively sheltered and quiet," he said. They put down their equipment and tried to make the area comfortable for sleeping. Alrion had difficulty getting to sleep, as it was only the afternoon. But sleep eventually found him when he least expected.

A firm hand woke him from sleep and Alrion noticed Certan standing over him.

"It's time, great," Alrion said with a start, jumping up. Certan and Lara were ready to go.

"I see you took the time to get yourselves sorted before waking me," he said.

"You need your beauty sleep," Lara said. Certan had a grin on his face.

"Sure, sure. I'll just need a minute," Alrion took his time preparing, not wanting to miss anything.

"Let's go," Certan said, heading out. Lara and Alrion followed close.

"How dark will it get?" Alrion said.

"Travelling by moonlight is possible, depending on its size. However, we may need additional light," Certan said.

"Just let me know," Alrion said.

"I will, although I suspect you won't need my prompting. We will be entering the desert shortly," Certan said, pointing at a spot in the distance. It was harder to see, but the grasses seemed to almost completely withered out.

"There's still some grass, or maybe shrubs," Lara said.

"Yes, that's normal. Not every part is completely sandy, although the overall effect is the same," Certan said. They walked on in silence, taking in the new environment. The ground was shifting more under their feet, gradually become less solid. Certan walked with purpose, but still regularly paused to get his bearings.

"I thought you were the desert master, we seem to be stopping a lot," Lara said.

"Realising the folly in having contempt for the desert is usually the last lesson one learns," Certan said and Lara laughed. Alrion stumbled on a small mound that he didn't spot and paused to create a ball of light. He visualised it attaching to an invisible string and floating above them. As he walked he looked at it, and monitored its progress, pleased that it seemed to be behaving as he expected.

"The light is a big help, it's not usually practical to have one," Certan said.

"Happy to help, and it'll stop me tripping as well," Alrion said.

"How can you make sense of these directions?" Lara said.

"They rely on markers and waypoints that only those familiar with the desert would understand. Whoever wrote these knows the place well. Many people would be unable to use these references to find the way," Certan said.

"Good thing we have you. I've been thinking and I want your opinion. Do you think this is a setup?" Alrion said.

"Do you mean are we walking into a trap?" Certan said.

"Yes exactly. We recently learned that Wraith as he calls himself now can communicate and coordinate a network of tainted. What if this lead is just to direct us how he wants?"

"This lead was definitely not from a tainted person," Lara said.

"Maybe not directly, but maybe it was planted with that person?" Alrion said. Lara felt confident that he was wrong, but was unable to prove it.

"I just don't see it," Lara said.

"Regardless, we can prepare ourselves and look out for signs. It would be very hard to hide that kind of presence in the desert," Certan said.

"Fair enough. Let's remain cautious," Alrion wasn't convinced that they would really find a wizard out here. Part of him was also anxious that maybe they would. How would a wizard react to him? Especially one that hates company.

The walk dragged on, but Certan kept a strong pace that made Alrion feel like they were at least getting somewhere. But he had no idea of the distances required, so just followed along. He played over scenarios in his head, for how he would deal with Blighters, another Shade or even a hostile wizard. The last one was the most worrying. He still felt like he lucked out when taking on Branthor, and wasn't confident he could handle himself with an experienced wizard.

This is all crazy. I shouldn't have to be worrying about wizards. The creatures of the Blight are supposed to be the enemy, Alrion thought.

Certan paused, reviewing the directions again. He held them up to Alrion's magical light.

"We are up to the last step. This is unusual. I was sure that nothing lay down this way, but perhaps that is why the instructions are correct," he said.

"If I wanted to be left alone, I would live in a desert in a place where locals thought nothing existed," Lara said.

"I still keep thinking what kind of person would do this? Can we even expect help?" Alrion said.

"We shall remain cautious, but there's no need to worry. All types live in the desert, let us give this wizard the benefit of the doubt," Certan said.

"You're right. This wizard is going to help, one way or another," Alrion said.

"I'll make sure of that," Lara said, flashing a smile at Alrion. The party turned off and took a right into an even more sparse area of the desert. There were no signs of passage, and nothing to mark the way. Yet Certan kept walking with confidence. Slowly but surely, they started going through their water supply. The journey became increasingly difficult, as there were no markers to show how they were progressing and they could see the sun beginning to rise in the distance.

"I hope we get there soon, otherwise we may be stranded in the sun," Lara said.

"We have ways of dealing with that, but yes let's hope we find him soon," Certan said. They trudged on, but soon they saw what looked like a small building in the distance.

"Finally!" Alrion said.

"It exists. The desert is so tricky, I'm relieved that we made it," Certan said.

"I thought you were more confident than that," Lara said.

"I was confident that we were following the directions properly, and that we were reaching the proper landmarks. However, this wizard is like a myth of the desert. There are many tales of him, but nobody you meet has actually seen him," Certan said.

"Don't speak too soon, we may be in the same boat. Does that hut look a little deserted to you?" Lara said. As they approached they could see inside the hut. It was tiny and sparse, with a mattress, some blankets and a table being the only pieces of furniture. A thin layer of dust covered everything, suggesting that the place had been vacant for some time.

Certan ran his hand along the surfaces, and examined the quantity of dust.

"This is not unusual for the desert. It could be that someone has just been away for a matter of days. We should not give up hope," he said.

"Any clues here?" Alrion gently probed the mattress to see if it hid anything, and looked over the table.

"I don't see anything to suggest that a wizard lives here. But maybe that's the point? He doesn't like to be visited after all," Lara said.

"What's that over there?" Alrion pointed at the lone window in the hut and what was visible in the distance. It looked like a tree.

"An oasis? That would explain why he chose this location and why he may not need to spend as much time here," Certan said.

"Oasis? Those are real?" Lara said.

"Yes, but they were quite rare and well-guarded secrets. There are very easily overwhelmed if overused," he said.

"I could use a drink, and maybe we will find the wizard there," Alrion said.

"It's worth a look," Lara said.

"Of course, but let us approach with caution. There could be traps." Certan led the way, stepping cautiously across the desert sand. Lara and Alrion followed close behind, looking around for signs of danger.

"Something seems off, but I cannot describe what it is. Stay alert," Certan said.

"I'm ready," Alrion said.

Lara removed her dagger from her jacket and twirled it in her hand. As they advanced they could see the tree was next to a small pond that was encircled by small green tufts of grass and shrubs. "Signs of life, that's promising," she said.

"We shall see." Certan walked closer and the other two kept pace. As they were about to reach the tree it started to shimmer. And once they stepped closer still, the tree vanished. Instead they were confronted with a stone wall.

"A mirage? Classic," Lara said.

"I suspected something was off. I didn't sense the amount of life that I expected from an oasis," Certan said.

"There's something to be said for an appreciation of the classics. How did you find this place?" a male voice said from behind them.

Alrion spun quickly to see who it was.

20

AN IMPORTANT LEAD

Vincent escorted Lara out of the inn, and made sure she was safe before returning inside. He navigated through the crowd and sat back down next to his wife.

"Things are escalating a lot faster than you expected," Celes said.

"I know. We have underestimated what we are up against. I did not think that Alrion would be intercepted like that," Vincent said.

"Hopefully after Lara tells them of Wraith's network, they can be more careful. At least they are near the desert now."

"Yes, it will be easier to hide in the desert and less chance of running into Tainted. I don't think they like it in there."

"Fingers crossed. So, what do we do now? Investigate here more or try and meet up with them?" Celes said.

"We're definitely on their radar, after that attack and the death of the Tainted guard. We would lead them straight to Alrion wouldn't we?"

"I think so. My gut tells me there's more here. I doubt that Wraith's network would end with one guard. Let's dig around here more, and see what we can find. Worst case scenario all we do is act as a distraction which still helps them."

"Sounds good to me." Vincent looked quite satisfied.

"You're just glad you get to do more blacksmithing. Do you miss it that much?" Celes said, making a face at him.

"No, but it does help me focus. I feel like we have been caught off guard, so I'm glad to slow down a little and feel our way forward rather than acting rashly. Banging a few things with a hammer is just a bonus," Vincent said.

"Let's head back then. It is safe to return, right?"

"Yes, there's nothing there," Vincent said.

"Good I would find it hard to sleep otherwise," Celes said and stood up quickly from the chair. Vincent walked ahead and they left the inn together.

The next morning Vincent went to find John, and made sure the blacksmith was distracted while Celes returned the armour she had borrowed.

"Why don't you start over there, I've got some pieces that need finishing. Here's a sample of how they should look." John handed Vincent a metallic cylinder that looked like it fit around the arm.

"Sure, I can follow that."

"Come grab me if you're unsure, we'll move on to the tricky stuff later," John said. Vincent walked over and placed the finished piece next to the pile of half-finished ones.

"I was pretty sneaky, wasn't I?" Celes whispered.

"You were, don't blow it now," Vincent said.

"I'll be around here and there, have fun," Celes said and quickly crept away. Vincent got to work on the first piece. He could see that it was a simple job and wouldn't require any input from John. He decided to lose himself in the work for a while.

After a few hours, he heard some commotion and walked over to investigate.

"I know for sure that you're selling pieces on the side. Don't even try and deny it," a female voice said.

"As I have said before, I don't do that. I value this contract, and I have no idea what you are talking about." John looked quite frustrated. As Vincent approached he could see a female guard standing over the blacksmith.

"We had a female impersonating a guard wearing a full uniform. We have checked and this is the only place it could have come from," the female guard said.

"I'll check again, but everything is here." John walked off.

"Yes?" the guard said looking at Vincent.

"I just heard an argument and came over. I'll leave you to it," Vincent said.

The guard instantly dismissed him with her eyes and returned to glaring at John.

Vincent walked back to his work area and looked around. "Where is she when you need her," he said, muttering to himself.

"Right here," Celes said.

"Good. Do you hear the argument over there?" Vincent said.

"Yes, hard not to."

"Do you think it is suspicious?"

"Definitely. Only the man we captured knew I was there. This guard must be Tainted as well."

"You're welcome," Vincent said and returned to his work.

"That's right, you go back to the blacksmithing and I'll follow her," Celes said.

"Sounds good to me," Vincent said grinning. Celes crept away and found a good vantage point to watch the guard.

John returned and repeated his story. The female guard spat in disgust and stormed off.

~

"Here we go," Celes said to herself. She started walking, keeping a safe distance between herself and the guard.

"Now where is she off to," Celes wondered. The guard had turned to the right, veering away from the guard building. Celes upped her speed, rushing to the corner so that she would not lose her lead. Once she reached the corner she peeked around it. The guard was looking back to see if she was being followed, but Celes managed to quickly hide herself.

Just as well I was cautious, Celes thought. A few seconds later she ducked her head out and saw the guard turning another corner. Celes quietly dashed down the street, slowing as she reached the corner and followed the same process. As before the guard was carefully looking behind.

"The cat and mouse game continues," Celes whispered. After rounding the next corner there was a long straight road. The guard walked quickly, not looking back. Celes made sure that she walked near other people, or buildings so that she could hide herself if required. But the guard seemed to have decided that nobody was following and just charged ahead.

Celes noticed a building at the end of the street. It had a high pointed roof, with lavish stonework on the walls and a series of steps leading into the entrance.

"That looks quite formal, this is interesting," Celes said to herself. There was a steady stream of people filing in and out of the building, so Celes upped her pace and entered alongside another group. Inside she found a large open room, with benches all around the sides. It looked like there were public officials working there, making notes, and having conversations. She looked around the room, trying to spot the guard. It was almost too late, but she noticed the guard turning into a room at the end. Celes quickly crossed the space and glanced up at the sign.

Council chambers, this just gets even more interesting. She stepped inside, and looked around. There was no sign of the guard, but a door slammed in the distance. Celes approached the source of the sound.

At the end of the hall there were two doors, one on the left and one on the right.

Which one? she wondered as she crept down the hall. It wasn't obvious as she progressed, but she did hear voices coming from one of the rooms.

This must be it. Celes checked the other door, and it opened. Nobody was inside.

"That was lucky," she whispered. But she wouldn't be able to repeat her trick of listening in, because the rooms were on opposite sides of the corridor. She looked up at the ceiling and didn't notice any obvious places to climb up.

I just have to risk it, she thought and returned to the hall. She left the door open for the empty room and sidled up to the other door to listen closely. As she pressed closer she could make out the voices more distinctly.

"So, you have no leads at all then," a male voice said.

"I'm sorry councillor. We have exhausted all the avenues. It's not apparent how the intruder got access to a uniform," the female guard said.

"Unacceptable! Wraith will not tolerate this kind of failure. We need to deal with this quickly. Do you understand why we are meeting in person?" the councillor said.

"Yes, because we don't want to broadcast the fact that we have nothing yet.

"Exactly. Questions are being asked, we need something immediately. What's the best lead?"

"I've cross-examined all the guards. Everything was accounted for and verified. It can't be a guard. It has to be the blacksmith."

"But he's adamant about not creating more uniforms? Do you believe him?"

"Yes, I do. But maybe someone accessed his stocks. It's the only explanation available," the guard said.

"Go back there, and be friendlier this time. Try and find out how someone could have gained access. Maybe ask about unfamiliar faces showing up. We need to really work this, you don't want to see what happens to people who fail," the councillor said.

"I understand, I'll go back to the blacksmith with a new approach," the guard said. Celes quickly backed away from the door and returned to the other room. She closed the door as quietly as possible and waited to hear what was happening next.

A minute passed by slowly, and another. But soon she heard the sound of the other door opening and footsteps proceeding down the corridor. Once she decided that it was relatively safe she slowly opened the door enough to catch a glimpse of the person leaving. It was the guard, as expected.

The councillor must still be inside, Celes thought. But she didn't have a name or a face to identify him. She had to decide when to confront him.

I can't do it here, it's too public. I'll have to tail him and find an opportunity. She wanted to go warn Vincent that there would be additional questioning, but this lead was too important She had to follow the trail further.

He'll be fine, I'll check in later, she decided and waited for the councillor to make a move.

Within a few minutes, she heard footsteps and a door slamming. She listened to the steps retreating down the hall then snuck a peek. There was a balding man in a long black robe about to exit the hallway. She quickly retreated back into the room in case he looked back, then entered the hallway.

He had already left, so she made her way down the corridor as quickly as possible. She took care leaving the council chambers to make sure she was not watched. It looked safe so she quickly mingled with a group wandering through the hallway.

Searching the crowd, she spotted the councillor nearing the exit. She sped up, ducking in-between people, and trying not to draw too much attention.

I'm just someone late for an appointment, Celes thought. She had to make sure she caught up with the councillor once he left the building to keep on his trail. As Celes left the building she slowed then stopped. People were walking in all directions, some of them wearing the same black robe. Again and again she looked everywhere trying to find the balding man. Finally, she saw him turn into a side street and rushed to catch up.

I'm probably going too fast, she thought but it didn't matter. It was fine for people to notice her, it was so important to find this councillor. He was clearly high up in the group of Tainted and would have valuable information. Celes reached the street he had entered and stopped to assess. She was just in time to watch him enter a house at the end of the street.

Hopefully that's where he lives. She walked with more care down the street, trying to fit in. She looked over the houses, and noticed that they were all quite large and had gardens. It was clearly a special street reserved for people of importance who also had strong finances. As she arrived at the house she noticed that it had a large iron gate in front. The gate wasn't locked but it looked quite noisy. Celes walked up and down and found a smaller section that could be climbed.

I wonder how many of these I have climbed in my life, she thought with a laugh. In seconds, she was up and over, landing softly on her feet. She rocked a little, and regained her balance.

"Not as easy as it once was," Celes said to herself. But she had entered the property without alerting anyone. Rather than entering through the front door, she walked down the side of the house and looked for a servant's entrance. About halfway down she spotted a plain door and tried the handle. It was unlocked.

"Here we go," Celes whispered and entered the house. She could hear people milling about, and the sound of clanking pots and pans. Avoiding the kitchen, she headed towards what she thought looked like more formal spaces. She passed through two sitting rooms and spotted a library at the end of the house. She couldn't hear anything but decided to investigate anyway. In her experience, rich people liked to pretend the help didn't exist, and libraries were set up for that quite nicely.

She padded quietly down the hall, using the long rug to hide her footsteps. She kept her eyes and ears open, but couldn't notice any signs of life. But her instincts told her this was the right place, so she persisted. She couldn't move on until she had eliminated it as an option.

As she reached the doorway she noticed that a large reading chair had been moved and there was a man sitting there looking out at her.

"Please, come in," he said.

Not again. I must be getting sloppy. Twice now she had been caught snooping by Tainted.

"Did you prepare me a chair?" she said, acting like she expected it.

"Sorry no, I had no time to arrange for additional furnishings. You'll have to remain standing where I can see you," he said. There was a hint of venom to his polite talk.

"What would you like to discuss?" Celes said, giving him a chance to open the conversation. He gave her a positively evil grin.

21

THE MIRAGE

The man before them was dressed in light sand-coloured robes. His hair was a mixture of black and grey, and was tied back but uncut. He had a wild beard and fierce green eyes.

"The desert wizard himself," Certan said.

"You have me at a loss. Yes, I am Ashra. Who are you? And I must repeat my question: how did you find this place?"

"We had directions. I'm Alrion and I am a wizard," Alrion said.

"I can see that. Very few people know how to get here. I'll need to find out more about those directions. But for now, why are you here?" Ashra said.

"We're heading to the desert temple, so that I can undertake the trial of the monks. I was hoping to get your help," Alrion said.

"Desert temple eh? I take it he's one of the monks. Looks a bit out of sorts though," Ashra said, pointing at Certan.

"Hello my name is Certan. I am accompanying Alrion to assist with his quest and will rejoin the monks," Certan said.

"Then who are you?" Ashra said to Lara.

"The name's Lara. I am a specialist in the art of acquiring hard to get things. I am also assisting with Alrion's quest," Lara said.

"A wizard, a thief and a monk. What an odd bunch. So, tell me, what is this quest you are all talking about?"

"I will cleanse the Blight from the world," Alrion said simply. Ashra was silent for a moment, then burst out laughing.

"Oh, that's cute. Cleanse the Blight from the world. You would sooner cleanse the air from it than accomplish that," Ashra said.

"My grandfather cleansed Avaria, I can recreate his spell. A key part of what I need is at the temple and guarded by the monks," Alrion said.

Ashra abruptly stopped laughing and started stroking his beard. "Granthion, yes I remember him. No doubt you want to master the power of Will, that's what the monks are known for. It would take great Will indeed to cleanse the Blight. Come back to the hut and tell me more about your journey so far and I will decide whether I can help you," Ashra said. He started walking off without waiting for an answer. Alrion looked at Certan and Lara for input.

"We've nothing to lose, let's see what he thinks," Lara said.

"Agreed. He seems to know about the monks, he may even be able to give us additional insights or advice in addition to any wizard training," Certan said.

"I hope he's not completely crazy," Alrion said and started walking. As they entered the hut they could see three glasses filled with water and a clear jug nearby also full.

"Drink your fill and tell me a story," Ashra said. He settled into some cushions in the corner. Alrion had to look again to trust his eyes. The hut seemed a lot nicer and much more furnished than when they had passed through.

"Just a parlour trick to confuse any that may stumble through here. Please sit," Ashra said. Alrion found somewhere to sit, and began to talk.

A few hours later, the three companions had shared their story. Ashra had been quiet and not asked anything.

"That's it?" he said.

"Yes," Alrion said.

"You're incredibly lucky, you should have died several times already," Ashra said.

"You're probably right," Alrion said.

"No, I'm definitely right. It's not just luck, there's something else at play here." Alrion didn't like the implication.

"What do you mean?" Alrion said.

"You have the mark of a wizard on you. Is Falric the only one you travelled with?"

"Yes."

"There was nobody else?" Ashra said. He stared intensely at Alrion.

"Just one thing," Alrion said reluctantly. He retrieved his notebook from his pack and showed it to Ashra.

"Ah, now this is interesting. It's a wizard communicator. You can share messages anywhere across the world. Where did you get this?"

"I found it in the wizard academy. As part of my initiation I was directed to select a relic at random from their store. This was it," Alrion said.

"And Falric knew about it?"

"Yes."

"When did you receive the first message?"

"After I visited the Pool of Knowledge. After Falric died. "

"Are you sure that Falric died? He was more of a thinker than a fighter. He would know how to use these quite effectively, and he might just continue to assist you with this," Ashra said.

"I have wondered, but I couldn't find any sign of him. But I can't help thinking that if these messages were from him, he would tell me," Alrion said.

"Perhaps, let's leave that as something to puzzle out later. But I definitely believe that a wizard is monitoring your progress. How did you get the directions to come here?" Ashra said.

"I found them," Lara said.

"Found them? Where?"

"Somebody was boasting that they had insider knowledge on the desert, and could find a wizard. I pickpocketed him," Lara said.

"No, that doesn't make sense. Show me the directions," Ashra said. Certan stood up and handed over the slip of paper.

"These are too specific meaning the person who wrote it must have knowledge of this place. Very few do, and they would not commit it to paper unless absolutely necessary. Something is wrong," Ashra said.

"Well that's what happened," Lara said, with an annoyed and defensive tone.

"If you insist, but I must wonder. Who really gave you these directions," Ashra said. He paused and stared off into the distance.

"Well, either way we made it here. Are you going to help us? We answered all your questions and told you everything," Alrion said.

"Maybe. I need to see something first," Ashra said.

"What?"

"I need to see you in action. Beat me in a fight and I'll consider helping you."

"Seriously? If I can beat you in a fight I probably don't need your help," Alrion said.

"Your journey of learning is never ended. I don't care if you drank from the Pool of Knowledge. There is always more to learn from others. There's a free lesson. But my requirement stands. You will get nothing from me until you beat me," Ashra said.

"If that's how it is, I'll just be leaving," Alrion said, standing up quickly. He had pinned so many hopes on finding this wizard, despite not really looking forward to it. But the wizard had just cast doubt on them all, and refused to help. He wasn't going to waste his time any further.

"By all means, show yourself out," Ashra said. Alrion stormed out of the hut and started walking. Lara and Certan quickly caught up to him.

"You're being impulsive, we need his help. You almost died fighting Branthor the first time. We couldn't really manage him the second time. What's your plan?" Lara said.

"She's right, Ashra must know a lot of useful information. Maybe there's strategies or special applications of your magic that will be key to our success," Certan said.

"He's just an arrogant loner who wants to show off. I don't have time for that. The sooner we get to the next trial, the sooner I'll learn something useful." Alrion increased his speed.

"We need to regroup, we cannot progress without proper water supplies and it's unwise to travel in the heat of the day," Certan said.

"I've left now, I don't want to go crawling back," Alrion said.

"We've come a long way, but we can't throw it all away now. Swallow your pride and don't risk our lives because of your childishness!" Lara shouted. She stopped walking. Certan stopped beside her.

Alrion stopped and looked back at them. He then looked ahead. Something was off. Alrion walked slowly forward. "Unbelievable," Alrion stopped and turned back to his friends. "Look at this wall. Does it look familiar?" Alrion said.

"That's the same wall that we came across at the mirage," Certan said.

"He's messing with us still," Alrion said.

"I'm impressed," Certan said.

"Clearly he doesn't want to let you go yet. At least talk to him again." Lara had calmed down and looked Alrion in the eyes.

He could see the concern on her face. "Looks like I don't have a choice," Alrion said, and turned to head back. The other two followed close.

Certan marvelled at the illusion as they walked.

Ashra was seated casually on a pillow, and he appeared surprised that they had returned.

"Welcome back," he said.

"Nice trick," Alrion said.

"It's not a trick. How do you think I've lived here all these years?"

"So, I figured you weren't finished. What else was there to discuss?"

"I know I'm a little unorthodox, and you do seem a bit unsettled by my approach. But this is a necessary step. I must test you in the heat of battle, and you must hold nothing back. Can you do that?"

"I can. I just don't understand why," Alrion said.

"It's not a big thing, you won't be hurt. Is there something else troubling you?" Ashra said. He stared at Alrion, which made him feel as if the eccentric wizard could hear all his thoughts. Alrion felt a cold shiver run down his spine.

"I'm just a little nervous about my power. It's a little wild, and I've had very little training." Alrion found that very hard to admit.

"Don't you worry, that's what I would expect. Do you see an academy around here?" Ashra said, gesturing at the barren desert.

"No."

"Exactly. Here's an additional piece of information that may interest you. I have been in the Vault of Silence," Ashra said. Alrion was dumbstruck.

"How interesting. I was not aware of anyone doing that," Certan said.

"It's not something the monks advertise, perhaps contrary to what you have been told. But that's all I can say," Ashra said.

"You win. Let's get this over with," Alrion said.

"Excellent, follow me please," Ashra said. He jumped up from his seated position with startling agility and left the hut.

"Come everyone," Ashra said, and continued walking. They walked past where the mirage was, and continued down a tight winding path between sand dunes. There were rocky formations holding the sand at bay.

Just as the sun was getting to Alrion, Ashra stopped suddenly. There was a fork in the path. There was a branch off to the left.

"Your friends should go left, it will lead to a vantage point up on the ridge. We will continue down," he said.

"We'll be watching," Lara said to Alrion, and started off. Certan slapped Alrion on the shoulders and followed close by. Once they had left Ashra spoke again.

"I have been where you are now. I have seen the academy and what it can offer, and it's a fantastic environment. But I wrestled with my power the same way you are now. With persistence, and experimentation and seeking whatever knowledge I could find," he said. He poked Alrion in the head. "I don't know how that works up there, but I can sense your apprehension. You have started to do things that you are not aware of, correct?" Ashra said.

"That's right," Alrion said.

"Don't worry, your mind will protect you. You have to quiet it, and let it do its work. Where we are going is a safe place and protected. Don't worry about me or the environment. You must treat this like you are in a life or death battle. Otherwise I cannot help you," Ashra said.

"If you insist," Alrion said, and followed Ashra down into the natural arena. He wasn't sure if he was more nervous, or more excited. But despite his reluctance he knew Ashra was right. He needed to test himself before his next battle.

22

AN OFFER

Alrion stood still, watching his opponent. Ashra stood with a relaxed stance at the opposite end of the natural arena. A gust of wind pushed sand and dust along the hard ground.

"Whenever you are ready," Ashra said loudly. Alrion heard the man, but wasn't sure how to start. He thought back to how they had launched their assault of the shade version of Branthor, and how ineffective it had been.

"Forget about that, just let go," he told himself. Shuffling his feet, he adjusted his stance and started to gather his Spark. It was time to begin.

Alrion began by throwing some ripples of force at Ashra, hoping to unsettle him or at least make him do some defence. Ashra must have seen them coming, because a wall of earth rose before him and easily absorbed the attack.

Earth too, how interesting. Branthor had been strong with that, and it had proven hard to deal with.

How about this then? Alrion thought, preparing a fire spell. He focused an intense beam of fire and force and projected it at the wall of earth.

There's no way it will withstand this, Alrion thought. He was curious how the other wizard would counter it. He didn't have to wait long for the answer.

As the fire began to hit the earth wall, it became wet. There seemed to be water seeping out of the wall, deflecting the heat, and turning it into steam.

How? Alrion wondered, confused by what he was seeing. He let the spell go and the area around Ashra was now covered in a haze of steam.

As Alrion was readying another spell the ground beneath him parted, causing him to stumble. As he looked down he saw a jet of water spray up. He had no time to dodge it and the force of the spray knocked him over. Alrion scrambled to his feet and watched the ground for more attacks. There was nothing else yet.

I have to do more, Alrion thought. He paused for a moment, then stoked his Spark once more. He channelled it into a huge wall of fire, completely separating both halves of the arena.

"That should buy me some time," he thought, and started to move slowly to avoid being a sitting target. As he moved he had an idea of how to attack. First, he created a large ball of fire and threw it into the air, holding it high above the wall of flame.

"Show yourself, or are you scared of my next attack?" Alrion shouted. He could see Ashra's silhouette standing on the other side of the wall of fire. Then it began to move. Alrion stared in disbelief, Ashra was walking through the wall of fire. When he emerged Alrion let out a surprised gasp.

The figure before him was no longer Ashra. It looked like a Shade. The figure shrugged off the flames that had come from the firewall and focused its gaze on Alrion.

"This is not possible," Alrion said to himself.

In a panic Alrion increased the intensity of the wall of fire, then flung down the fireball at the Shade. The fireball flew fast, but stopped suddenly as if it were being held by another force.

"Now you go down," Alrion whispered to himself. He concentrated all the flames, heat, and power of the wall of fire into a wave that was half as high but twice as powerful and sent it forward. He saw his fireball deflected aside, but his wave of fire continued unrestricted.

This may actually work, he thought, ready to disperse the flames once they started to get too close to him. However, the flames passed through the shade and did no discernible damage. As Alrion prepared to extinguish the flames, a huge shift in the ground occurred. A large amount of earth rose up towards him. It was a dome of reinforced sand that not only smothered the flame, but quickly enclosed Alrion within.

Alrion furiously threw waves of force at the sand structure, trying to break a hole in it. But the sand absorbed each attack and stayed resilient.

This is not happening.

"You have lost," Ashra's voice said from outside the dome.

"No!" Alrion shouted. He channelled everything he had into one last attack. He poured his fear, frustration and embarrassment and the rest of his Spark into a modified wave of force. It started as a white hot glowing orb above him, and it expanded out quickly. It shimmered and exploded outwards, obliterating the sand prison and everything in the area. Alrion fell to the ground, exhausted. As the dust settled he looked around him at what had just happened.

A spherical shape was neatly cut out of sides of the arena and the surface was now perfectly flat like it has been swept and polished. On one ridge Alrion could see Ashra standing tall, and Lara and Certan were crouched behind him.

What did I do? Alrion rose to his feet, and stumbled, so he dropped back to the ground and sat down, waiting for his friends to return.

Lara and Certan had concerned looks of their faces. Ashra had a blank look, that was undecipherable.

"You are not ready," he said to Alrion.

"I know."

"I don't think you do. Where did you learn how to craft a lightbomb?"

"I don't know, it must have come from the Pool." Alrion shrugged, it was as good a guess as any.

"Partial knowledge is incredibly dangerous. You very nearly killed your friends. Such a spell is not taught lightly, and much caution is used in its practice and application. You don't even know what you did do you?"

"I know enough to recreate it, but you're right. It was all instinctive."

"You have good survival instincts, that attack would certainly have destroyed your enemy or forced him to retreat. But the cost is too great. If I were not here to shield your friends, they would be gone," Ashra said. Alrion let that sink in.

"I'm sorry. But what are you?" Alrion said.

"I'm a wizard. What did you expect?"

"But the Shade?"

"An illusion to test you. It caused quite a stir I can see. I was actually up on the ridge with your friends for the majority of the battle. My instincts are pretty good too," Ashra said.

"He was commenting on what was happening, which helped us follow along. Lucky he was there to protect us. What about next time?" Lara said.

"I am really sorry. Maybe I can work on controlling this spell better for next time," Alrion said.

"You will not!" Ashra shouted.

"Why?"

"It's too dangerous, it cannot be easily controlled. You should forget that you even know it."

"What do I do then? I have no effective spells against Wraith, the creature that Branthor has become." Alrion felt incredibly frustrated.

"I will train you and show you how to harness the power of earth and water. You have too few tools at your disposal."

"You will then?"

"Yes, on one condition."

"Which is?"

"You never use a spell you don't understand when there is the potential for friendly casualties. I never quite understood what the legends of the Pool of Knowledge were about, but now I know for sure. You have everything ever used and recorded stuffed into that mind of yours. Anything could come out. You cannot let yourself lose control. The risk is very high. This is why I will train you. It would be incredibly irresponsible otherwise. Who knows what you could do," Ashra said.

"I accept your condition. But first I have a question."

"Yes?"

"How did you do water spells? And how useful will they be in the desert?" Alrion said. Ashra laughed and even Certan chuckled.

"There is much water in the desert. Some in the air, but most of it is deep underground. You just need to know how to harvest it. I imagine the desert wizard is quite adept at that," Certan said.

"You are quite correct. It's also a rather important ingredient in my illusion spells."

"Illusion spells require water?"

"Of course. Once I explain it will make perfect sense. But for now, let's return to the hut and rest," Ashra said. He leaned down and offered a hand to Alrion. The young wizard accepted it and rose again to his feet, a bit more steadily this time.

"Do you need assistance?" Certan said.

"No, I'm alright now. Each step I regain some strength," Alrion said.

"Very well, we are here to help," Certan said. They walked together, following Ashra back to the hut.

The hut was cool and comfortable compared to the intensity of the heat outside.

"How long have you lived here?" Alrion said.

"Many years. I don't fit in well with society. Your grandfather approached me back in the day and offered me a place in the academy. But I declined, and stayed here, living out my days in peace. Refining my spells and helping the odd traveller. Secretly of course," Ashra said.

"The stories are true!" Certan said.

"Yes, well some of them at least."

"What stories?" Lara said.

"Tales of travellers who are lost, thirsty and unable to move. They find themselves in a mysterious oasis and a voice tells them to refresh and guides them on the path out. They've even given a name to the voice."

"Which is?" Lara said.

"Caretaker of the desert."

"That's you? The man who doesn't like people?" Alrion said.

"I didn't say I helped everyone. Just the ones I come across that I can't avoid helping. It gives me a way to practice my craft," Ashra said.

"On your own terms," Alrion said.

"Exactly. I don't want every man and his dog wandering out here and forming an orderly line at my front door. It's more fun this way."

"When does training start?"

"Tomorrow. I know you are in a rush, but you need to recover today so we can do it properly."

"That's fine, I understand. Maybe you can at least explain a bit about the illusion spells then?"

"I may as well, and it may benefit your friends to know a little about it too. Have you ever seen a rainbow?" Ashra said.

"Yes."

"They're created by the light passing through water and splitting into distinct colours. Building upon this basic principle, you can make the light do whatever you want. With a few tricks to complete the illusion you can fool people into believing that your image is real."

"Wow, I hadn't thought of it that way."

"Knowledge is so important, as you are discovering. It is the gateway to the formerly impossible," Ashra said, giving them a wry smile.

"Sounds like something I could use," Lara said.

"I'm sure you could. Unfortunately, there's very little that can be accomplished by knowledge and will. You need the power of Spark to fuel these spells. But knowing the principles may help you to see through the illusions of others, and understand the limitations of what Alrion will be able to do," Ashra said.

"True, but I'm definitely disappointed," Lara said.

"Sorry, that's just how it is. The wizards get the interesting toys," Ashra said.

"Why don't you come with us? You can train me on the way and escort us to the desert temple," Alrion said.

"Absolutely not," Ashra said without hesitation.

"Why not?"

"This is my home here, and I feel a responsibility for aiding in your training. But I will not be pulled into your quest. It is yours alone. Besides, as I mentioned before I think there is already a wizard following your progress."

"I can't convince you?"

"No. This is the way it must be. If you want more help figure out who that wizard is that's already involved," Ashra said. He gave Alrion a cryptic smile.

"You've figured something out, haven't you?" Alrion said.

"Maybe, maybe not. But all of you should rest and prepare. Tomorrow we begin," Ashra said. He gestured at the room, pointing out food, water, and cushions. Then he walked out of the hut.

"Such a strange man," Certan said.

"But he will help, in some way. That's what counts." Alrion pondered what kind of training he would receive. From early impressions, it would be quite different to what he received from Falric.

23

IMPENDING DANGER

Vincent put down his tools and wiped the sweat from his brow. John was sure working him hard.

I guess he's trying to get back into the good graces for the guards. They seemed pretty persistent with their questioning before. Thinking back, he realised that he hadn't seen Celes for a while either.

It's not like her to dally. Maybe she actually found something? Vincent mused. He wandered around to see what John was working on.

"Hello there Vincent, how are you going today?" he said.

"Great. I finished up those pieces you asked for." Vincent pointed over at his completed work.

"Really? You're pretty fast, I must admit I wasn't sure what to expect."

"I have a lot of experience, just not in these. It's been a good exercise," Vincent said.

"You've done way more than I thought. I'll have to give you some gold to compensate you."

"Don't be silly, you're letting me stay that's payment enough. Earlier, was everything alright? What ended up happening with that guard?"

"Oh, I really don't know what their problem is. Everything here is business as usual. I didn't like their tone either." John seemed quite hurt by the accusatory manner of the conversation.

"Yeah, they didn't seem particularly friendly, lots of accusations being thrown around. Are they always like that?"

"No, not generally. Now they aren't the friendliest folk, but generally politer and by the book. Something must have really stirred them up." John heard footsteps nearby and turned to look at who was approaching. "Speaking of which," he said and stepped forward.

Vincent looked over and noticed a female guard approaching.

"Hello again blacksmith, how are you?" she said. She flashed a smile that Vincent was certain was purely false.

"Same as before, busy. To what do I owe this pleasure?" John said.

"I realised I was a little harsh earlier, and wanted to come apologise. You have been a trusted partner to the guard for a long time, and I didn't give you due respect. To explain my actions a little more, I would just like to add that we're under a lot of pressure. It doesn't excuse my actions, but I hope it provides some context," she said. John looked to be swayed by her words, but Vincent was more sceptical.

"That's good of you, not enough folks take responsibility for their actions these days," John said.

"Absolutely. I don't think I was properly introduced to your colleague before," the guard said.

"Vincent, nice to meet you," Vincent said, offering his hand. The guard took off her gauntlet and shook his hand. Her grip was firm, a little too firm. Vincent was used to strong shakes, and with his strength could crush a hand if he wanted. But he was surprised.

"Tanya, nice to meet you also. You are new here?" she said.

"Yes, he joined recently, helping me get through the additional work. He's been a big help," John said.

"Been in town long?" Tanya said.

"Not that long. Looking to pick up some new skills and work on some more interesting pieces. I've done enough horse shoes for a lifetime," Vincent said chuckling. Tanya smiled but continued her questioning.

"Of course. Have you seen anything suspicious around? Maybe you've left things where they shouldn't have been?" she said.

"Can't say I have, it's been quiet here. John, have you seen anything left where it shouldn't be?" Vincent said.

"No, everything's been where it should. I even double checked today just to make sure," he said.

"Of course. I just need to make sure I leave no stone unturned, this is quite a high-pressure environment right now," Tanya said. John nodded sympathetically.

"Tell me about it. I've got huge orders to fulfil, and no time to do it. The work is detail orientated so it's incredibly time consuming," he said.

"I understand. Please think about it and let me know if you hear anything. You can come to the guard station and ask for Glinda," Glinda said.

"Will do. Thank you for coming back, I really value a good working relationship with the guards," John said.

"And we value your work too. Good day," Glinda said and left.

"What did you make of that?" Vincent said.

"She's had to change her tune, probably due to someone higher up getting annoyed. She was almost convincing, but you could see through it all."

"I agree completely. She clearly could care less about you but had to come back and be politer. One to watch out for."

"Wise words. You had enough for the day?"

"Yes, if you don't mind I'd like some time to explore the city and rest." Vincent scanned the background and took note of the direction in which Glinda had left.

"Not a problem, you've done a day's work anyway. Let me get you a few gold to enjoy yourself." John reached for his pouch.

"No, I insist. If you're really adamant at the end we can figure something out. But for now, I'm happy with the experience. It's invaluable," Vincent said.

"As you wish. Have a good rest, see you tomorrow," John said.

"Thanks, you too," Vincent said and returned to his work area. He put everything away and changed clothes.

If I rush I can catch up to her, Vincent thought. He was worried about not seeing Celes again, and decided that Glinda was his best avenue. He jogged along the street, trying to catch sight of the guard again. She wasn't headed towards the guard station, but in the opposite direction. He considered trying to follow her, but decided that it wasn't the best idea. Being direct would suit him better.

Once he was within range he shouted.

"Glinda, have you a moment!" Vincent said. The female guard stopped and turned around. She had an annoyed look on her face, but forced it away when she saw Vincent.

"Yes, of course," she said.

"Great, I was thinking about what you said and thought of something that may help. I did see a woman around the other night. I didn't think anything of it, but since I saw her more than once I remembered her face. It could be nothing but..."

"That is a fantastic lead. Let me think for a moment." Glinda seemed to stare off into space for a while. Suddenly she refocused on Vincent. "Would you be able to recognise her if you saw her?" she said.

"Absolutely."

"Come with me then, we could definitely use your help," Glinda said.

"Happy to help," Vincent said with a smile. The guard walked off with purpose, and Vincent followed close behind.

"Do you have this woman in custody?" Vincent said.

"No, but we have a suspicious woman that is our main suspect. You could provide the additional verification we require," Glinda said.

This is not good. What is Celes mixed up in? It could be a coincidence, but it really seemed like they had Celes and wanted to confirm she was the one they were after.

That strange pause and look from the guard, maybe that's what they look like when they communicate, Vincent thought. It was a good theory, and they suspected the guard was Tainted. Now he just had to think about what to do if his suspicions were right. He was definitely walking into a dangerous situation.

He mused over that scenario as they walked. Vincent noticed a disruption up head. There was a shape moving fast through the crowd of people. From the reactions of the people shifting and complaining it was coming towards them. Suddenly a shape broke out from the crowd and leapt at Glinda.

It was a tiny girl with short brown hair. She tackled Glinda and the guard caught the girl and swung her into a more comfortable position.

"Baby girl, I'm working right now. Where's the rest of your friends?"

"Over there with the teacher. They're talking about the trees, it's so boring!"

"If you pay attention you may learn something interesting. I have to escort this gentleman somewhere, so please rejoin your friends and I will see you after work!"

"Sorry," Vincent said, shrugging his shoulders, and apologising to the young girl. She responded by playfully poking her tongue out at him.

"Alright, I guess I can do that. See you later!" the girl said, jumped back to the ground and tore off with fantastic speed back through the crowds.

"She's quite energetic, that's good. Such a nice age," Vincent said.

"Thanks. I take it you have kids?" Glinda said.

"Just the one. But he's older now, doing his own thing. No more running hugs," Vincent said with a chuckle.

"Yeah those can't last, can they?" Glinda said. Her tone of voice had changed, and she was silent for the rest of the walk.

Maybe we've all misjudged her? What would an ordinary person do when put in an extraordinary situation? What if she had to play along to keep your daughter safe?

"He's with me," Glinda said, and Vincent broke out of his inner thought. They were in front of a manor house with a large gate and guards.

This looks like trouble. He started to focus on the job ahead.

Glinda led him down a side passage and into the house. Vincent could tell the house was home to a very important person. It was richly furnished and had extremely elaborate floorings and paintings.

I hope she's here.

"In here please," Glinda didn't even look at Vincent while she opened the door. He stepped inside and saw it was a drab grey room with no furnishings. He could see Celes sitting in the corner. He rushed over immediately.

"Did they hurt you?" he said.

"No, I'm fine. I refused to talk so they threw me in here. I think they were planning something else, but they suddenly changed their minds."

"Good. When you didn't return, I told the guard that I saw a woman sneaking around so that they would bring me in. It worked," Vincent said softly.

"I see you recognise her, perhaps even know her?" a sarcastic voice said from the doorway. Vincent looked up and saw a well-dressed man in ornate robes addressing them. Glinda had retreated into the corridor and had turned to leave.

"And who might you be?" Vincent said.

"None of your concern," he said.

"He's a councillor," Celes said.

"Corrupt official? That's a bit of a cliché, isn't it? Couldn't help yourself?" Vincent said. The councillor pursed his lips but suppressed an outburst.

"I'm quite pleased. We have the spy and her accomplice in our custody. Wraith will give a lot to have his hands on you," the councillor said with a dark laugh. He continued to smirk then slammed the door. Vincent stood up and examined the room. It looked solid and the door was heavy and metal. There was a keyhole though.

"Do you think you could pick this?" he said to Celes.

"Probably. But I don't want to try just yet, we haven't gotten the information we need."

"That councillor runs the show around here?"

"Looks like it. That guard reported in to him, she's a piece of work, isn't she?"

"I had thought that too, but we ran into her daughter on the way here. It showed another side of her. Maybe she's just caught up in this?"

"But she's Tainted, I know that for sure." Celes looked adamant and quite irate.

"Yes, but do you think that's by choice? Especially with a daughter to look after," Vincent said.

Celes started to speak, but stopped. She looked thoughtful. "I hadn't considered that. You could be right," she said.

"I think I am, at least on this. Do you have a plan?"

"Yes. Let's appear like we can't escape, and see what they have in store for us. They appear quite confident, they didn't take anything from me," Celes said.

"Sure, we can give them a hard time if they are asking for it. I just hope we get something out of this."

"Did you have anything better to do?" Celes said with a laugh.

"I don't suppose that I do. At least we're here together." Vincent was all jokes and comfort, but he didn't feel right. These people were more dangerous than they appeared. But for now, he would wait, and see what opportunities were presented.

24

SAND AND WATER

Alrion followed Ashra out into the oasis.

"As you know, this is all an illusion. I'll demonstrate," Ashra said. He snapped his fingers and the lush scenery disappeared and was replaced by the desert, some rubble, and a stone wall.

"It's still amazing to see," Alrion said.

"Yes, it's a neat trick. But very difficult to do. We're not going start with that, and we may not even get there. But at least I will help you understand the principles at work and how to get started with manipulating water. The first thing we need to do, is to tap into your senses," Ashra said. He said down on the ground and directed Alrion to join him.

"It's really hot," he said.

"It is, but it's not dangerous. Your reaction to the heat can be managed, it's just another sense. Something that will come easier once you complete the Vault of Silence." Ashra paused for dramatic effect.

"Can you tell me more about that?"

"No. Concentrate on what we are here to do. Place your hand on the ground like this," Ashra said, demonstrating by placing his own palm on the ground.

"Done."

"Now there is a large reservoir of water below us, but it's deep. You need to visualise a drop of water falling from your palm, through the earth and re-joining the water below. Imagine that single drop rippling through the calm surface of the water, and sounding like the toll of a high-pitched bell," Ashra said. Alrion concentrated hard but struggled to do so. The only water he could imagine leaving his palm was his sweat from the extreme heat.

"I can see that you are struggling. I'll help a little," Ashra said. He snapped his fingers again and a large tree put them in shade. Alrion felt cooler and more focused immediately.

He focused again, visualising the droplet of water passing through the layers of earth and dripping into a large reservoir. He could hear the bell-like chime of the water echoing in the space and his mind filled with the awareness of the body of water.

"Yes! That's it. Draw it up into your palm!" Ashra said.

Alrion didn't know how to do that, but he could imagine it. He pictured himself scooping a handful of water and saw it materialise in his hand. "Wow! My hand is wet," Alrion said with surprise. He lifted his hand and saw the water below it sink back into the ground. He felt the wetness of his hand, and was amazed. "But how? Can anyone do that?" he said.

"No, you need Spark for that. But the heavy lifting is done by your mind and visualisation. How are you feeling?" Ashra said.

"Refreshed, which makes me wonder where this shelter came from," Alrion said, looking around.

"It's all in your mind," Ashra said, snapping his fingers. The shade and shelter vanished and the sun was beating down on Alrion again.

"Do you believe that I can create shelter and destroy it with merely a thought?"

"No." Alrion could almost believe it though. But he would have felt silly to admit that.

"Then how did I do it?"

"An illusion?"

"Precisely. But how did you feel when I did it?"

"I felt like I was cooler, sheltered and I could focus better," Alrion said.

"Exactly! And yet the same amount of sun was hitting you, and the ground was just as hot. But your perception changed. So, you felt more comfortable. Let that sink in," Ashra said. He stood up and paced around the area. Alrion was amazed by the revelation.

"Seems like there's a lot you can do with illusions," Alrion said.

"There certainly is. But they are very difficult. We'll only be able to lay down the groundwork before you leave."

"Why?"

"I can't keep you long, a day or two at most. And we also need to work on other things. For now, I want you to fill this bowl," Ashra said. He retrieved a plain circular bowl and placed it down in front of Alrion.

"Fill it with water?"

"Yes, you can draw it, so let's gather it," Ashra said.

"Sure, let's give this a go." Alrion concentrated once more and began the visualisation.

Hours passed and Alrion had finally filled the bowl.

"I feel like I have sweated enough to fill it twice over," he said.

"You also lost some to the heat of the desert," Ashra said.

"That makes me feel a bit better."

"Good. You did well, now drink it and let's move on." Ashra pointed at the water.

"Drink it? Isn't that a waste?"

"Do you see any other water around here? We can't have you fainting on me," Ashra said, laughing. Alrion drank the water, and it seemed particularly refreshing.

"You can work on that more as you travel, but water is an essential element in many different spells. Next, we will work on earth manipulation. You need to understand how to use it, and how to counter it," Ashra said. He walked away and made a motion with his hands like he was pulling up the earth. A small mound of dirt piled up in front of him.

"This should be easier for you. It's developing an affinity with the earth, then using force to manipulate it. You seem to be pretty good at using force through the air, this is just a different application," Ashra said.

"Sounds sensible," Alrion said.

"It is. Try it now. Focus yourself and gather up a pile of dirt like mine," Ashra said. Alrion looked at the ground and gathered his Spark, fuelling the fire within. He sent his force at the ground and imagined drawing out the earth into a mound. However, the opposite happened. He managed to fling the dust everywhere. He could hear Ashra laughing amidst it.

"That's an effective escape tool, but not quite what we were after. Pull, not push," he said.

"That's what I was trying to do," Alrion said. Annoyed with himself.

"You need to think about what you are doing, and not just assume that a simple change in your thinking will alter the result," Ashra said patiently. Alrion thought over what the older wizard had said, and decided to try again. He broke down his actions into smaller steps. It was working. He could sense that the process was working differently, and slowly but surely, he created a small dust pile.

"That's better. See what I mean?" Ashra said.

"Yes, there are fundamental steps that are different that I didn't alter the first time."

"Yes. Your instincts are good, but you can't shortcut everything. But you see this pile, it's not useful. It has no strength of structure," Ashra said, kicking his pile of dirt. It dispersed without effort. He focused again and created a small wall of the same height.

"Come and examine this," he said. Alrion walked over and felt the wall with his hand.

"It's solid," he said.

"Good. And what else?"

"It's not as dry, is there water within it?"

"Good. The sand and dirt here is so dry it is harder to maintain forms with it. A bit of water to bind it works wonders. Now you try to build a wall," he said. Alrion looked unsure, but looked back down at the ground and started to concentrate.

He started to assemble the pile of dirt, and placed his hand on it to assist with drawing the water. And it worked, but not the way he had hoped. The water pooled into the middle of the pile, muddying it, and not assisting with any structural integrity.

"That's quite a common problem," Ashra said.

"How do I fix it?" Alrion said.

"Less water and more distributed. You need to find a way to draw the water with more finesse. A pool of it doesn't help, as you can see."

"Is there a trick to it?"

"Of course, but it's something you need to puzzle out," Ashra said. He disassembled his wall and created himself a chair to sit in. He sat back, crossed his legs, and watched Alrion work.

Show-off! Alrion thought. He had to figure out how to make the wall work. He could see how useful the technique was. "I need to first figure out how to draw less water," Alrion said to himself. He started by practising variations of how he drew the water, but instead of the water forming into a greater body, he imagined thin wispy strands of it travelling through the air. He used the strands to define blocks and bind them together. It started working. His pile of dust and sand started to form into something with more structure, even though it wasn't particularly neat.

"That's the way," Ashra said. Once Alrion had finished, the desert wizard stood up and walked over. He kicked the wall and it practically disintegrated.

"Needs a bit more strength," he said with a chuckle.

"Just a tiny bit," Alrion said, sharing a smile.

"You've done well, let's rest for a while," Ashra said, heading back to his little hut. Alrion followed closely, pausing to look back at the remnants of his small wall.

They found Lara and Certan lounging in the hut, avoiding the heat.

"Aren't you hungry? We ate hours ago," Lara said as they approached. Alrion hadn't even realised how much time had passed.

"No, although I can definitely eat now. Too much concentration required," Alrion said, flopping down onto one of the cushions.

"How's he doing?" Certan said to Ashra.

"Fairly well, I don't have a comparison because I don't teach others. But I think he's getting the principles which is the most important part. We will practise more today on what we have learned, and try a few new things tomorrow," Ashra said.

"How long will it take?" Alrion said.

"Years, but you get two days with me. You'll be leaving tomorrow evening."

"How is that going to be enough?"

"Time is against you. Your enemy has been one step ahead the entire time, and knows everything you do since he has also drunk from the Pool of Knowledge. Have you considered that?" Ashra said. Alrion felt defensive immediately.

"Sure, but I still need to prepare. He's practically invincible!"

"There is always a way. All I can do is help you start down the path. You must follow it yourself. Be prepared for anything is my best advice," he said. Alrion ate quickly, and took the opportunity to rest out of the heat. Just as he became comfortable Ashra abruptly stood up.

"Time to get back to work, you have rested enough," he said.

"Have fun!" Lara said.

"You too, I hope I don't miss anything," Alrion said, trying to make a joke.

"We shall keep a detailed log," Certan said, getting in on the joke. Alrion shook his head at the lameness of the reply and followed Ashra back to where they had been training.

The hours passed quickly once more, and Alrion refined his ability to draw water and form the earth into a simple wall. He felt pleased by that, but wasn't sure if it would be effective for anything useful.

"That's enough for today, let's join the others," Ashra said.

Together they walked back to the hut and found Lara and Certan in the same spots. It looked like they hadn't moved at all.

"Having a nice time?" Alrion said.

"It's not too bad, I could get used to this. I'd get bored though I think," Lara said.

"Some additional time to rest and recover is quite important. I would advise it for you, if we had the capacity to spare it," Certan said.

"Someday perhaps. I've been meaning to ask, where do you get this food from?" Alrion pointed at the various breads and biscuits and other food that was available.

"I do leave the hut occasionally you know, but I do also have to provide for myself quite a bit," Ashra said. He walked over to a corner of the hut and lifted the dirty brown rug there. Underneath was a trap door.

"This is interesting," Lara said jumping up immediately. Ashra opened the trap door and revealed a ladder going down into the ground. He started to descend and the others followed close.

Alrion found himself in a giant cavern. There were stores of food on shelves carved into the walls, benches, and other furnishing. Two fire pits were in the middle of the room.

"This is your kitchen then," Certan said.

"That's it. I use a few shortcuts, but otherwise it keeps me busy. I usually sleep down here as well when it gets particularly cold."

"This is incredible!" Lara said walking around the room.

"Thank you, I appreciate that. This is my home, so I need a few things. I can't live off the wind and sand you know," Ashra said. Certan laughed.

"Alrion, recover as best you can, we have an early start tomorrow," Ashra said, starting to prepare a meal for dinner.

Alrion awoke suddenly to Ashra's face in close proximity.

"Time to start, we eat later," Ashra said. Alrion rose quietly and they left Certan and Lara asleep. A short walk later they were back to the training area.

"First thing today, I want you to build a curved wall. Same principles as yesterday, but more complexity in the construction," Ashra said. He demonstrated by building a wall that curved slightly towards him.

"You used something similar to enclose me in the fight," Alrion said.

"Exactly. That's the end-game for a technique such as this. It can be used for many different things. Enclosing an enemy, shielding a target, hiding things, or protecting them from harm. I don't expect you to master it now, but I want you to understand the principles," Ashra said. Alrion could see the benefits, and threw himself into the practice. His few two attempts were barely curved at all. When Ashra chided him for being too cautious, Alrion changed his approach and made a wall that couldn't stand at all. But the extreme curvature did teach him something about the technique. He ended up with something similar to what Ashra had built eventually.

"I think you're beginning to understand. Still lacking strength," Ashra commented, collapsing the wall with his palm without exerting any effort.

"What can I do to improve that?" Alrion said.

"More compacting of the sand, injecting more Spark into the binding process. It takes a bit of experimentation to understand how it works." Ashra did another quick demonstration.

"I see," Alrion said, preparing to try again.

"Leave that for now, I have one other things you must learn. Wait here a moment," Ashra said. He walked off back to the hut and returned soon after. He was holding a large red cushion. The colour was a little faded, but it was still a bright red.

"You're going to make this cushion blue," Ashra said.

"Really?"

"Yes. Observe," Ashra said. He waved his hand over the cushion and it looked a vibrant blue colour.

"Wow, that was quick!"

"Come over here," Ashra said. Alrion walked around and Ashra directed him to look at the cushion from behind.

"It's red," Alrion said.

"Yes, it is. The first rule of an illusion is that you need to understand how it will be viewed," Ashra said.

"Is it possible to completely cover something?" Alrion said.

"Yes, but it requires you to consider all the angles and prepare appropriately. The spell becomes much more complex. It's a trade-off between the quality of the illusion and the effort of creating and maintaining it."

"So, you can't just create it and leave it?"

"You can, there are ways. But it lacks the nuance that your mind brings to it. Suitable for things that would not get close scrutiny, but the effect eventually fades. For now though, let's just focus on something that you must create yourself," Ashra said.

"How do I do it?"

"You draw water, like we have practised. But you imagine it as a light spray intersecting with the air and the light, bending the rays. Then you inject your vision into the water, and create the illusion."

"Sounds tricky," Alrion said, doubt entering his voice.

"It is, but it's incredibly useful. Just try to make this cushion green," Ashra said.

"I'll do it!" Alrion reminded himself that he had come a long way, and already learned some new skills. This was just another one. He concentrated and found the underground water reservoir, drawing the water once more. He tried to disperse it and use it as a fine blanket in front of the cushion.

"It looks like you're wetting it, finer again and not so close," Ashra said. Alrion doubled his efforts, and kept trying. He kept the vision in his head completely clear, the cushion was not blue it was green.

"You're getting it, keep going," Ashra said. He could see that the pillow was starting to appear green in places, where Alrion had been successful. As he watched the cushion slowly alternated between the two colours in constantly changing patches. Then all of a sudden it locked in, and the cushion was green.

"That's it, now just open your eyes," Ashra said. Alrion opened his eyes and saw that the cushion was still blue.

"Come around here and look," Ashra said. Alrion walked slowly, trying to maintain his focus. As he took the last step he cautiously looked over at the cushion.

"It's green!" Alrion shouted in excitement. In that instant, the illusion dropped and the cushion was blue once more.

"Well done. Now you just need to practise some more. By the end of the day I need you to be able to make this cushion appear any colour I specify from any direction," Ashra said. Alrion felt exhausted already from the effort. It wasn't just a case of drawing on his Spark, the focus and concentration required were huge.

"I just didn't expect it to be so tiring," he said.

"That's why Will is such a key component of magic. The more you train and enhance it, the less effort it takes to create and maintain all these spells that require your mind's focus. Raw power is not always the answer, as you are no doubt finding out," Ashra said. Alrion nodded with understanding. He had discovered vast tracts of power, but Ashra had easily beaten him. Defeated by the desert wizard's superior Will and training. Alrion had to improve in all areas if he was going to succeed.

"Almost there," Alrion whispered to himself, then threw everything back into his training.

25

BUNKERING DOWN

Alrion stumbled twice while walking back to the hut. Extreme exhaustion was making every step a challenge.

At least the heat is dropping, he thought. The relative cool of the hut was incredibly soothing, and he quickly dropped down onto one of the pillows.

"Tough day?" Lara said. Alrion just nodded.

"He did well, but you'll need to let him rest a few hours before you leave," Ashra said.

"What did you learn today?" Certan said.

"Basic illusions. I can make that cushion appear a different colour," Alrion said, pointing at a cushion at random.

"Can you show me?" Lara said. Alrion just groaned.

"He's a little tired, I'm sure he will perk up and give a demonstration later," Ashra said.

"You seem fine," Lara said.

"I have a little more practise. Alrion has been doing this the hard way. The burden of that extreme focus has worn him out. I'm sure Certan understands what I mean." Ashra gave Certan a knowing look.

"Yes, until you achieve competency then mastery, exerting the

Will is very draining. We had a little exercise demonstrating that a few days ago," Certan said.

"And I was the winner!" Lara said.

"That doesn't surprise me," Ashra said with a laugh. He disappeared downstairs and Lara followed him.

"Don't worry it will get easier," Certan said.

"I don't doubt you, I just can't understand it right now," Alrion said.

"Yes, your mind is too tired. But you are strengthening it every day, so don't worry. Maintaining your Will is a constant effort, you cannot just achieve a milestone then ignore it."

"But you're a monk, surely you just have it now?" Alrion said.

"In some ways yes, but in others no. Let me show you something." Certan removed a small flask from his robes and handed it to Alrion. It was metallic and had the symbol of the monk order on it.

"What is this?" Alrion said.

"It was made for the monks by a craftsman who they had saved in the desert. It was originally intended for water, but it was too heavy and impractical for daily use. So, it was instead filled with a strong alcoholic spirit and kept in storage."

"And you took it? When you left?"

"Yes, I don't know why. It seemed like an even worse thing to do on top of everything else. And I drank from it nearly every day, just a drop to make sure I could keep it as long as possible. But since I met you, I stopped." A lightness broke up the sadness on Certan's face. He looked hopeful.

"You haven't drunk from it since then?"

"No, there's still some left. Every day I look at the flask, and I am tempted to drink from it. Just for a taste. But every day I stop and remind myself, that this symbol of my failure can be a sign of my success. If I can return to the monks and show that there is still alcohol left in this flask, then I can prove to them that I overcame my weakness and strengthened my Will," Certan said.

"Thanks for sharing that story. I never realised that this was still such a struggle for you." Alrion handed back the flask.

Certan carefully returned it to within his robes. "I suspect I may never be clear of it, but perhaps I can forgive myself one day and it will become easier. Ah, it looks like the food is now here." Certan rose and helped Lara and Ashra distribute the bread.

"Eat well, you will need your strength. You must leave tonight so you can make good time. Certan, are you familiar with this area at night?" Ashra said.

"Mostly, it will not be an issue," he said.

"Good, you all eat your fill I will pack you some supplies," Ashra said, and disappeared again downstairs. Alrion and the others started to get ready, and soon they were standing at the entrance to the hut, packing away the food provided by Ashra.

"You've been such an incredible help. I was a little resistant, and I'm sorry," Alrion said.

"Don't worry, we are all under our own pressures. You did well here, good luck on your journey," Ashra said.

"Are you sure I can't convince you to come with us? Just to the temple? You wouldn't need to leave the desert," Alrion said.

"Not a chance. This is your journey, and I have played my part. Everything will be fine, just remember what I have shown you. And trust your companions, they are quite resourceful."

"Alright then. Goodbye and thanks again," Alrion said.

"It was enlightening to meet the legend himself, and to confirm your existence," Certan said.

"You keep that conformation to yourself. It's too troublesome diverting large numbers of visitors," Ashra said.

"I think you'd secretly let some in, you aren't as bad as you make out," Lara said.

"I'd appreciate if you don't share those sentiments," Ashra said.

"Don't worry, we won't send anyone here," Alrion said, and waved as they set off.

"Good luck young man. You have the slimmest of chances, but maybe you will succeed," Ashra whispered, then retreated to his hut. He looked out into the desert, and felt a chill run down his spine. Something bad was coming.

Certan lead the way, making as much haste as possible. He wanted to capitalise on the available light. Alrion was a bit slow, but once they worked into a rhythm the steps flowed easier.

"What a strange man, I don't know how you could live in such a place all by yourself," Lara said.

"There must be a story behind that. Something significant changed that man," Certan said.

"I wonder why," Alrion said. From what he knew of wizards, Ashra seemed positively brilliant. He would be remarkable in any setting, but had chosen to stay in such an isolated and remote place.

"We shouldn't stop yet, but the light is fading. Can you assist?" Certan said. Alrion created three orbs of light, and placed one above his right shoulder and positioned the other two with Certan and Lara.

"A bit brighter," Lara said. Alrion increased the intensity slowly.

"That's it," Certan said. Alrion took a moment to stabilise the spell and make it easier to maintain, then continued on.

They trekked down minor paths which wouldn't be visible unless they were known. But the path ended soon, and they had to traverse up and down sand dunes.

"Is there no other way?" Alrion said, struggling to keep up. He was already tired and had to keep up the light spells as well.

"There is, but it is a much further distance and would result in more effort. This is definitely worth the additional fatigue," Certan said.

"Fine," Alrion said, and persevered. With each step, he felt like he was sliding back ever slightly, which increased the strain and the feeling that he was not progressing.

"A bit further," Certan said, then they suddenly passed over a dune and down onto a nice flat surface.

"Can you illuminate the distance?" Certan said. Alrion repositioned and repurposed Certan's light, casting rays into the distance. Before them spread an expanse of desert. There was nothing as far as they could see.

"We have arrived at the plain of despair," Certan said.

"That's a lovely name," Lara said.

"Yes, it's named because we are relatively central to the desert and there is nothing for a long way. Just flat desert. Many get stuck here and lose their sense of direction, and despair. It is the despair that kills, the feeling of helplessness. If you keep a cool head and keep travelling in a single direction you will get somewhere in time," Certan said. Alrion could believe the despair, he couldn't see anything that would serve as a landmark.

"Definitely not sure I would like to get stranded. How much further should we go tonight?" Lara said.

"As far as Alrion can make it. There's nowhere to take shelter here, and we can rest during the day if we can find somewhere suitable," Certan said.

"Shelter from what?" Alrion said.

"Dust storms. They're relatively rare, and don't last long. But you can be sure if we are caught up in the middle of nowhere we will get one. Best to move along as far as possible."

"You've convinced me, let's get moving. Can you keep up Alrion?" Lara said.

"For now, let's just get on with it." Alrion let the light dim to assist with his concentration. He had to concentrate more on walking faster and more carefully.

They continued in relative quiet for the next few hours. Alrion had no idea how long had actually elapsed, because the dark and the bare surroundings didn't offer any idea of how far they had travelled.

"How do you keep us on track?" Alrion said.

"You learn to develop a good internal compass. There are minor clues spread around, and also our footsteps are a good marker," Certan said. Alrion paused and looked back. There was definitely evidence of their passing.

"How long do they stick around?" Lara said.

"It depends on the winds. Hours probably, not more usually. There's not as much shifting around here unless there's a storm so it can be longer if the weather permits. Are you worried about us being followed?" Certan said.

"Not really, I was just curious. I like to know what kind of trail we are leaving."

"That's quite wise. It would be easy for someone to follow us right now. We would probably see evidence of their light if that were the case, but you never know," Certan said. Alrion started to imagine people tracking them through the desert then dismissed the thought. He quickened his pace to catch up to Certan. Just as he drew close, Certan abruptly stopped.

"Alrion, magnify the light again please," he said. Alrion complied, giving Certan a good view of the distance.

"Do you see that?" Certan said, pointing.

"No, what is it?" Alrion said.

"Is that a storm?" Lara said.

"Yes. Quite a big one if you can see it from this distance in the dark," Certan said.

"What do we do?" Alrion said.

"We look for shelter, we can't take any chances. I don't like the way it is moving, it seems unnatural." Certan started to look around at the area. As before, there was nothing around just the flat expanse of sand.

"I can build something," Alrion said.

"It's our only chance. I just hope you can make it strong, this is going to be a nasty storm," Certan said.

"No pressure then. I've just been training all day and walking all night," Alrion said with a sigh.

"Dig deep please. I've heard of these storms and they're awful," Lara said. Alrion tried to shake off his exhaustion and concentrate.

"It's approaching quite fast. You've probably got five minutes," Certan said.

"That will do," Alrion said, trying to sound confident. He had made a slightly curved wall, but that wasn't going to be enough. He needed to completely cover them.

"Here goes," he said to himself, and started gathering his Spark. It seemed to be in good supply, which was reassuring. It was the mental exertion and fatigue that he had to combat. He first detected a body of water nearby, then began to draw together his wall. Rather than just go with the curve, he visualised it extending further in the shape of a dome. Several times he had to stop, and reform a section because it wasn't right. But he seemed to be getting the structural integrity right.

"I don't mean to alarm you, but it's almost upon us. If we don't have a complete shield we're going to be buried alive in sand," Certan said. Alrion increased his efforts, but also increased his mistakes.

"I think you just need to finish this," Lara said. Alrion didn't look up but he heard the fear in her voice. His dome was only three-quarters completed, and they were all hunched over to stay within it.

"Get down now! Alrion do what you can to finish," Certan said. Lara lay down quickly, and Certan joined her. Alrion slowly sank down as he held his concentration. He could hear the whistling and howling of the wind, and the sand flying everywhere. It was almost upon them. He extended his dome, just as the first wave of sand hit it. He could feel the impact of the wind and sand on his creation.

"It's not going to hold, do something!" Lara said. Certan half stood up and braced the weak section with his hands. Alrion infused the sand with his Spark, trying to reinforce it. He felt the structure of the dome altering and re-forming. It was hardening in a way that he had never achieved in his practise. "Over there, is that another storm?" Lara shouted above the howling.

Sand was entering from the not-quite closed rear of the dome. Certan lay down, blocking the gap with his body and Alrion rushed to complete the dome. As he was extending it he was trying to strengthen it. He collapsed to his knees, and released the spell. The three of them sat very quietly, listening to the storm rage around them.

"I think you did it," Certain said with caution. Lara crept around the whole structure, listening carefully, and feeling it with her hands.

"I think it will hold, for now," she said, looking at Alrion with concern.

26

KEY FINDING

Keys jangled and the lock creaked and groaned. The heavy metal door slowly opened, making even more noise than anything else. Vincent looked up with interest to see who was coming in.

"Glinda, lovely to see you," he said.

"I'm here to ask more questions," she said, closing the door behind herself and making sure it locked.

"Don't trust us?" Celes said.

"Not at all. As you may be aware, you are being held here for Wraith," she said.

"Oh, he's not nearby? Where might he be?" Celes said.

"Not here. Only the councillor would know his location and plans," Glinda said. The tone of her voice was the same, but Vincent noticed something odd. She seemed to be giving them more information than was actually necessary.

"So, it may take a while for him to get here?" Vincent said.

"Not sure, probably. That's why it's worth me asking you some additional questions," Glinda said.

"I'm not sure what you would want to know," Celes said.

"We want to know where your son is. Where is Alrion?" Glinda said. Her tone was very formal and stiff.

"I don't actually know," Celes said.

"And you? What's your answer?" Glinda said to Vincent.

"Sorry, I also don't know." Vincent showed his open palms.

"Unfortunately, they are not going to accept those answers," Glinda said.

"That's a shame now isn't it. Will that look bad for you?" Vincent said. He didn't have any malice in his voice. He was more interested in getting a real response from the female guard.

"Yes, it will. They will escalate to more extreme methods of questioning," she said.

"All we know is that he was here recently, but have no idea where he is now," Vincent said, offering her something.

"He was here? Tell me more," Glinda said.

"He didn't enter the city, you had it all locked up. But he managed to get word through to us regardless," Celes said.

"I see," Glinda said, staring off into space.

"Perhaps you could satisfy a curiosity of mine. You seem to have that far-away look when you are communicating with your...colleagues. Is that something that you must concentrate to do, or do you always overhear each other?" Vincent said. His comments snapped Glinda out of her apparent daze.

"You have been somewhat accommodating so I'll answer. It is a conscious communication. You must purposefully broadcast, and the others must be listening out. But there are some who can dominate with their message regardless of the listeners," Glinda said.

"I see, like Wraith," Vincent said.

"Exactly." Glinda nodded.

"They only know what you tell them? They can't spy on you?" Vincent said.

"No."

"Good. So, if you were to help us, nobody would have to know," Vincent said. Celes looked at him and realised that Vincent had been working towards this.

"Why would I help you?" Glinda said.

"Because you have a child. You don't seem like a bad person. I don't know how you ended up in this situation, but it's not something you can easily escape. Can't we help each other?" Vincent said.

"I don't see how you could help me. I would risk everything for nothing," Glinda said.

"I'm sure there is something we can do for you right now. But what our son is doing, is cleansing the Blight from the world. You won't have to live with this forever," Vincent said.

That got Glinda's attention. "He can cure us?" That's not possible," Glinda said.

"It happened to Avaria, there's your proof that it's possible," Vincent said.

"But that was twenty years ago. And it was a spell cast by the greatest of all wizards," Glinda said.

"Yes, my father and Alrion's grandfather. If you help us, you are helping that future." Vincent could see that he had the guard's attention. He could see the struggle in her features, as much as she tried to hide them. His assessment had been correct, she wasn't willingly a part of this. But she looked afraid. He needed something to offer her right now. "I know that sounds like a long shot. But what if we took care of the councillor. He seems to run things around here. If he were gone, would you be able to disappear? Or at least fade into the background?" Vincent said.

"You don't know what you are suggesting," Glinda said.

"Yes, we do. We are offering to remove the man who is controlling this city, and freeing you up to make your own decisions," Celes said. Glinda seemed to be weakening.

"You just need to give us the opportunity and we will do the rest. We won't divulge your involvement at all, so you won't be under suspicion. Can you help us?" Vincent said. Glinda appeared conflicted. Her fear was obvious. But a look of resolve crossed her face. She had decided.

"I will help you in this. But if anything goes wrong, I will side with him. I must," Glinda said.

"Perfectly fair. Celes, do you have a plan in mind?" Vincent said.

"Yes, let me explain it to you both," she said, a smile breaking out on her face.

Glinda locked the door behind her and strode down the corridor. Her involvement was minimal, but she couldn't afford to make any mistakes. The trickiest part was just ahead of her.

She didn't run into anyone else in the hallways, which was a relief. She didn't know the others that well, and there was little chance that they would notice anything different. But she was glad to not have the encounters, they were a possibility for throwing her off her guard. As expected she found the councillor in his library.

"Any news?" he said, looking up from a pile of papers.

"They won't talk," she said.

"And have you tried persuading them?" he said with annoyance.

"No, I really don't have the skill for it and I thought that you would have better luck. I figured that in the meantime I could search their accommodation," she said.

"They wouldn't talk but you know where they live?" the councillor said with suspicion. He had put his papers away and was focusing entirely on her. Glinda cursed herself inwardly. She had embellished too much on the detail with real facts she had been told.

"They made a mistake, a slight one, then retracted it. But I believe I know where they have been staying and wish to investigate it as soon as possible," Glinda said.

"I see, that's wise. There may be evidence of their plans there. Go look into it, and I'll let you know if I learn anything or confirm where they have been staying," the councillor said. He rose from his chair slowly.

"If only you were more resourceful, I wouldn't have to do these things myself," he said.

"My apologies, hopefully I can make up for it," Glinda said.

"Yes, let's hope so. Go on, get out my sight before I make you join me. I haven't forgotten your reluctance for proper interrogation, and may just change my mind and attempt to instruct you further," he said. Glinda bowed quickly and left immediately.

Almost there. She went directly to the side entrance of the house and left the door ajar as she left. Finally, she made her way around the perimeter to the front.

"You are relieved, I'm taking over until shift change," she told the guards.

"Really?" But there's not long left until changeover. Why?" the first guard said.

"I have to wait around anyway, figured I could cut you a break. Hurry up before I reconsider," Glinda said.

"That won't be a problem. Thanks!" the second guard said, and almost dragged his companion away. Glinda watched them leave and waited. She had to stop herself from tapping her foot. The nervous energy was almost too much.

"They better know what they are doing," she said to herself.

Vincent heard the steady footsteps outside the door, and stepped to the side, ready to strike. As the door opened, he rushed over and threw an elbow at the man entering. He saw the attack coming, but couldn't react in time and crumpled to the ground.

"Ugly, but effective," Vincent said.

"Let's get him somewhere else," Celes said. Vincent picked up the councillor and Celes helped carry him out into the hallway. One of them held the man up under each arm, and Vincent freed a hand to close the door behind them.

"She better be right about the patrols and servants, because we look mighty suspicious right now," Celes said.

"She's trustworthy. Let's just be quick," Vincent said. They slowly navigated around several corners, ending up back in a small private library. "This looks like the place," he said. They shuffled inside and dropped the councillor down into his large reading chair. "I'll watch him while you review the material there," Vincent said pointing to the pile of papers.

Celes quickly leafed through, scanning each page. "Not much of interest, it's pretty mundane. Maybe they don't put anything dangerous down on paper?" she said.

"Anything at all out of the ordinary?" Vincent said.

"They have a note about trade routes through the desert," Celes said.

"Isn't that unusual? We should ask him about that," Vincent said.

"Good idea. Give me a moment and I'll prepare the elixir." Celes retrieved a few vials from her cloak and mixed them carefully.

"Down the hatch," she said, as Vincent helped her open the councillor's mouth. He coughed suddenly and woke up, looking around the room.

"What's happening?" he said. His voice was a little slurred, and his speech slower than usual.

"You're drugged, and you're going to tell us exactly what we want to know," Celes said.

"The prisoners? How can this be?"

"You underestimated us. Don't even think about calling for help, the concoction you drank has dulled your senses," Vincent said.

"You think you're clever, but you won't get away with this," the councillor said with considerable effort.

"If you're so sure, just tell us what we want to know," Celes said. The councillor looked conflicted and confused. His confidence was still there, but he was a little unsure of himself.

"What could you possibly want to know anyway?" he said with satisfaction. Like he was both showing off and resisting at the same time.

"We want to know what Wraith is planning. He's organised you all - for what purpose?" Vincent said.

"Oh, I can't possibly tell you that. But I can share something. Something that you will find interesting," the councillor said. He had an odd grin on his face.

"Did you know that Wraith is in the desert? He's heading for an old temple to destroy it before a certain someone gets the chance to visit," he said, attempting a slow chuckle that sounded horrible.

"Wraith is in the desert? How long as he been there?" Vincent said.

"Oh, I don't know. But he's got an army with him. I sure hope your son isn't there, he'll be in for some trouble," the councillor said again. He couldn't contain his awkward laughter.

"Time to end this," Celes said. Vincent belted the councillor in the jaw and the man slumped down in his chair, unconscious.

"What do we do with him?" Celes said.

"I was going to ask you what the plan is. I think we can discredit him enough to neuter his authority." Vincent saw Celes's face light up with the possibilities.

Celes scouted ahead while Vincent half carried half dragged the councillor along. They had stripped him of all his clothes and soaked him in the expensive liquor they found in his library.

"I can't handle the stench from here, not sure how you're managing," Celes said.

"Just moving forward," Vincent said.

Celes laughed and went further ahead once more. She stepped out and made eye contact with Glinda. Glinda nodded, left the gate unattended and stepped out onto the street. "Coast is clear, let's finish this." Celes returned to help Vincent and they rushed out of the grounds as quickly as possible and eased the councillor down onto a wooden bench across from his house. "I hope this does the trick," Celes said.

"You can stick around and monitor the situation. I must go after Alrion," Vincent said.

"But that's suicide! You don't know the desert!" Celes said. Her eyes pleaded with him.

"No, it's fine. I can manage, I have the directions. Take care, I'll find our son." Vincent gave Celes a quick kiss and ran off into the street.

Celes watched him go, all the elation of their escape and victory dispersing all at once.

27

THE DESERT TEMPLE

As the storm settled in Alrion began to relax a little.

"We should take turns remaining on watch, so we can warn Alrion if there's danger of the shelter breaking," Certan said.

"That sounds wise, I'm not sure if I could sleep otherwise. I don't trust this, no offence Alrion," Lara said.

"None taken, I'm a little amazed it actually worked. How about you both sleep first, I can't sleep immediately anyway, I need to monitor this a bit more and try to relax," Alrion said.

"No problem. Make sure you wake me before you get too sleepy. Then I'll wake Lara for her shift," Certan said. Then he and Lara slowly prepared to sleep, laying out some blankets to lie on. They took additional care to not bump into any of the walls protecting them.

Alrion couldn't sleep yet, but needed something else to focus on. He decided to review his spell book, and that strange notebook he had been receiving messages in.

I wonder if it's Falric sending them? He still wasn't sure of Falric's fate, although he secretly wished the wizard had survived. Alrion still carried the guilt of not being able to help his mentor.

Next time, I won't fail. He saw the notebook first, and reached for it. Leafing through the pages, he found a new entry.

You must use time to your advantage.

"That's odd," Alrion whispered, and turned to the next page. There was no other message, just that one. Alrion had the distinct feeling that someone was watching him.

Does this wizard know that I am trapped in a storm? Maybe it's Ashra, Alrion thought. There were some aspects that made sense, but he never met Ashra until recently. The advice seemed timely, but it was too neat.

There has to be something else to this, but what? I am using my time as effectively as possible. We kept my training short so that I could make my way to the temple as soon as possible. Is there something I'm missing?

Alrion worked through all the interpretations of the message. He was still missing something, but decided to capitalise on the fact that he was stuck in a storm and reviewed his spell book.

With delight Alrion noticed that the spells he had practised with Ashra were now documented in the book. Reading about them from a different author provided an additional perspective and helped his understanding. It was as if what he read resonated strongly with him.

Somewhere in my head, I have this knowledge already. It must be the act of joining the lines from something I instinctively know, to something I actively know. It was an interesting perspective that he would have to try out on someone.

"Next time I go to Paperton I'll have a lot of questions," Alrion said to himself. But first, he had other things to focus on. He used the time to do some minor reinforcement of his walls, and rework small sections to learn some of the slightly different techniques in his spell book.

As his confidence climbed, and the protective dome retained its strength, Alrion felt sleep coming on.

It's safe now, and I have no energy left. It's time, he thought. He shuffled over and shook Certan. At the slightest touch the monk's eyes darted open and he was completely alert.

"Time for my shift? Great. Have a good rest." Certan sat up carefully and inspected the walls and listened carefully. "This will be set in for a while, but I think we are safe. Don't worry I will wake you if required," he said.

"Thanks, I'm exhausted." Alrion laid out a blanket and collapsed onto it. Sleep was close, but it was a restless sleep.

He awoke by himself, and was quite groggy and confused.

Lara and Certan were up and talking quietly.

"Welcome back. I would ask how your sleep was, but I could tell from all the tossing and turning that it wasn't great," Lara said.

"I'm not sure, maybe I was overtired. Is everything alright?" Alrion started to test the walls.

"Seems fine, storm has died down a bit. It's still too much to go out yet, but I think we are over the worst. Eat and we shall keep an ear out," Certan said. Alrion drank some water and ate some biscuits and bread. He felt a bit better than the day before, even his restless sleep had done the job.

"Have you ever experienced a storm like this?" Alrion said.

"No, nothing quite this bad. It's suspicious," Certan said.

"In what way? It's unnatural?" Lara said.

"Yes." Certan didn't elaborate but he looked concerned.

"So maybe a wizard is behind it?" Alrion said.

"I don't know what's possible, but it seems likely. We should be very careful during the rest of our journey," Certan said.

"You know, it seems like a crazy spell, but it's plausible," Alrion said after a moment of consideration.

"At least if that's the case, they don't know where we are. It's not very targeted," Lara said.

"Agreed. We just need to remain cautious and prepare ourselves," Certan said.

"Sure. I'll review my spells and do some training," Alrion went back to the spell book and tried miniature versions of his spells within the dome. By practising at a very small scale, he would not disrupt their shelter and he could focus more on how he was controlling the spells.

Hours passed, and Alrion felt in more control of his new techniques. He built a tiny dome that surrounded Certan's foot and he kicked it away.

"Aww that was cute," Lara said with a laugh. Certan was about to respond when he stopped suddenly and pressed his ear against the dome wall.

"Something has changed. I think the storm is dying down," he said. Lara and Alrion became still and tried listening as well. The howling seemed more distant, and less enthusiastic.

"I think you're right," Lara said softly.

"How long until we can emerge?" Alrion said.

"Let's wait a bit longer," Certan said. They all waited cautiously. Alrion stopped practising his spells and Lara sat still, occasionally trying to listen through the wall. After a while Certan broke the silence again.

"Can you open a tiny part of the wall? I want to test the environment outside," Certan said. Alrion concentrated, and thought about how to adjust the wall. He couldn't just attack it, he needed a way of altering the structure in just the right way.

"I need a minute to figure this out," Alrion said, and began his work. It was almost like building the shelter again, but this time looking for places that he could remove. He projected an invisible framework over it, then tried moving a section out. The wall shook, but then settled and a rectangular chunk shuffled over along the sand. Alrion was just about to cheer when a rush of sand blocked the gap he had created.

"Something must have gone wrong," Alrion said, confused. He was sure he had done it carefully.

"It wasn't your mistake, I think we are quite buried. Have you noticed the air going stale?" Certan said.

"Now that you mention it. But why now?" Lara said.

"I think it took a long time to build up, but we are quite buried. I have been monitoring it but didn't say anything in order to prevent panic. The last thing we needed was to unnecessarily waste the air," Certan said.

"What do we do?" Lara said.

"We need to take a chance that the storm has moved on. Alrion will need to clear a path for us," Certan said.

"That can be arranged. Let's pack up then give me the word," Alrion said.

The three of them took care in packing their things, working methodically.

"That looks to be it," Lara said.

"So, I just clear a path in front of us?" Alrion said.

"Correct. Just be careful of sand coming in." Certan shuffled over to behind Alrion, and Lara joined him.

Alrion considered his options. "I should clear and build at the same time, that's safer," he decided. He drew in a deep breath, then built up his Spark. He prepared a tightly compacted ball of force, and held it ready. Before he unleashed it, he prepared himself to build up some walls.

"I hope this works," he whispered and let his spell loose. The ball of force rocked ahead, displacing a huge curtain of sand. Alrion had not expected so much to come back to him. He quickly brought up a protective wall in front of them and extended the dome roof to try and prevent additional burial by the sand.

"More sand is coming in," Certan said. Alrion tried again, but altered his technique. Instead he built a moving sand wall, and advanced it ahead. The length of their dome kept extending. With a sigh, he stopped it and paused, letting the wall in front of him drop down.

"You've extended our space. What's the plan?" Lara said.

"We have to assume the sand cover is extensive. I am hoping that if I poke a hole up, if we have enough space we can reinforce an exit before we get buried for good," Alrion said,

"Worth a try, I will advise you if the situation is worsening," Certan said.

This better work. Alrion had underestimated the seriousness of their situation. He shuffled closer, and picked a spot in the ceiling. He gathered his Spark, and prepared another ball of force. But this time he packed more and more power into it, and tried to compact the energy as much as possible.

"Here goes," he whispered and put everything into the spell. There was an explosion of force above them, displacing the sand everywhere. But the intensity and power of the force pushed most of the sand out and they saw the daylight finally.

"Quick, reinforce!" Certan shouted.

Alrion created walls either side of the relatively small hole and only minimal sand dropped back in.

"We have an exit, if we can get there," Lara said, looking up at the daylight.

"Maybe I can build a ladder," Alrion said, thinking out loud. He shuffled over then examined his new reinforced vertical walls. With some experimentation, he managed to create some bricks sticking out of the wall. Lara tested on.

"It's a bit crumbly, can you do better?" she said. Alrion tried again, putting more water into the mix and compacting the sand further.

"That'll do. Keep going," Lara said. Alrion built additional blocks, and Lara kept climbing.

"Keep it up, I'm almost there," Lara said. Soon her head disappeared into the hole and she dragged herself out.

"Wow. Get up here," she said. Alrion let Certan go next, and watched carefully to ensure the makeshift ladder held. Once Certan had reached the top, he called down to Alrion.

"Can you throw the bags up?" Certan said. Alrion picked up the bags with waves of force and gently carried them up to Certan's waiting hands. Once they were taken, Alrion started climbing by himself. The rungs on his sand ladder were stronger than he had expected.

I'm getting this finally. He took care and soon his head poked out of the opening. He had to take care to ensure his sword didn't get stuck as he climbed out of the hole. He dusted himself off and took a look around. There were now sand dunes where before they were none.

"The whole landscape has changed," Alrion said.

"Yes, an unimaginable amount of sand has settled here. I have a bad feeling about this," Certan said.

"How will we navigate now?" Lara said.

"Don't worry, I can look at the position of the sun and adjust our course. Eventually we will start to see landmarks that I can use as a guide," Certan said.

"Good. Let's get started?" Alrion said.

"Certainly. This way." Certan walked off with confidence, and Alrion followed close behind.

Lara lingered, looking back at the mostly buried shelter. "Shouldn't you close that up? What if someone fell in?" she said.

"Good point, it's useful but more likely a person would fall in unexpectedly. I'll close it in." Alrion reached out and visualised the structure of the wall, as he had done previously when taking out a small piece. However, this time he started to crack and destabilise the entire wall. The sand shifted suddenly and the mini dune next to them sunk swiftly into the ground. Alrion stepped back with a start, surprised at the speed of the movement.

"Lucky you weren't standing any closer," Lara said.

"I know, I won't miscalculate that again," Alrion said.

"The sand is a dangerous and often misjudged element," Certan said, then he turned back and started walking again. Lara and Alrion rushed to catch up.

Up and down they went, navigating the new dunes. Certan only paused occasionally to check they were heading in the right direction. There seemed to be a lot of sand and dust still in the air, which helped reduce the sun's rays a little. But it was hot and slow going.

Hours later, Alrion was tired and hot. He couldn't see that they had made any progress at all. But Certan seemed confident, so he kept going. His mind started drifting off when suddenly, he ran into Certan. The monk had stopped completely.

"What is it?" Alrion said.

"That should be the temple in the distance. Take a look," Certan said. Alrion squinted and looked where the monk was pointing.

"All I can see is the haze. Is that smoke?"

"That's definitely smoke. I take it you don't have massive bonfires at the temple?" Lara said.

"Not at all. I believe the temple is under attack," Certan said. Alrion didn't know what to say. Despite everything they had done, they were too late.

28

WAVERING

Certan started walking again, increasing his speed.

"What are we doing? What's the plan?" Alrion said.

"We must get closer and assess. Don't you agree?" Certan said.

"Sure, we don't know what we are dealing with," Alrion said, although he felt quite rattled. They had been so quick in travelling here, and only paused for a while.

"Maybe we shouldn't have stopped," Alrion said.

"We may have been caught in the storm anyway, and you wouldn't have had the required training. Besides, you needed that to take on Wraith," Lara said.

"Maybe it's not enough? My spells did nothing last time. I should have focused on learning how to use this sword, that seemed to work," Alrion said.

"Don't second guess yourself, everything you did was the best choice. You weren't going to be an effective fighter in such a brief time anyway, so it's best that you worked on being a better wizard. Don't you agree Certan?" Lara said.

"Absolutely. You need the right focus and mindset to fight effectively. Some of that you have already from your previous encounters so you are at an advantage. But the body has many secrets, which take time to master. Your sword may be an effective weapon against Wraith, but you are not ready to wield it properly. There is time for that," Certan said.

"You both make sense. I just feel a bit lost now that it seems as though he is here and ahead of us. I secretly thought that we could get there first, so I could use the second trial to be better prepared for him," Alrion said.

"You beat him once with even less training, don't let yourself get defeated already," Lara said, giving him a big smile. Alrion couldn't help but smile back. His doubts were still there, but he could push them back. For a time.

They continued on, gradually through the burning hot desert. The addition of the new dunes made the going tougher, and Alrion frequently wanted the flat wasteland back. At least it was less work. The route seemed to be slowly taking them higher and higher. Lara mentioned it first.

"We seem to be slowly ascending. Is that normal?" Lara said.

"No, this is not natural. I suspect it because we are getting closer to the source of the storm," Certan said.

"Let's say Wraith or someone near the temple created the storm?" Alrion said.

"That would be my guess," Certan said.

"Lucky we weren't any closer, we would have struggled to get out from that much sand," Lara said. Alrion stopped and looked back. When he looked for it, he could see the gentle slope of the sand all the way back. The amount of sand displaced was staggering. He thought about the power required to fuel such a storm and a chill ran down his spine.

Don't think about it, you're fine, he thought, and took some quicker steps to catch up.

"We are getting closer, I think we shall see better once we reach the top of this dune," Certan said.

"You would hope so, that thing is massive," Lara said. The incline was steeper than anything they had traversed yet, and it was obviously towering over the rest of the area.

With more measured steps, they ascended the giant dune. The sand still shifted considerably, so they had to take care with each step forward. Alrion found this section very frustrating. His footing was constantly sliding back, and he felt like he was making very little progress. But each time he paused and looked back, he could see how far they had come. Not as far as he would have liked for the effort expended but at least he could see.

"If I'm right, we should be able to see the temple once we reach the top. Very close now." Certan increased his speed, his urge to see the temple once more spurring him on. Lara also sped up, but Alrion let them go ahead. He wanted to conserve his energy.

The monk reached the top first, and crouched. He said nothing. Lara joined him shortly after and let out a quiet gasp. Alrion was intrigued by what they were seeing, and pushed on to look for himself. He crested the top of the dune and almost toppled over, the ridge was actually quite narrow. Once he steadied himself he looked out.

The desert temple was in clear view. The large blocks of stone covered in sand looked like something from a long-forgotten time. But that was not what took his breath away. The smoke was a sign of danger, as Certan had pointed out. But the horrifying thing was the black mass of seething Tainted swarming the temple and surrounding it. As far as he could see, they ground was covered with Tainted. He could pick out Blighters, Tainted Ones and even several Shades.

"This is bad," Alrion said. It was a lot more than that, but he couldn't put the words together.

"It is probably the worst-case scenario, given the circumstances," Certan said.

"We can't take that head on," Lara said.

"We can't take that period," Alrion said.

"There are ways and means. The temple is not yet overcome, so our quest is not in vain." Certan was studying the scene with a thoughtful look.

"You're just getting sentimental over returning to your home. Lara and I took on a tiny fraction of the force here, and I used the entirety of my Spark. She had to save me at the last moment," Alrion said.

"We wouldn't have to fight them all," Certan said.

"There must be another way into the temple," Lara said.

"No, stealth takes time. By the time, we enter it will be too late. The monks will be defeated, the temple will be taken and the Vault of Silence will be destroyed or locked away. This is a no-win situation," Alrion said.

"You've dealt with long-shots before and succeeded. We can't give up, not at this stage," Lara said.

"I won't allow you to falter now. We have come too far, and the monks need our help. You have an important responsibility that you cannot give up," Certan said,

"I can find Ashra, and he can teach me instead. He has passed the trial, he understands how it works and what it teaches. It won't be the same, but at least I can prepare in safety. I can't deal with this, it's too much too soon. No amount of power can overcome these odds," Alrion said. Certan stood up and walked off the dune. He stood in front of Alrion, blocking the way back.

"To retreat, you must go through me," Certan said.

"Don't make me do this. Just let me go," Alrion said.

"Don't be silly Alrion, let's just figure this out." Lara reached out for Alrion's arm, but he shook her off.

"Move, Certan," Alrion said. The monk shrugged and shook his head. Alrion sent a wave of force at the monk's feet. Certan was moved, but regained his footing and resumed his stance. Alrion threw another wave, this time at Certan's chest. The monk absorbed the force, moving slightly, but without losing his ground.

"You will need more than that," Certan said.

Alrion started to get frustrated. "Just leave me be," he said. He prepared a fire spell, and as he readied it Certan moved. He dashed with incredible speed, knocking Alrion to the side and disrupting the spell. Alrion recovered, and went all out, throwing waves of force at Certan from all directions. The monk seemed to anticipate most of them, and either dodged or blocked the force with minimal impact. Alrion kept up the onslaught and prepared another spell.

Since Certan was within a smaller area, Alrion raised a large block of wet sand and formed a powerful seal around Certan's feet. As the sand solidified it contracted, binding the monk's feet tighter and tighter. Certan noticed it happening, and started to struggle with increasing force. But it was too late. Alrion managed to strengthen the block so much that the monk was completely trapped.

"So, it has come to this," Certan said. There was a sadness and regret in his voice.

"I'm sorry, but I can't do this," Alrion said. Certan nodded, and reached into his robes. He retrieved the metal flask, and held it out.

"What's what?" Lara said.

"My saving grace." Certan unscrewed the lid and held it still in front of him.

"Don't drink it, it's not worth it," Alrion said. Certan chuckled quietly.

"You misunderstand," he said. He tipped the flask over and poured it out into the sand. Quite a bit flowed out. Each drop was one that Certan had avoided drinking.

"They will never know," Certan said wistfully.

"What is he talking about? What did you make him do?" Lara said.

"He took that flask from the temple when he was banished. He swore that he would not drink from it again, no matter what happened. So that one day, he could return and show them that had regained his honour and mastered his weakness," Alrion said.

"Why Certan?" she said.

"If all hope is lost for you Alrion, then it is for me also," Certan said. Alrion was shocked. His fear at his powerlessness had not only turned him away from his quest, it had damaged his friend's chances at being accepted again by his people.

"Why would you do that?" Alrion said.

"Because you need to learn. Will is not something you use. Will is a part of how you live. Will means persevering no matter the odds. I will find a way to succeed with an empty flask, just as you will find a way to succeed now," Certan said.

"I...I don't know what to say." Alrion dispersed all the sand around Certan's feet and dropped into a crouch. He buried his head in his hands, trying to think.

"You have come a long way. You have been putting on a big front, and showing off with the use of your new-found power. But you still carry fear for your enemy. And healthy doses of self-doubt. This is normal, especially given the situation. But you mustn't give it power. Acknowledge it and move on. There is much more you must achieve," Certan said.

Alrion looked up. The monk was right about a lot of things. He had been trying to compensate with his magic, to bluff about his confidence and mastery. But it had been a front, and had crumbled spectacularly in front of overwhelming odds. Would that realisation change anything though?

"But where do we go from here? Acknowledging my fear and uncertainty is not going to make that ridiculous army go away," Alrion said.

"Who said anything about fighting them all. There is another way," Certan said.

"I'm all ears, I don't want to deal with that," Lara said, jerking her thumb over her shoulder towards the teeming mass of Tainted.

"You don't take me as the type to just saunter in the front door. Do you think the monks don't have other ways of getting around?" Certan said. A wry smile broke out on his face.

"You have a way of getting us in?" Lara said.

"Yes. Provided you have the courage to join me."

"I'll go. Maybe there's a chance," Alrion said.

"Me too. I need to see this place for myself. Maybe even liberate some treasure," Lara said with a wink.

"Follow me," Certan said, shaking off the sand around his feet and walking off with purpose.

29

ENTERING THE TEMPLE

The trio walked with renewed hope. Certan took them along the newly formed ridge and they tried to avoid looking at the black mass of enemies. They started to approach the temple in a round-about way, avoiding danger.

"We can't do this the whole way, it will take all day," Lara said.

"I agree, just a bit further," Certan said. Lara didn't respond, and decided to see what the monk had to show them. A few minutes later he stopped quickly, and crouched down. He motioned for Lara and Alrion to do the same.

"This is as close as we can come without the need to approach directly," Certan said.

"The front door perhaps, but you said there was another way," Lara said.

"There is, but not for us. You yourself said, it will take too long to take the long way in. If I show Alrion the way, he can enter the temple from the secret passage and we can create a diversion so that he doesn't get noticed," Certan said.

"Hang on, you want us to go into that?" Lara said.

"I said we had a chance, not that it was safe," Certan said.

"Why are you smiling? This is terrible!" Lara said.

"Nothing is certain, except death. We don't know when it will come, but that it will claim us eventually. I don't want it to be today, but it wouldn't be the worst end, would it?" Certan said.

"You monks are crazy. Alrion say something," Lara said.

"I don't know the area well, and I certainly don't want to sacrifice anyone today. But Certan must know that I can't sneak in unnoticed. If there's a way for you to enable that and survive, it's not a bad idea," Alrion said.

"Lara is quite resourceful, I've noticed she has a few interesting things hidden up her sleeves. I'm not sacrificing myself just yet," Certan said.

"If you're going to do this, I'll promise that I'll make it to the trial. One way or another," Alrion said.

"I guess it's up to us then," Lara said.

"I'll leave you to ponder about our chances of survival, and I'll show Alrion where the entrance is." Certan led Alrion aside, and they crept down the ridge on the other side.

"The entrance is marked by a statue of a cat. The cat' tail is actually a lever, and if you pull it the entrance will be revealed. But you must close the entrance immediately. If the enemy notices it, the temple's defenses will be overrun in no time," Certan said.

"Understood," Alrion said.

"See that curve in the ridge down there?"

"Yes, I see it."

"Make your way down there as quietly as possible. You should be able to see the cat statue from there. Await our signal, then make a run for it. I'm not sure how much time you will have."

"I can do that. Thank you Certan, I wouldn't have made it this far without you. Now go survive so I can repay you," Alrion said.

"That's my intention."

"What's the signal?"

"I'm not sure, but knowing Lara, you will know it when you see it," Certan said.

"I'm sure you are right about that," Alrion said, and held out his hand. Certan shook it firmly then headed back. Alrion started working his way down. He wanted to get his bearings and locate the statue before he noticed the signal. It would be a disaster if he didn't get there in time.

The ridge was quite steep, and following it without going over the top was hard going. He was walking on an angle and each step threatened to have him toppling down the slope. But he persevered and made consistent progress. Soon he reached the spot that Certan had pointed out and paused for a rest.

Once he had composed himself, Alrion crept up the ridge and looked out. They were around the side of the temple, but there was still a large mass of Blighters and Tainted milling around. It seemed as though they were looking for another entry.

Not just a large mass, they're coordinating. This is bad, Alrion thought. He could see why a diversion was required. There was a decent chance that Alrion could make it to that entrance, and get inside. But there was purpose behind the enemy's actions. If they got wind of a secret entrance hidden here, and thought to investigate the statue it was only a matter of time until they managed to open it.

I won't be able to do a single thing. Certan and Lara are on their own, Alrion realised. He dismissed the thought and focused on what he could do himself.

He noticed strange movement out on the ground, and tracked it with his eyes. Something was moving really fast, but wasn't being noticed by the enemy. That is until it started attacking. It was like an invisible whirlwind of death, carving a path through the mass of Blighters. It took them seconds to figure out what was going on, and in that time at least twenty of them had fallen.

As they began to react in anger, a large explosion went off a bit further away. A wave of Blighters was sent flying, sending the whole group into disarray. The deathly blur that was Certan changed direction, moving towards the explosion. The confused and angry Blighters started to follow, the Tainted spurring them on.

Alrion watched carefully. That was definitely the signal. But there were still one or two Blighters that had not followed. He had to make a call. Should he wait more, or take them out?

I'll wait a tiny bit more, just in case. Despite the commotion and damage that Certan and Lara were causing, the few straggling Blighters were not going over. Either they were oblivious or reacting to different orders.

They're not that close to the statue, maybe I can creep past them. It was worth a try. He didn't want to draw any attention, because it would detract from what was being done by his friends.

Alrion cautiously crested the ridge and slid down the other side. He rose quickly and kept an eye on the Blighters. There were three worth worrying about, and two of them were roving around and not too close to the statue. However, there was one patrolling around that was a danger. If Alrion was careless he would get spotted for sure.

He kept low and ensured his hood was up over his face. He slowly moved along, watching all three Blighters. As he closed in on the cat statue he realised that the timing wasn't going to work. The roving Blighter would be too close, and Alrion had nowhere to hide. He had to take care of it.

Alrion altered his path, and closed in on the Blighter. He wanted to get close, to make things easier. He stalked behind it, waiting until it reached what appeared to be the limit of its patrol. Alrion carefully prepared a wave of force and directed it at the creature's neck, providing a powerful spin to quickly and efficiently break its neck. The Blighter dropped silently, and Alrion stalked back to the cat statue.

So far so good. I hope the other ones don't notice. As he neared the statue, he kept an eye on the other Blighters. They didn't seem to notice anything unusual, and in the distance Alrion could still hear the noises of fighting and explosions.

"I hope they're alright over there. Better take care of this now," he whispered. As he examined the cat, he could see the amazing detail. It looked ancient too, but was quite well preserved considering the circumstances. He found the tail without trouble, and gave it a yank. Nothing happened.

Alrion held onto the tail and tried manipulating it in different directions. Down, side to side and diagonally had no effect. He tried lifting it up and it started to move. Throwing more effort into it he managed to force the tail up, and heard a nearby clunk. Then nothing.

Alrion's eyes darted back to the other two Blighters. It may have been his imagination but they seemed like they were heading over. They seemed to be moving with a bit more purpose than before.

"Come on statue, let's go," Alrion whispered. The Blighters were still a way off, but if they came too close he wouldn't be able to hide. Suddenly the ground beneath him shifted, and he almost toppled over. He saw steps appearing in the sand, descending into a dark passage. Alrion ran down as quickly as he could, almost slipping several times. Once he reached the bottom he created a light above his hand and looked everywhere for another lever. He found one on the wall, and yanked it as hard as possible.

Another clank, then silence.

Where are those Blighters? I hope they're not too inquisitive. He was completely exposed if they came close and noticed the stairs down. He strained his ears but couldn't hear anything. With a start, the stairs began to move. They shifted back and up, forming a neat wall where there was once an incline.

I guess that's closed. Time to investigate this passage.

Certan was beginning to get overwhelmed. Lara's explosives had helped thin out and confuse the Blighters. But the Tainted that were controlling the horde had recovered from the initial shock, and were sending wave after wave at them. He knew from counting the explosions that Lara was almost out of her bombs. He made his way closer to the latest one, hoping to find her.

Spinning and rolling he made his way through the throng like a scythe, cutting down Blighters left and right. He couldn't keep this up forever, but at least he could hold his own. He was waiting for another explosion, but it didn't come.

"Lara!" Certan shouted. He needed to have an indication of where she was, or even if she was still alive.

"Over here, bit busy!" she shouted back. Certan redirected his efforts and headed in her direction. A deadly claw strike interrupted his train of thought, almost catching him in the neck. A last-minute reaction saved him, and he took the offending Blighter down quickly.

I'm slowing, getting sloppy, Certan thought. Time was running out. He found Lara surrounded by a wreath of Blighter corpses. She was in the centre, alternating between slicing with her dagger and throwing knives with pinpoint precision.

"Out of bombs?" Certan said as he joined her.

"Yes. How much longer do we need to do this?" she said.

"Enough time has passed. We are no use to him dead. We need to get into the temple," Certan said.

"I'm with you there. Any ideas?"

"There are columns holding up the main entrance. They may provide a narrow corridor for us to fight through, where numbers won't be as big an issue." Certan pointed in the general direction.

"If we can get there." Lara threw two knives, taking down two Blighters who had managed to get close. Another was right behind him, its eyes beaming murder and its mouth was slightly open. Lara could see the drool running down its chin and its sharp fangs.

Certan was contending with three others, and had not noticed. Lara panicked. She wasn't sure she had the right space to fend it off without taking a serious injury. As she was awaiting its move she noticed the creature slow then fall down, splitting at the middle as it fell. A blade of Runesteel emerged and Lara finally smiled.

30

___

THE TRIAL

As Alrion became accustomed with the passage he increased his speed. He needed to enter the temple as quickly as possible and find the trial. There were no guarantees as to what would happen, but at least he had a chance. It didn't look like the temple was overrun yet.

He had heard nothing behind him, so it appeared as though he had entered without attracting any attention. If the Blighters discovered their fallen friend, they would not know where to look.

The passage was long and winding. Luckily there were no turns to take, so he could move fast and not worry about losing his way. But that was about to change.

The passage ended in a set of stairs. Alrion ran up as fast as he could without risking a fall. He looked up and could not see the end of the stairs. Finally, he reached the end, which was not an exit. It was a dead end. Alrion examined the walls with his light, and could see nothing of use. The ceiling at the landing was very low, so he tried pushing on that instead. It moved slightly.

Encouraged by the movement, Alrion pushed more and a piece of stone above him rotated, acting like a trap door. Alrion felt around with his hands and found something. It was a rope of some kind. He tugged at it, and a simple rope ladder fell down and landed on his head. He pushed it away, then tested it.

Feeling satisfied, Alrion climbed up and hauled himself out of the hole. He was in a tiny room with no other furnishings and only one open doorway.

"Here we are," Alrion whispered. He dusted himself off and left the room immediately. He found himself in a corridor with the option of going left or right. It was well-lit, so he let his light vanish.

This isn't good. I'll try the path on the right. He walked quickly down the corridor, hoping to establish if it was the right way. He passed several rooms that looked like they were sleeping quarters. But nobody was around.

Makes sense, everyone will be out fighting. But that didn't help him. He had no idea where the trial would be. He came to another cross-roads and had another decision to make.

"Right again," he decided, and headed off. This time he emerged in a large hall. Weapons lined the walls, and there was a square marked out in the centre of the room.

"This is not it," he decided. But he did notice another doorway at the other end of the room and kept going. He pressed through and found a staircase going up.

"May as well try it," he whispered. He was trying to keep up-beat but felt so frustrated at not knowing what the Vault of Silence even looked like.

I probably should have asked Certan or Ashra more about it. They could have at least told me where to look, he thought. But nobody had expected there to be such trouble.

The staircase wound up and up and rays of daylight stole through the occasional slit. Alrion didn't bother trying to look through, he had no time. He noticed a doorway at the top bathed in light. He ran for it, and burst through.

Alrion emerged onto a rooftop of some sort. The sun blinded him for a second, and he had to adjust. There was a lone monk on the roof, firing arrows down at the horde of Tainted. His tall build gave him a good vantage over his targets. From this view, Alrion decided that things looked even worse.

"Hello!" Alrion shouted as he approached. The monk looked back in surprise, but resumed his attacks. "I need your help," Alrion said when he reached the monk.

"Whatever it is, we are in greater need. Are you a wizard?" the monk said.

"Yes, I'm here to do the trial of Will. It's vital that you take me there as soon as possible," Alrion said.

"If you don't help me, there won't be a temple left to do the trial in," the monk said. He motioned with his head and Alrion looked over to see what he meant. There were streams of Blighters climbing the walls, using the nooks and crevasses built up by the passage of time.

"If I help with this, you'll take me to the trial?" Alrion said.

"I'll escort you myself and introduce you. My name is Graem," the monk said.

"Let's work together then Graem. I am Alrion. Is there a leader here?"

"I would say so. Look over there, see that lone Tainted One?" Graem said.

"Yes, you might be right. First, we can deal with these Blighters who are advancing and see his reaction," Alrion took up a position next to Graem and started building up his Spark. He formed up many spheres and infused them with fire and hurled them down at the Blighters. There was a punch of force behind each one, so not only did the affected Blighters catch fire but they also lost their hand-holds and tumbled down, taking others with them.

"Where have you been? This is much faster," Graem said.

"Trying to get here. We had to bunker down during the storm." Alrion launched another volley, taking out the next row of hopeful Blighters.

"Must be the work of a wizard. Someone has to be coordinating all these Tainted and Blighters. Haven't seen anything like this in my entire life. The only edge we've had over the Tainted is that they weren't organised. This is too much." Graem launched another arrow, and took out a Blighter that had been hiding and had dodged the previous attacks.

After that attack, there seemed to be a lull.

"They're planning the next move. Look at that Tainted One," Graem said, pointing out the same one as before. He was waving his hands and seemingly talking to himself.

"I think you're right. I'm not sure how effective my spells are at this range. Hard to aim and he will probably see them coming," Alrion said.

"You ever worked with projectiles before?" Graem said.

"Yes, I've sped up daggers over short distances," Alrion said.

"Let's try that, only with an arrow. I can aim true, but I can't shoot that far either. But if I line up the shot properly and you can provide enough force and ensure it flies straight, we can nail their leader," Graem said.

"Worth a try, give me a moment." Alrion prepared a lance of air that he could catch the arrow within and propel forward.

"Are you ready? You have to act quickly, I won't be compensating for height," Graem said.

"Ready, just let me know when you're firing," Alrion said.

"Now!" Graem shouted. Alrion let loose the spell in anticipation and focused all his attention on the archer. He saw the arrow launching and caught it with his lance of air. The arrow increased in speed and hurtled towards its target. However, the aim was slightly off, and all the arrow did was graze the ear of the Tainted One.

He screamed in pain and looked over. When he noticed Alrion and Graem standing together, he paused then started running.

"Not bad for a first, if you can repeat that same level of force I can aim the next shot better. But it's going to be more difficult with a moving target." Graem already had the next arrow nocked and was aiming at the Tainted One.

"Just a moment." Alrion prepared another spell and watched Graem closely.

"Any minute now. There!" Graem said and launched his arrow.

Alrion repeated his spell, but this time tried to have less impact on the arrow's path. It flew away with rapid speed, toward the target. Alrion tracked its progress, and was unsure if it would hit. But Graem had aimed true, and the arrow struck the man in the head and he dropped immediately.

"Wow, great shot," Alrion said.

"Thanks, but I had help. If you wouldn't mind assisting again," Graem said. Alrion looked back and saw another wave of Blighters preparing to climb over the temple walls. He prepared and launched another wave of fireballs, this time completely incinerating all those that had reached the top.

They waited patiently for another minute, but no more Blighters followed their fallen.

"I think we've done enough here, let's go and I'll settle my end of the bargain." Graem put his bow over his shoulder and ran towards the stairwell.

"Do you know Certan?" Alrion asked as they descended.

"Yes. Great monk with an even greater weakness. He will be missed," Graem said.

"He has returned, he guided me here and showed me the secret passage," Alrion said.

"I've never heard of anyone returning after being banished, and betraying our secrets too. I'll be glad to see him again, but I am not sure if he can rejoin us," Graem said.

"That would be a shame." Alrion knew his friend had pinned so much on being able to return to the temple. He would do all he could to help that become a reality.

As they weaved through the various passages and rooms Alrion realised that he would never have found his way in time. The temple was a maze, and he had trouble keeping track of the way they had gone.

"This place is huge," Alrion said.

"Yes, it's been extended constantly over its lifetime. It's a great deterrent for attackers. Something that will be tested today," Graem said.

"Do you know anything about the trial of Will? The Vault of Silence? Have you seen it?" Alrion said.

"I only know of its location. Unfortunately, I can offer no other help, but that's all you need." Alrion appreciated the monk's straight forward approach.

"I appreciate it, time is of the essence."

"You are welcome, you have helped us greatly already. I would be interested to hear your story at another time. It would be a curious one for sure. You would need a special reason to turn up here at such a time and still require to take the trial."

"It is an impossible quest, one that I hope to achieve regardless," Alrion said.

"Sounds like a challenge. I wish you luck, Alrion. I cannot stay, but I hope we meet again." Graem left the young wizard standing before an impressive set of doors. Unlike the rest of the temple they were made of a strange metal.

Alrion pushed them open and they floated inwards with ease.

Inside was a great chamber, which looked like it had been carved out of rock. There were four monks sitting cross-legged on the ground.

"Close the doors behind you Alrion," one of the monks said. Alrion followed the instruction immediately, then continued to approach.

"I'm sorry, this is such a rush. I need to take the trial immediately," Alrion said.

"We know who you are and why you are here," the second monk said.

"Great. How do I start it?"

"Why do you deserve to take this trial?" The third monk said.

"I need to, to fulfil my quest. I need the power of Will to succeed," Alrion said.

"All could use it, but few can use it. Why you?" the fourth monk said.

"I just told you. I need it to cast the spell. The spell to end the Blight," Alrion said.

"And why do you deserve that responsibility?" The fourth monk said.

"It was given to me," Alrion said.

"Responsibility is not given, it is taken and borne," the fourth monk said.

"I accepted this quest, and all it entailed. Yes, I have faltered on my way. But I have made it here today. Isn't that proof enough?" Alrion said.

"Why do YOU deserve it?" the fourth monk said.

"I don't have time for this. Enemies are at the gate, an army bigger than you have ever seen. Why all the questioning?" Alrion said.

"Only those who are deserving can perform the trial," the first monk said.

"Why are YOU deserving?" the fourth monk said. Alrion was getting increasingly frustrated. He didn't have time for this, Wraith and his creatures could break through at any moment. He racked his brain, for the right response. He needed a way to convince them.

Suddenly he remembered Certan's words. Yes, that was it.

"I am deserving because I have encountered many setbacks on the way here. I have been almost killed, turned away by people, and almost buried alive in the sand. But I persevered. Because Will is about persevering no matter what. Getting up and trying again. It's about knowing that eventually you will succeed," Alrion said. The monks did not respond. Minutes seemed to pass. Alrion did not try to add anything, he knew nothing else would affect them.

"You are deserving. Go forth and perform the trial. You may enter the Vault of Silence," the first monk said. He gestured with his hand and a glowing portal opened in-between the four monks. Alrion walked closer, and was amazed by what lay within.

31

THE VAULT OF SILENCE

Alrion was in a completely white room. As soon as he entered, he turned back to look at how he had entered, and the entry was gone. He was completely sealed in.

That's a little unnerving. But the wonder of the space he was in overcame that. With care, he walked around the vault, examining all the walls. They were perfectly smooth and white, built from a material he didn't recognise. There were no seams anywhere. It was as if the whole space was one surface.

The Vault of Silence. It certainly is impressive, but very minimal. There's nothing here, Alrion thought. He reached out and touched the wall. It felt cool to the touch, but was impossibly smooth. He ran his hand around the wall, feeling for any inconsistencies in it. There were none.

I suppose the trial is to find a way out. As he walked through the vault, his mind was telling him that something was wrong. He stopped, trying to puzzle it out.

"My footsteps are not making any sound," he said. But no words came out. He tried to call out. No sound was made at all.

This vault is actually silent. That seems impossible, Alrion thought. But no matter what he did, there was no sound. It was a bit overwhelming, so he sank down and sat on the floor, leaning his back against the wall.

I'm here, I can't make a sound no matter what I do and I need to get out. But it's a trial of Will, so that has to be the key. As Certan said, perseverance is vital. I'll examine every part of the Vault to see if there's any weakness or secret. He stood up and walked around the room, taking his time to feel the entire surface.

It took a long time, but he managed to complete a circuit, with only the ceiling and other high places unchecked.

I'll try a spell. He gathered his Spark and prepared a wave of force. He spread it out like a blanket and ran it across the ceiling and other areas he could not access. He didn't notice any resistance to the spell. It seemed that the surfaces were all identical and there were no imperfections or secret nooks.

"At least my magic works here," Alrion said to himself. He sat down again and thought about how to pass the trial. He had one other tool to try. He unsheathed his sword and examined the diamond. It wasn't glowing at all.

Wherever I am, is not close to the Blight monsters. That may mean something, he thought. Holding the sword, he tried several times to pierce or damage the walls. As before, there were no signs of damage.

Maybe it's a matter of breaking down the wall, without anything external. That would take willpower and persistence. I have an advantage because I'm a wizard, Alrion thought. He was happy with the plan and gathered his Spark once more. He systematically hit the entire room with waves of force, then rotated into pinpointing an exact spot. Since the vault didn't seem to take any damage, he increased the intensity slowly to a level he didn't normally try.

This is good training, if nothing else. Soon he tired though, and the room appeared perfectly untouched.

This will require further thought. But his mind was not at ease. He kept thinking back to his friends, and the assault on the temple. Time was not something he had ample supply of.

~

"Vincent! It's a relief to see you here. How did you find your way?" Certan said, as he knocked down another Blighter and stood back to back with Lara.

"You gave me directions remember? When we found out that there was going to be an attack on the temple I rushed here immediately," Vincent said.

"We'll have to hear the story later, when we're not about to get killed!" Lara said.

"I'll cover us, you two make a path through to the temple," Vincent said as he sliced through another two Blighters.

Certan took the lead, using his attacks to knock the Blighters away as far as possible, and Lara stood close behind, taking out any trying to attack from strange angles. As a unit, the three of them managed to slowly work their way to the temple entrance, and take cover between the vast columns of the entrance area and the temple walls.

"If we make it back there will the monks let us in?" Vincent said.

"They should, if we can make it safe enough to risk it," Certan said.

"That's quite an ask," Lara said, slashing at another Blighter. The reduced space meant that there was less space for the Blighters to attack them. But it also meant it was harder to strike back.

"Do you have any other interesting things to throw?" Certan said.

"Only a few, and I'm saving them for later. But I have something that should help us get inside," Lara said.

"We'll need it," Vincent said, cutting down another Blighter and kicking the lifeless body away. As they neared the main entry they saw the monks shooting arrows and throwing metal discs through a rectangular slit in the massive metal doors.

"Here's the plan. I'll create a space, you do some sort of diversion, then we'll get the monks to sneak us in," Vincent said.

"That sounds possible, but we need to tell them the plan. We may be stranded otherwise," Certan said. They fought their way closer, so that Certan could speak with the monks.

"Friends, if we can make a safe opportunity can you open the doors?" Certan said.

"The banished one returns, interesting timing," one of the monks said.

"I am here to help. Let us in so that we may recover then fight again," Certan said.

"Let them try, if they can create a gap we can manage the doors," a second monk said.

"Very well, do your best," the first monk said and ducked to let his companion fire another arrow.

"When you're ready!" Certan shouted to Vincent.

The blacksmith waved his hand to signify that he understood, then started advancing. His blade whirled with skill as he stepped forward, pressing the Blighters back with his fury. In their surprise, he managed to cut down a Tainted one and push the offensive even further.

Lara followed close behind, watching Vincent's progress. She needed to wait as long as possible, so that they would have time and space to enter the temple.

The Blighters started to rally again, the initial surprise wearing off. Vincent saw some Shades in the distance moving in, and knew that his attack was losing its effectiveness.

Lara noticed too, and lobbed a glass vial into the crowd just past Vincent. It broke and released plumes of thick black smoke.

That's the signal, Vincent thought, and quickly retreated. As he ran he heard the giant doors begin to open. Some of the Blighters were ignoring the smoke and starting to advance.

I hope this works, Vincent thought, looking back. He wouldn't have nearly as much time as he had hoped for. Certan and Lara were at the door, just inside and waving him in. A monk pointed to three Blighters running ahead of the pack, trying to intercept Vincent.

"That's not a problem." Lara snatched three metallic discs off a nearby monk and let them loose. Just as Vincent reached the doors, the three Blighters sank to the ground and the great doors closed once more.

Another monk said, "Now that you are here, you can make your-selves useful,"

"Just let me catch my breath," Vincent said with a laugh.

"We are not by any means safe, but we have earned a small breather," Certan said.

"Very small breather. I saw some Shades advancing before I came back. These doors will not hold them. We need to ensure the temple is ready to be defended."

"We are already taking care of that," one of the monks said, steel and fire in his eyes.

Alrion woke up. He looked around in amazement.

How did I fall asleep? He reviewed what he remembered happening. He had inspected the entire vault, and cast multiple spells testing the integrity of the walls. He had even tried fire spells too. Nothing had worked.

Then I was exhausted and sat down to take a break. How long as I asleep? Alrion wondered. He had no time for sleep, or resting. But something was strange indeed. If he had slept, what had happened outside? Was there a chance that his friends had defeated Wraith?

This just doesn't make sense. I have no idea how much time has passed. Wherever he was, he was completely sealed away from the outside world. There were no signs of passing time whatsoever.

No time for solving that, I'm rested so I must keep trying, Alrion decided. He stood up and did a quick lap of the room. There was nothing new.

He had tried his main spells, but he hadn't tried his new spells.

"Maybe Ashra was on to something. Maybe earth spells are effec-tive here," Alrion said to himself. He focused his mind, trying to feel a source or water or earth nearby. But nothing resonated at all. There wasn't even any in the walls.

The walls aren't made of earth, I'm confused, Alrion thought. He had tried force, he had tried inspection and care and nothing had achieved any result.

Maybe I just need to Will a door? It was a bit of a crazy thought, but perhaps some out of the box thinking was required to escape this vault. He approached a wall, closed his eyes, and imagined a door opening in it. The door shimmered and glowed, and was big enough for him to step through.

Alrion opened his eyes and observed the wall. It was unchanged.

Maybe it's a trust exercise too? He repeated his visualisation technique and instead of opening his eyes, stepped through his newly imagined door. The wall smacked him in the face and he stumbled.

Not quite there. But at least he had a new avenue to try.

Bang. Bang. Bang. The great doors of the temple were under assault by three Shades. Nothing the monks could throw through the slits in the door had any effect of them.

"The door is lost, it's just a matter of time," Vincent said.

"Time is everything. If what you said is true and your son is in the Vault of Silence he needs as much time as possible," said Rengin, the seeming leader of the monks' defences.

"Have you undergone the trial?" Certan said.

"I cannot say," Rengin said.

"I guess we keep annoying them then," Lara said, hurling more discs through the slits in the doors. One of the Shades bent down to peer through the slit and Lara let loose another disc that hit it between the eyes.

"Oh, I think he's angry," Lara said, judging the reaction of the Shade. The blows against the door stopped.

"Maybe you convinced them to go away?" Vincent said.

"Listen carefully," Certan said. Amongst the general clamour there was the sound of heavy footsteps.

"Are they charging the door?" Lara said.

"Everyone move back, defensive positions around the entry,"

Rengin said. The monks all stepped back, and moved their ammunition to further back in the room. With a gigantic crash the doors bent, and one of the three Shades pushed through and emerged in the room.

"Now the real fight begins," Vincent said.

Certan and Lara moved next to him, and all three readied themselves.

32

TIME AND TIME AGAIN

Alrion bashed the wall in frustration. As always, it made no sound and had no impact ruining any possible satisfaction from the act.

This is insane. How do I get out? I don't even care about this stupid trial, I need to help my friends, Alrion thought. He had no idea what was going on outside, everyone could be dead for all he knew.

There's that one spell. The light bomb that he had been forbidden to use. There was nobody else here, and it had seemed ridiculously effective.

I've nothing to lose. Let's try it. He built up his Spark cautiously, and remembered how he had built it. He combined the light, fire, and force into the unique combination, and let it build and build. Once he had injected all of his power he let it go. He planned for it to explode once it reached the furthest wall.

As the bomb impacted, the walls began to shimmer, but instead of being destroyed they were absorbing and repelling the force.

Oh no, Alrion thought before his world was enveloped in light.

"We need to keep them separated if we have any chance of doing this," Vincent said.

The three Shades were fighting together, and any time there seemed to be an opening, more Blighters flooded into the entryway.

"We will try and contain the rest, if you focus on that one." Rengin pointed at the Shade nearest the wall.

"Excellent choice, we may be able to steer him into the corner." Lara grabbed a handful of the monks' metal discs and started to advance.

"As we discussed, Lara and Certan you create the opportunity and I'll capitalise," Vincent said.

Lara dashed forward, launching more discs at the Shade. *If only Alrion were here to make them more effective*, she thought. She did miss him, and wanted him by her side. But he was the reason they were fighting, and chances were he had made it to his trial by now.

Just make it back safely, she thought and continued her assault on the Shade. The discs bounced harmlessly off, but the Shade was annoyed and focused his attention on her.

Certan dashed in, raining blows on the Shade's stomach, then disappearing. The Shade whirled quickly to counter attack, but Certan was gone. As it turned to face Lara again it noticed too late that Vincent was there, swinging his sword. The Shade moved quickly to block with its right arm, but it had made a critical mistake. The sword cut cleanly through and the severed arm dropped to the ground. The Shade howled in pain, a strangely muffled and muted sound despite the high volume.

"Nice one," Lara said as Certan and Vincent retreated.

"We weren't fast enough, so the surprise is lost. It will be more cautious now," Vincent said.

"True, we will need to be more cunning. Lara, is your blade made of the same material?"

"Yes, thanks to Vincent."

"I see where you are going with this. It won't expect her to attack up close. Let's try that," Vincent said.

This time he advanced upon the Shade, whirling his sword in

large arcs, capturing its attention. After having a taste of the Runesteel, it was keen not to have another.

With the Shade occupied, Certan moved in to attack from the side. He got in several quick blows, which unsteadied the Shade. It didn't move to counter though, as it was carefully watching Vincent. The Shade wasn't going to make the same mistake twice. However, it had made another mistake, in not looking for Lara.

While the fight had carried on, Lara had crept through the other concurrent battles, and sliced the occasional Blighter in her path. But now she was positioned behind the Shade, and it had no idea of her location.

I don't think I can kill it from behind, but I can do some major damage. When she saw the Shade was completely occupied she quietly stalked behind it, leapt, and drove her dagger into the creature's neck.

The Shade lurched back in pain, grasping for the dagger. Lara pulled it out and rolled away. As the Shade lost its balance Vincent lunged forward with his sword and pierced the Shade through the heart. The strike was precise and deep, and within a second the Shade perished. It fell to the ground, lifeless.

The other two Shades recoiled in pain, and looked over. One of them became quite enraged, and grabbed a nearby monk who was momentarily distracted by the commotion. The monk cried out in pain, communicating the anguish that the Shade now felt.

"I think somehow things just got worse," Lara said.

"You could be right," Certan said. Vincent removed his sword and turned his attention onto the other Shade.

Alrion slowly regained consciousness. His body ached, and he had no strength. As his eyes opened fully, he sat up and examined his body. Everything was fine, he just felt incredible pain. Once he had done that initial check he looked around the room. It was exactly the same as before. Nothing had happened.

Nothing except almost killing myself. He reached for his Spark and found that it was not available. He had used up all his power.

I keep failing. Why? He lay down and looked at the ceiling, hoping for a breakthrough. What he did attain though was sleep.

Alrion awoke, not knowing how long had passed. But his back was stiff and his muscles restless.

I must have been asleep for hours. But everything is still the same, and I'm still here. What does this all mean? Alrion thought, running his hands through his hair. There was only one possible explanation. Time had to act differently within the vault. It was the only way he could think of to explain how long he had been toiling with no answer.

Shouldn't I be hungry? But he wasn't hungry, or thirsty. He was just in this place, unable to leave.

I have recovered my strength, I am going to train while I think of another way out, Alrion decided. The decision triggered a memory, of the notebook message that he had recently received.

Time is always against us. Use it to your advantage.

*I thought the message was about being stuck in the sandstorm, or my training. But maybe it's about this?*Regardless, it seemed practical. He would find a way out, but while he pondered the solution he would use the time he had available to train. If he had additional time here, he would put it to good use. He was going to emerge more capable in many ways, not just one.

Vincent and Certan stepped back, exhausted. They had managed to defeat another Shade, capitalising on its anger, and finding an opening. But they were quite spent. Lara looked around at the monks. Many had fallen, and many were wounded.

"This doesn't look too good," Lara said.

"No, this space is becoming too hard to defend," Vincent said.

"I was going to say the same thing, but I wanted to wait until you toppled that second beast. It's time to pull back," Rengin said.

"Something else prepared?" Vincent said.

"Of course, we're just not sitting on our hands while you take down Shades." Rengin let out a piercing whistle with his hands and the monks started to retreat. Vincent and Lara followed closely, and Certan was helping another monk get away. Once they all passed into the main passage Rengin directed them around a corner. "Now!" he shouted. Two monks hit a wall with a coordinated strike and it started to fall over, blocking the passage. "This will buy us some time, fall back," Rengin said, directing the monks to retreat even further. "This is our home and it's a maze. We can use that to our advantage."

"And the Vault of Silence?" Vincent said.

"At the heart of the temple. It's where we make our last stand."

"Let's hope it doesn't come to that," Certan said.

"You have fought with honour today, brother. I will stand for you, when this is over," Rengin said.

"That is a great honour, coming from you. I will continue to be worthy of your praise," Certan said.

"Take a position in one of these rooms. You can rest a little until they break through, then ambush them," Rengin said. The rooms he pointed to were all tiny, single occupant nooks. Vincent took the first one, Lara the second and Certan the third. The other monks distributed themselves down the passageway, similarly hidden and waiting.

A giant crash and the sounds of rubble echoed down the passageway.

"They're making progress, get ready," Rengin shouted while he was standing in the middle of the passage, monitoring the enemy's progress.

"Here they come!" he shouted. He ran down past the first set of rooms and waited. A stream of Blighters ran down the passageway, heading straight for Rengin. As soon as the first one attacked, the defenders emerged from the nooks and cut down the Blighters from the side. The whole encounter was over within seconds.

The next wave was not as hasty, and the third Shade was standing behind them.

"It's probably directing them, springing the traps. They're crafty," Lara said.

"Yes, it's a shame they're not just dumb beasts. They're certainly strong enough to qualify. At least the narrow passage here helps us with numbers. But we won't be able to flank the Shade, so we may need to retreat again," Vincent said.

"You're right. Rengin will call it, just keep up the fight," Certan said.

"I never said I was going to stop, it's just more challenging." Vincent stretched his shoulders and prepared for the next wave of Blighters.

As predicted the narrow corridor suited the defenders, and the Blighters were unable to make a dent in them. Seeing this, the Shade began to advance by itself. Two monks tried using the rooms to ambush the creature, but it knew they were coming and they didn't have enough space to manoeuvre. They were crushed quickly.

"It has the advantage here for sure," Certan said.

"Let's go back to Rengin," Vincent said.

The three of them retreated and joined the monk leader.

"Unfortunately, this isn't a simple change of tactics. Much of the ground we will retreat to is the same layout. We need to balance safety and time. If we retreat too soon, we will be defeated too quickly," Rengin said.

"I saw your monks topple a wall, isn't there a way we can make a better space?" Lara said.

"There could be something. You come with me, Certan hold here. Retreat as you need to." Rengin dashed down the passage with Lara and showed her a few spaces further down.

"I think this could work. But we would need these two walls knocked down. And these over here," Lara said.

"That can be done, I'll task some monks to assist. Hopefully we have enough time," Rengin said.

"Is it possible to have them one strike away from falling over?" Lara said.

"Should be. Why?"

"I think that could work better. Bring the monks and I'll talk you through it." Lara had a smile on her face. *This might just work*, she thought, the smile her reaction to imagining the last remaining Shade go down.

33

A LOSING BATTLE

Certan threw a punch at the Shade, then rolled away before it could retaliate.

"Fall back!" he shouted, and lead the retreat. They had held up the Shade as best as they could, but it moved forward with relentless power and they couldn't use their numbers to overwhelm it.

"Don't worry, Lara will have a good ambush cooked up," Vincent said.

"I'm not worried about that, I'm worried about them having enough time to prepare it," Certan said.

"If that's your concern perhaps I can help," Vincent said. As they turned the corner he waited instead of joining the rest. As he heard the Shade lumbering through he sliced low and fast, aiming for the feet. He managed to connect, slicing off one of the Shade's feet and causing it to tumble. Vincent hesitated, wondering if he could get in a fatal blow.

"Don't risk it, come back!" Certan shouted. His friend's advice tipped the scales in one direction and Vincent ran off to join the rest.

"That will certainly help," Rengin said.

"Should slow it down a little. How's things back there?" Vincent said.

"Almost ready. Don't lose too many up here, we will need them to spring the ambush."

"It's your command again, just give us the orders," Vincent said

"Just follow my lead. Here it comes," Rengin said. The Shade walked slower, but it seemed otherwise unfazed by the loss of a foot. It walked on the stump instead, losing a little of its balance in the process.

"Harrying strikes only, we need to annoy and slow it down," Rengin shouted. Many of the monks used arrows or discs to pester the Shade, and it began to stop trying to block them. One monk got a little too greedy with the arrows, and the Shade suddenly closed the gap between them and grabbed the monk with its right hand. Rengin loosed his bow immediately, putting the monk out of his misery.

"Retreat!" Rengin shouted. He led the group back, into a slightly wider room with multiple rooms off it.

"You need to get him into the middle of this room," Rengin said.

"Done. Leave it to us." Vincent stood at the entry of the room, to ensure the Shade saw him. Once it arrived it charged immediately at Vincent. "Good to see I have its attention," Vincent said, stepping back, and parrying the Shade's attack. It put Vincent off balance, and he struggled to block the next attack.

Certan circled around, trying to find an opening to capitalise on the creature's compromised balance. It was wise to his tricks, whirling and stepping to keep its distance while still keeping Vincent its focus. Vincent kept retreating, leading the creature closer and closer to the middle of the room.

The Shade increased its onslaught. Vincent desperately parried attack after attack, losing ground faster than he had wanted.

"You're too close! Get away!" Lara shouted. Certan retreated instantly, but Vincent could not. If he gave the Shade any opening at all, it would have him.

"Just do it anyway!" Vincent shouted. Lara did not hesitate and gave the signal. The walls to either side of Vincent shook and started to collapse inwards. Vincent dived to the ground, trying to stay clear of the rubble. The Shade paused its attacks, and focused on batting away the debris from the collapsing wall.

Two additional walls came down behind the Shade, and as they fell monks emerged from the dust and attacked the Shade from behind. It quickly turned to face these foes, angrier than ever.

Vincent stood up, and navigated the unstable ground. He was joined by three other monks, who could now attack the Shade in greater numbers. As they started to land blows, it wheeled around and lunged at them. The monks darted back, only one of them receiving a glancing injury.

In all this commotion Lara dashed in, and dodged the monks, the crumbled walls and the Shade's flailing attack. She manoeuvred in-between it all and planted her dagger squarely in the creature's heart. It shuddered and released a muted cry. Certan stepped up and slammed the dagger with his palm, forcing it the rest of the way and killing the Shade. It toppled to the ground with a crash, surrounded by the broken walls and stones.

The victory was short-lived. As the Shade fell more waves of Blighters entered the room. They were followed by Tainted Ones, clearly giving the orders.

"It never ends," Lara said.

"It will eventually," Certan said, not elaborating. But they were all thinking the same thing. There was only one way this fight could end. They needed a miracle.

"Reinforcements coming through. Change over," Rengin shouted as he came up to the front. The injured and tired monks fell back, and others took their place on the front lines. The room was bigger and full of hazards, but it was still tighter than the entry hallway, so they had a chance at holding it.

Lara stood back, aiming for the Tainted Ones. She took down two before they caught on and stood much further back, directing the Blighters from afar.

"This might sound crazy, but if we can continue this rotation, and there's no more Shades, we can hold this," Vincent said.

"Until we have no energy left yes, but for quite a time. Let's hope there's nothing else to throw at us," Rengin said. It was clear the leader was tiring, despite not fighting as much as some others.

The strategy worked for a little while, the scores of fallen Blighters helping by providing additional barriers and hazards for the enemies to traverse. But the defenders slowed, and little by little they were whittled down.

Their front line retreated. Before long they were holding at the end of the room.

"Why don't we fall back again, use the narrow corridor?" Lara said.

"It's hard to reinforce, and we are getting closer and closer to the Vault. Any setback at all would have us practically running backwards," Rengin said.

"So, we're going to hold here as long as possible," Lara said.

"Exactly." Rengin was about to shout out again but abruptly stopped. Vincent noticed it too. The Blighters were all moving to the sides of the room, filling the space but leaving a passageway through the middle. The Tainted Ones too.

"I don't like the look of this," Vincent said.

"It's an odd arrangement." Certan leaned against a wall to catch his breath.

Stomp. Stomp. Stomp. A shape was slowly advancing from the distance. Each step was measured and powerful. Deliberate and strong. Designed to cause fear. The monks looked at each other. A mixture of curiosity and anxiety crossing their faces. Rengin was resolute, overly so. Vincent could see him putting on a brave face for the other monks. As the shape advanced, it began to take shape.

"No," Lara said softly.

"Is it him?" Vincent said, peering into the distance.

"Definitely," Certan said, clenching his fist. The shape continued to advance.

"What is it? You seem to recognise it," Rengin said.

"You'll see soon enough. It is our enemy," Lara said, spitting onto the ground. In answer to her question the creature arrived and stood in the middle of the room.

"It's a Shade?" Rengin said.

"And here we are at last. Thank you for the welcoming party," Wraith said. His voice still had the muted and shrill harshness of a Shade, but it was more controlled and understandable.

"It speaks?" What are you?" Rengin said.

"I am Wraith. I am the epitome of the power and majesty of the Blight. I have come here to destroy your pathetic little trial and claim the wizard for myself," Wraith said.

"I've never seen this before," Rengin said to Certan as quietly as possible.

"It's a wizard turned into a Shade. He's managed to overcome this form, and use it to his advantage. When we encountered him he was still wrestling with it, but he seems in control now," Certan said.

"Are you going to be smart and give in, or are you going to die horribly?" Wraith said.

"You will not reach the heart of this temple, you foul thing. We have already dealt with three of your kind," Rengin said. His monks rallied behind him.

"Don't underestimate him, we don't know how powerful he is," Lara said.

"I won't. I expect I won't survive this encounter either. I will make a stand here. Certan, stay with me and learn what you can to aid the monks. Vincent and Lara, you should retreat and prepare to fight him again. I fear you will have the best chance against this monster," Rengin said.

"Are you sure?" Certan said.

"Of course, the rest of you go now," Rengin said. Vincent and Lara turned and ran swiftly out of the room and into the dark corridor beyond.

～

"Leaving already? I'm glad someone has the courage to stand here. What's your answer?" Wraith said.

"You will die here!" Rengin said. Before Wraith could respond the monk charged ahead. Rengin quickly feinted an attack, then dashed behind to try an additional strike. None of the Blighters or Tainted Ones moved to protect their master.

Wraith let Rengin's attack connect. He moved slightly with the blow, but was otherwise unharmed. Rengin darted back to his waiting monks.

"Was that it?" Wraith said, mockery in his voice.

"Just an initial attack," Rengin said.

"Charming. I'll allow this for now, but I can't let it drag on. I have other business to attend to," Wraith said.

"I need to prepare something. The rest of you, attack in constant waves. Test all of his body for weak areas. But don't stand around, dodge away after each strike. Let there be no cheap deaths." Rengin sat on the floor, legs crossed and eyes closed.

The monks attacked as ordered, landing blows all over Wraith's body. Mostly he let them land, others he swatted away. But subsequent attacks to that area left no mark.

A Shade would have felt at least some impact; his form can't be that different. He must be using some sort of spell, Certan thought. He looked back at Rengin, intrigued by what the older monk was doing. It had to be something more than his own technique of gathering energy into a single strike.

"Ugh," a monk said, rolling away, nursing a broken arm. He had been a little sloppy and Wraith had punished him.

"I tire with these simple attacks. Show me something else, or I'm moving on," Wraith said.

"It is now time for you to answer for your actions," Rengin shouted. He stood but his feet were not on the ground. He was hovering.

"Watch carefully then retreat. My final act is a gift to you. A gift of time, and also a demonstration of what is possible. Farewell Certan, and good luck." Rengin gently placed his hand on Certan's shoulder.

"Thank you for your generosity and leadership," Certan said.

Rengin nodded and readied his stance. "I call this the seven strikes of salvation," Rengin said. Wraith just laughed and waited. Rengin dashed forward at incredible speed. Certan could not follow him. It was if Rengin appeared next to Wraith and delivered a stunning blow. The sound of the impact reverberated around the room. Wraith was knocked back slightly, but showed no other signs of damage. Before he could recover, Rengin appeared behind Wraith, and circled around again at great speed hitting the same spot a second time. This time Wraith lunged out with his arm, but was too slow and Rengin slipped away.

The super speed monk appeared above Wraith, and dove down, striking this time with a foot on the same spot. The impact was so great, that Wraith was forced to stumble backwards. Clearly the attacks were beginning to have an effect. Wraith created a wall of stone around himself, to prevent the next strike. But Rengin came again, and passed through the stone as if it weren't there, landing another crushing blow. Wraith dropped to one knee, then quickly stood again.

The older monk appeared back with the others, but before they could see anything he was off again. Wraith held his arms out to block the strike. Rengin, dodged under, and with two successive palm strikes hammered the same spot again.

Wraith was knocked over, skidding along the ground. He rose, and dusted himself off. There was a small crack in his skin, where Rengin had been attacking.

"That was only six. Is that all you have?" Wraith said. Rengin was frozen in the pose of his last attack. He was motionless as a statue.

"Maybe you can't move anymore? Oh well, I'll enjoy this!" Wraith said, he ran forward leading with his right arm. As he connected with Rengin's head something strange happened. An explosion of light appeared at the point of impact, knocking Wraith back to the end of the room. Rengin dropped to the ground. The monks rushed to his aid.

"Bring him with us, and let's retreat," Certan said. Rengin had bought them some time and space, but it looked like at a great cost.

34

THE CROSSROADS

Alrion let the spell dissipate and sank down with frustration. He had made the most of his confinement in the Vault, but it was time to get out. He had tried many things, none of which had worked.

He knew that spells would not be the answer, so he tried many different tricks to use his Will to alter the situation. Nothing had even looked like working.

What am I missing? This Vault doesn't seem to be a real space, everything is wrong about it. The monks must have something to do with it. Maybe they are using their Will to keep this place as is, and prevent me from leaving. That must be what is happening, Alrion thought. If that was true though, how could he counter that?

He let his mind wander, to imagine the construction of the Vault. How would he build it, if it was his own creation? He designed the entire construction in his mind, down to the smallest detail. A model so impressive that if he could just flick a switch in his mind it would become reality.

Why can't I just do that? There was no reason why not. He took his model of the Vault, and implanted it on the surroundings. There seemed to be some sort of resistance, but he ignored it. His reality was fact, and it had the construction of the room in a particular way. He felt the walls vibrating and moving, as if they were alternating between different extremes. Finally, they settled, and he knew that the Vault was as he designed.

Time for a change. He walked over to a wall, and redesigned it. He added a doorway to the outside world. The wall reshaped itself to his command. He could see out into the room. There was a great battle going on.

Time to make my grand entrance. It wasn't too early, or too late. It was the perfect timing.

~

"There's no time!" Certan said as he reached the heart of the temple. Vincent and Lara were in a defensive position in front of the four monks. Certan and the rest of the monks moved to the front of the room. They could hear Wraith stomping down the corridor towards them.

The monks bearing Rengin placed him down carefully at the rear of the room and joined their companions.

"Any weaknesses you can help us with?" Lara said.

"No, he seems almost impervious to harm. Rengin managed to create a small hole in Wraith's skin, but that was after repeated attacks of amazing power. He seems stronger than when we first encountered him. I think he is using his spells to somehow shield his body further," Certan said.

"Maybe Alrion will be able to counter. But there's still a good chance Runesteel will work," Vincent said.

"I hope so. Good luck to all." Certan turned to face the sound of Wraith entering.

"Here we are, everyone together at last. We never met officially, but I assume you are Alrion's father?" Wraith said, pointing at Vincent.

"That's correct. And you are Branthor the monster?" Vincent said.

"Actually, we did meet a long time ago. Back when you were following your father around like a puppy," Wraith said.

"I don't remember, I guess you weren't that memorable without your costume," Vincent said.

"Are you still disappointed that you couldn't cut it? Don't take that out on me. Anyway, I'm more interested in your son. Where is Alrion?" Wraith said.

"He'll be here when he's ready."

"I've come all this way, it would be rude not to wait. You can entertain me instead," Wraith said. He raised his arm and sent spirals of earth and fire at Vincent.

"Look out!" Lara shouted, pushing Vincent to the side. He rolled to the ground and held up his sword, blocking the last trail of fiery death and knocking it aside. "Certan would have a decent attack, if we can buy him some time and opportunity," Lara said.

"Seeing Rengin's attacks I am not sure how effective it will be, but it is worth a chance," Certan said.

"Very well, let's see what we can do," Vincent cautiously advanced on Wraith.

Lara let loose a series of discs which bounced harmlessly off Wraith's chest, but did get his attention.

"You can't possibly hope to hurt me, I have become something more than any other wizard," Wraith said.

"That may be, but there is nothing that Runesteel cannot cut through," Vincent said, twirling his sword with menace. Wraith watched the blade very carefully, which confirmed Vincent's suspicions. Despite his improved power and control, the blade was still effective.

Wraith raised a wall of earth right in front of Vincent, but he sliced it in half and kicked it down. A wave of force tugged at his feet and a spear of earth flew through the air, but Vincent used the momentum of force beneath him to roll to safety.

Vincent quickly rose and kept walking, closing the distance between them. Lara crept forward from another angle, waiting for an opportunity.

He doesn't know that my dagger is also Runesteel, he may give me an opening. As Wraith focused on Vincent, she stalked closer and closer.

This is it! she thought and stepped forward with a quick slice. Wraith noticed at the last moment, and moved just enough. The slice became a light graze, but it did break the skin. Wraith looked at her in horror.

"Too slow!" Vincent said as he swung his sword. Wraith managed to blast Vincent back with a wave of force, slowing his strike and increasing the gap between them.

Out of nowhere Certan appeared, and struck with his charged palm. The blow exploded with power and knocked Wraith back. He paused to examine his body. The crack created by Rengin was larger now, and appeared to be an open wound, albeit minor.

In a fury, Wraith whipped through the air with his arm. It created a diagonal wave of shearing force, striking all of his three opponents. All the surfaces that were hit suffered deep cuts, and all three limped back to a defensive position.

"That was our best shot, and he just blew us away," Lara said.

"True, I'm not sure how much more we can do," Vincent said.

"What's that?" Certan said. They looked over and saw a shimmering doorway appear at the rear of the room, in-between the four older monks. All they could see on the other side was white. A man stepped through. It was Alrion.

"Sorry to keep you waiting," he said.

"Alrion!" Vincent shouted. He staggered to his feet and ran over to his son.

"Easy there, you're hurt." Alrion accepted the hug, then guided his father to crouch down. Alrion gathered his Spark and used his healing spell, knotting the skin back together. "That's different," Alrion said, but said nothing further.

"I feel like I should be saving you, not the opposite," Vincent said.

"Sorry, this a once-off. You can save me again later," Alrion said.

"Good, that's better. Did you pass the trial?"

"Yes, otherwise I wouldn't be here. Lara and Certan come over here," Alrion said.

"You look different. Better and stronger." Lara gave him a hug too.

"Good to see you," Certan said, slapping Alrion on the back.

"Let me patch you up a bit." Alrion healed their wounds in the same way. "Anything I should know?" Alrion said.

"He's terribly strong, but the Runesteel seems to work a bit. Do you have any ideas?" Lara said.

"I think we should just leave, Rengin mentioned a secret passage in this room," Certan said.

"Find the passage, I'll deal with Wraith," Alrion stepped forward and looked at his enemy.

"Alrion, finally. We've all been waiting so long. What took you?" Wraith said.

"I was busy. I see you have been too. Do you have any humanity left?" Alrion said. Wraith just laughed.

"Maybe you have just misplaced it. Why don't you just leave?" Alrion said.

"Clearly, I can't do the trial, not with you all here and it relies on those pesky monks. But you are here, so I'll settle for that. I made you an offer before, and it's still available. If you're feeling a little shy, I'll just accept on your behalf. It's easier that way," Wraith said.

"I won't join you, there's nothing you can say to convince me."

"Who said you needed to be convinced?" Wraith said, and launched a rolling wave of earth at Alrion. The young wizard concentrated then stopped the earth in its tracks, letting it settle back down into the ground.

"Oh, learned a few new tricks? That won't be enough." Wraith let loose with a stream of fire and earth, attacking in a criss-cross pattern.

Alrion extinguished the fire and knocked the earth back down to the ground.

"My turn," Alrion sent wave after wave of force at Wraith. Nothing happened, as each one hit. Alrion did the same again, but alternated with fire. Again, Wraith let each attack hit and nothing happened.

"You thought that would work?" Wraith said. Alrion did not respond, but tried again. This time the waves of force alternated with waves of fire and earth. Like before Wraith let them crash against him. But something was different.

The ground around Wraith's feet sucked him in like quicksand. It quickly solidified, binding him in place. As he struggled to break free, Alrion fired an intensely bright white-hot rod of fire directly at Wraith's chest wound. He roared in pain and broke his feet free.

"That smarts, it really does. But it's not enough." Wraith was trying to shake off the pain, but it seemed to linger.

"Alrion we found the path. Come with us," Certan said.

"No, I have a chance. I can beat him," Alrion said.

"It's too risky. Just come with us, it'll be fine," Lara said.

"She's right Alrion. You've done enough, let's regroup and move forward," Vincent said.

"No, I'm sorry. I can't have this thing following me around forever. I need to deal with it now, so I can focus on the next trial. Just go on ahead, I'll catch up." Alrion felt his friends had not moved, so he turned to face them. "Please go, I need to do this. I promise I'll come find you," he said.

"Very well, let's go. Don't keep us waiting," Vincent said.

Alrion watched them go, then turned back to face his enemy.

"I see you are now alone. Such a pity," Wraith said.

"You sure do talk a lot," Alrion said. A grin stole across Wraith's face and suddenly hundreds of projectiles flew towards Alrion. They came from every direction and were incredibly fast. He dove for cover and built an earth shield around himself. As fast as he could reinforce it, dents embedded in the surface at an alarming rate. In seconds the whole thing would collapse. Alrion threw up more walls, opened an exit and ran. With a crash the whole thing toppled and Alrion was scrambling for breath.

"You were saying?" Wraith said.

"That you don't talk nearly enough," Alrion said, chuckling.

"I think I should be honest with you, it's only fair. You got a good attack in, I have to admire that. It's the least I expect from you. However, you can't possibly win."

"Why is that?"

"The Blight has a power all its own. I can break the rules, enhance this already strong body even further, and employ a bag of tricks so large I can't even begin to tell you all about them. No spell you throw at me will be enough."

"So, what do we do then?"

"You come with me and we leave. And I bring you into the fold. I have great plans for us," Wraith said.

"For the last time, no," Alrion said. As much as Wraith was a liar, there was probably some truth in his words. Alrion drew the Runesteel sword, and the diamond glowed bright blue.

"You're definitely a piece of work, but I can cut you down to size," Alrion said, readying himself.

35

INFECTED

Alrion knew he had neither the skill nor the strength to wield the sword properly. But he knew it was effective, so perhaps he could create an opening that anyone could exploit.

Wraith eyed the sword carefully, which told Alrion he had made the right choice. The creature must have remembered losing its hand. Alrion had one chance to make this work, so he prepared himself. Wraith wasn't ready to wait, and sent multiple waves of fire and earth before following them in himself.

"This is my shot," Alrion decided. He would not dodge the attacks, he would use them as a shield. As the attacks came in Alrion did not move, he readied his sword in a lunge position, the blade pointing out at Wraith. Alrion gathered his Spark, and deflected or destroyed all the attacks that would hit. When the last wave of earth came, and Wraith was right behind it, Alrion pierced a small hole in the wave and thrust his sword through. He let the rest of the wave hit him, committing everything to enhancing his single strike.

Wraith thought that his attack had succeeded, and was committed to grabbing Alrion. He noticed too late the sword emerging from the rock straight for his chest. All he could do was twist slightly, which was just enough.

The Runesteel sword pierced Wraith in the chest, but missed the heart. It sunk in right up to the hilt. Wraith reached out and grabbed Alrion by the neck.

"So near, yet so far," Wraith said. His second finger turned ash-black and he jabbed Alrion with it. Alrion recoiled in surprise, and fell back.

"It is done. You are mine now," Wraith said with glee, removing the sword, and tossing it aside.

"No!" Alrion cried, reaching for his neck. He could feel the wound pulsing.

"You are infected, it's only a matter of time now," Wraith said. Alrion backed away, stumbling over the littered rocks. He made it over to his sword and picked it up, rocking with the weight. "You are weak now, it is overcoming your system. I must say you seem to be handling it well, some become unconscious immediately," Wraith said. He slowly advanced towards Alrion.

"This can't be happening," Alrion said, shocked. How had he let this happen? He could have left with his friends, as they had wanted. But he had chosen to stay, and he had failed.

"Try and use your Spark, I dare you," Wraith said. Alrion reached for it, hoping to find something to throw at his enemy. But the fire was tainted. It wasn't the pure heat he was used it, there was already a smoky black mass over it. Alrion recoiled again. "Ahh that's right. By all means reach through the filth and use the Spark. You may as well speed things up, and you need to get used to it. The real magic happens when you learn to accept it," Wraith said.

"No, never. I'll die before that happens," Alrion said.

"Impossible I'm afraid. If you die it just completes the process. The Blight has you now. Welcome."

"I'll find a way, there's always a way."

"Oh, there's that ritual you are looking for, but good luck casting that while infected. Not going to work too well is it?" Wraith said. He was right, and Alrion was scared. But deep down, he knew something else. But he couldn't put his finger on it. As Wraith came closer and closer, Alrion scrambled for that thought in his brain, the one that had hope attached to it.

He put aside all the fear, and emotion and worries that coursed through him and focused on that thought. He found it and spoke it out loud.

"I have passed the trial of Will, and left the Vault of Silence. The power of will is exercised by persistence, and getting back up. This is not the end, this is another step on my journey. I will not submit to you, in life or in death," Alrion said. Wraith stopped, puzzled by the outburst. Before he could move further Alrion had already decided what to do next.

Magic was not available to him, and his strength was quickly fading. But he had the power of Will, which was not constrained by those things. He tapped into the reality around him, and remade it into his design.

The ground underneath Wraith suddenly dropped hundreds of feet, and sand filled its place. It was if it had always been so, and the change was instantaneous. Wraith was now trapped within a prison of sand.

Alrion didn't revel in the victory, he stumbled over to the back of the room. He found the secret passage and tumbled down the stairs. With great difficulty he picked himself up, and dragged himself forward, using the sword as a walking stick.

Just ... have ... to ... get ... out, Alrion thought. He pushed on for as long as he could, before collapsing on the ground.

Please, help me, he thought finally.

36

RECOVERY

Vincent started to slow down, and Certan did the same. The rest of the monks continued their escape. Lara stopped suddenly, looking at the other two.

"What is it?" she said.

"Something has happened." Certan paused and listened carefully.

"I can't explain it myself, I just felt like Alrion needed us," Vincent said.

"Let us just wait a bit, we are far enough for relative safety," Certan said. The three of them waited in silence, staring back at the darkness behind them.

The tunnel they were in was long and straight, with no indication of how far it went. As the footsteps of the monks ahead became softer and softer they were surrounded by true silence as they waited patiently under the earth.

A strange sound surrounded them. It was like an immense amount of sand just shifted incredibly quickly.

"That shouldn't be possible. We must head back." Certan looked at the tunnel ahead, and back at where they had come from.

"Go to the monks, they may need your assistance. The two of us can handle this. Just keep the door open for us at the other end," Vincent said.

"Thank you, I will accept your offer. Hurry back, I will see you soon." Certan ran off into the darkness and Vincent and Lara ran back the way they had come.

"What do you think happened?" Lara said.

"Some sort of gigantic shift happened, that's what we heard. It doesn't matter who did that, it is bad news. Certan seemed to have felt it too, and he seemed quite shaken," Vincent said.

"He was definitely spooked. But was equally worried about the other monks."

"We don't know where that shift happened. He is right to be concerned."

"I have a bad feeling about this. Let's keep quiet and see what we can find." Lara increased her pace and Vincent kept up.

The going was tough as the only guide they had was the tunnel wall. There were no lights and they weren't going to try and create any. Lara's pulse quickened as they ran, more from worry than from exertion. Alrion had seemed off, like it was his last chance to do something. She hoped he hadn't run into more trouble than he could handle.

He managed to survive last time, maybe he's fine, she thought. The start of the tunnel was approaching, and a thin light crept in from the room above. "Is someone there?" Lara said. As they continued they could see better.

"It's Alrion?" Vincent said. He fell to his knees and cradled his son in his arms.

"He's alive, but he feels cold. Help me get him up," Vincent said.

Together the two of them hauled the young wizard up onto his feet, but he couldn't stand by himself.

"He seems a bit out of it, and his forehead is burning up. This doesn't feel right," Lara said.

"Let's just get him out of here," Vincent said. Together they moved forward at a fast walk. "Alrion can you hear me?" he said. There was no response.

"He must have passed out. It's like he's sick. You don't think?" Lara said.

"We don't know, let's not jump to conclusions. Whatever has happened, he got away. Our responsibility is to ensure that he gets to safety," Vincent said.

"Of course, let's see if we can pick up the pace," Lara said. `

Alrion felt himself be picked up, but his body was so heavy. He couldn't help whoever was helping him. He had brief flashes of awareness, but it was so dark he couldn't distinguish them from when he blacked out.

There were more voices soon, some calling his name. But they seemed so distant, so far away. He didn't have the energy to respond. He could sense the concern, but he couldn't address it. All he could do was what he was already doing which was letting them take him.

He could feel the light and heat building around him, but he couldn't open his eyes. It was too difficult. The more he tried to exert himself, the more he felt the strange thumping in his heart. Better to rest, and not stir that unwelcome addition.

Finally, he was laid down, and he felt like he could finally rest. He let himself sink into the depth of sleep, and forgot all his worries. They were for another time, when he had the strength to deal with them. For a while, he was at peace.

Alrion could sense the light, and it was annoying him. He tried opening his eyes. They did as instructed, and the room slowly became visible. His surroundings were familiar. He was in Ashra's hut.

He sat up too quickly, and nursed his head.

"Alrion, you're awake. How are you?" Lara said. She was sitting by his side. The concern in her eyes was obvious.

"I've been better. What happened?"

"We found you at the entrance of the secret tunnel. And we brought you here as quickly as possible. You're safe now," Lara said. Vincent walked over and crouched by Alrion's other side.

"Welcome back to the land of the living. You did well son. Everything's alright now, although you probably need more rest before you can get back on your feet," Vincent said. Alrion nodded. He thought back to what had happened. He remembered the infection, and quickly felt around his neck. "The wound has healed, but you have been tainted," Vincent said.

"This, this isn't right," Alrion said. The memories came flooding back.

"There is a cure, you're working on it right now remember?" Ashra said from the other side of the room.

"But I can't learn the spell like this?"

"There's always a way. But in the meantime, you need to know a few things. The Blight travels different speeds in different people. Some change overnight, for others it is a gradual process. I have done what I could do to slow it down, and I feel like time is on our side. But it cannot be stopped with the tools we have at our disposal," Ashra said.

"What can I do?"

"Have you felt your Spark?" Ashra said. Alrion thought back and remembered the feeling when he tried to access it before.

"Yes, I tried immediately. Wraith was quite pleased with himself at my reaction," Alrion said.

"Then you know not to touch it. Not under any circumstances. Not only will it speed up the transformation, but it may also put the cure at risk. We don't know how it works," Ashra said.

"I understand."

"This is very important. It's not worth it, you must find another way of dealing with things," Ashra said. Alrion looked around the room.

"I have your sword, if that's what you are after," Vincent said.

"Now's as good a time as any. I'm not particularly skilled with it," Alrion said.

"We can work on that, when you get your strength back. Can you tell us what happened back there?"

"I passed the trial, and I fought Wraith. Even with my best spells and tricks all I managed to do was injure him with the sword. But my aim was off, it wasn't a fatal strike and he had the opportunity to infect me," Alrion said.

"It was an achievement for you to keep up with him in battle, he had us all beaten," Vincent said.

"From what I have been told, he is a formidable foe. An unnatural fusion of Shade and Wizard. How did you get away after he infected you?" Ashra said.

"I had only one tool left, my Will. I remade the structure of the temple, trapping him in a deep pit below the ground. I doubt it will kill him, but it was enough to escape," Alrion said.

"Remarkable that you mastered your Will so quickly," Certan said as he joined them.

"I can't really talk about that, it's called the Vault of Silence for a reason," Alrion said, forcing out a shaky laugh.

"You are talking like one of the masters already," Certan said, chuckling.

"Are you able to do the same here?" Ashra said. Vincent shot Ashra a strange look and was about to speak up, when Ashra signalled him to be quiet. Alrion focused on his will, and tried to replicate what he had done at the temple. It didn't feel the same though. He couldn't seem to tap into the fabric of reality the same way.

"No, it's different. Maybe I don't have the same strength," Alrion said.

"It's not that, although I'm sure it is a factor. I believe the temple itself is either built in a unique way, or sits upon a unique location. The temple facilitates the use of Will, and the bending of reality. It would explain why it's in the middle of the desert. That's my theory at least, and your experience cements that in my mind," Ashra said.

"So, what happened to the temple?" Alrion said.

"Scouts have suggested that all the Tainted have left. The temple is still intact, although heavily damaged. The remaining monks will be returning and building it back up," Certan said.

"Will you be joining them?" Alrion said.

"I'm sorry, but I must. With the loss of Rengin and many others, our numbers have dwindled. It is my first responsibility to help repair what was done."

"It sounds like they have accepted you back though," Alrion said with a smile.

"Yes, the flask didn't even factor in. It turns out, my behaviour is not unique. In many cases, it is expected. Thank you for convincing me to return. I would like to believe that I would have returned eventually, but how many years would have passed?"

"You are welcome, in fact I should be thanking you. With your guidance, I made it in time, and completed the Trial of Will."

"You are now my senior. I will catch up to you, and I'll find you again to help with the completion of your quest," Certan said, bowing to Alrion.

"I look forward to it. Please, don't hang around on my account, if you are needed there please go," Alrion said. Certan approached Alrion, and kissed him on the forehead.

"Where I come from, that is how we say goodbye to family that we will not see for a long time. Take care young wizard, when we meet again I will be your equal." Certan bowed again and left the hut.

"Bye, Certan, I'll always consider you my teacher," Alrion said quietly, after the monk had left.

"For now, you need to rest more. You will be safe here until you are ready to leave," Ashra said.

"I don't even know where to go next," Alrion said.

"We'll figure it out, don't worry. That's not a job for today." Lara stroked his arm softly.

"Are you hungry?" Vincent said.

"I think so?"

"Let's get you some food and rest. You need to build up your strength for our journey," Vincent said.

"If you insist," Alrion said, and rearranged himself to be in a better seated position. He had to focus on his recovery first, and worry about the next steps later. And with sleep, came dreams.

A NEW DREAM

A lrion dreamed. Again, the rush of images and scenes, a massive blur. Everything settled, and he saw his grandfather once more sitting at a desk. Alrion walked over.

"Grandfather, I need your help," Alrion said.

"I cannot help you. I am merely a guide to the knowledge within you," Granthion said.

"I am infected with the Blight. Can you show me the cure?" Alrion said.

"I already gave you the spell. You will know it when you are ready."

"How can I be ready when I am tainted?" Alrion said with frustration. Granthion thought carefully, then responded.

"How can you cure others, before you cure yourself?" he said.

"That's exactly what I am talking about!" Alrion said.

"You have the knowledge and you have the Will. What's missing?"

"Well, the third component would be Spark. But I already have that."

"No, you have only half."

"What do you mean?" Alrion said. Granthion stood up from the desk and gestured into the distance. A shimmering doorway opened and Alrion ran through without a moment's hesitation.

He was cold, really cold. Snow was falling, and covered the ground. It was so thick as he walked he seemed to be sinking into it. Alrion instinctively went to cast a fire spell, but stopped himself.

Even if this is a dream, I can't use it, he thought. He trekked forward through the snow, towards what looked like a summit. As he stepped onto it, he saw a woman with black hair and purple robes standing with her back turned to him.

"Hello!" Alrion shouted over the wind. But there was no response. She raised her hands and looked to be casting some sort of spell. Her body shimmered with magic, and within her pulsed a strange glow. Alrion walked closer fascinated. As he approached he noticed a strange heat within himself. He looked at his own body, and noticed a fierce core burning inside. If he concentrated he could also see a black tinge on the edges.

He looked again at the woman and noticed she was different. Within her was a core of pure water, still and at peace. As he stared, she suddenly turned and looked directly at Alrion. Her eyes glowed an icy blue and she reached out for him.

Alrion awoke suddenly, feeling the heat of his surroundings immediately. Part of him wished for that cool to return.

"Did you have another strange dream? You seemed unusually restless," Lara said.

"Yes, I think it's a clue for my next step or trial," Alrion said.

"Let me hear it," Ashra said, coming over and sitting down. Alrion looked around.

"Where's my father?" he said.

"He went to visit the monks to see how they were doing. I think he was restless sitting around here doing nothing. Don't worry he will return soon. What was in your dream?"

"My grandfather told me that Spark was only half of what I needed for the spell. He created a doorway that took me to a wintery place, a snowy mountain. At its peak, I found a woman who was casting some sort of spell. Only where I had a core of fire, she had one of water. And when she turned to look at me, her eyes were glowing blue," Alrion said.

"That's very interesting. I think you have your next goal," Ashra said.

"You know where this is?" Lara said.

"There are stories, but not confirmed, of a group of women. Some call them witches, others refer to them as mystics. They can cast magic of a different sort, from a different source. I had never really taken much stock in the stories, because I had no need to. But it seems plausible," Ashra said.

"Do you know any more about them? Where do they live? What can do they?" Alrion said.

"Well you already know where they live, deep in the north amongst the mountains. Although there are stories that they travel and are hidden in many places. In plain sight. In terms of what they can do, it's hard to really distinguish fairy tales from the potentially real."

"Give some examples?" Lara said.

"Healing, fortune telling, granting wishes, and mind control for example. Fairly outlandish don't you think?" Ashra said.

"That's useful, even if most of it is nonsense. It will help us find women who fit that description," Alrion said.

"Indeed, you may even find one on your way there. I think this is the right path for you, there is enormous potential. They may be able to assist you with the Blight's taint, or even show you how to harness their power," Ashra said.

"I have a goal and I have a direction. How long will it take?" Alrion said.

"You need more time to heal, because the journey is harsh. After you cross the desert, you need to travel quite a distance north. You should have horses for that. Then the trek into the mountains is not for the faint of heart."

"Have you been there?"

"No, I haven't. Perhaps if I had, I could offer you more guidance. But you will have able companions, so you will be fine. The only other issue is the Blight," Ashra said, pointing at Alrion's chest.

"What do I do about it?" Alrion said.

"Don't use your Spark for starters. Just use your Will and whatever skill you can muster up with a sword. I also recommend meditating every day. The body resists the Blight by itself, any effort to assist will buy you some more time."

"Thanks, for everything. Are you sure you won't come with us? You can see the women of the north for yourself, these mystics," Alrion said.

"No, as before. My place is here, and your quest is your own. Come visit me again, and I will hear your tales of them," Ashra said.

"As you wish, but if you change your mind..." Alrion said.

"I will not, but thank you for the offer. If you apply yourself, you can leave in a week," Ashra said.

"A week? Not sooner?"

"That's up to you. But I won't let you leave here until it is safe. I have my ways," Ashra said with a grin on his face.

"Yes, I've noticed," Alrion said, remembering the last time he had tried to leave without Ashra's blessing. The idea of meeting the women magic users, and the possibility for a new type of magic filled him with hope. But there was a nagging doubt below it all. He pushed it away, but knew it would return. For now, he just had to keep his focus on recovering his strength and beginning his journey.

EPILOGUE

Ashra waved goodbye to Alrion, Lara and Vincent and wished them well. Alrion had recovered incredibly well over the last week, although Ashra could see that the Blight was having an effect on the young wizard. He had taken Vincent aside and mentioned it specifically. Vincent would monitor the situation and keep Alrion's spirits up.

I hope he makes it, but it's such a tall order. How can he reach them in time? Ashra thought. He had seen many suffer the Blight's taint, and even the ones that resisted the most had turned in time. Alrion had a long journey ahead of him, one that would be a race against the infection.

"Better he keeps his hope up. Any dark thoughts will work against him," Ashra said to himself. It was his justification for hiding from Alrion the true timeline he was fighting against. In some cases, ignorance was definitely the better option.

The desert wizard had a restless afternoon, and evening. He tried to get into his normal routines and carry on as normal, but he couldn't settle down. The events that had just occurred were momentous.

A young wizard accessing the Pool of Knowledge, conquering the Vault of Silence, and surviving against a Shade born from a Wizard. It's unheard of. It excited him in a way that he had not been for some time. He felt a little disappointed that he hadn't taken Alrion up on his offer, although he absolutely could not tag along. Some journeys could not accept extra passengers.

As he pondered the entire situation he noticed movement out of the corner of his eye.

"Such simple tricks won't get past me," Ashra said, calling out to the intruder.

"I didn't expect so, but you can forgive my caution in coming here," a voice said from the shadows. A man emerged, wearing a dark hooded robe covering his face.

"So, you're the mysterious wizard following young Alrion around," Ashra said.

"Yes, the very same."

"I take it you don't need an update from me then," Ashra said.

"No, I do not."

"So why have you come?" Ashra said, about to say the man's name.

"Call me Aydan," the man said.

"Aydan? What's that mean? It's in the ancient language, isn't it?"

"Yes, it means The Lost One," Aydan said.

"Very well Aydan, I will keep your secret. What brings you to my humble home?"

"First, I wanted to thank you for assisting Alrion."

"Of course, but no need to thank me. I may be an outcast, but I can see what's in front of me."

"An outcast only by your own making. That was my second reason for seeing you."

"Yes? You have my attention," Ashra said.

"I want you to return to the Academy, they need a new leader. You did wonders with Alrion, think of what you can contribute to the rest!" Aydan said.

"I don't think you have the authority to make that request."

"All the same, what do you think? Can you really stay here in the desert, knowing events are happening out in the world?" Aydan said. Ashra didn't have a response ready.

"Maybe not," he said finally.

"Then consider it as a possibility."

"I will indeed. What about you?"

"That's not my place, I gave that up. Alrion is my responsibility," Aydan said.

"I thought as much, but thought it worth asking anyway. Thanks for coming to see me. I appreciate it," Ashra said.

"I know that I can trust you, and I think you are wasted here. You're not as much of a loner as you think. Why have you saved all those lost idiots over the years?" Aydan said. Before Ashra could respond Aydan turned to leave and blended into shadows.

"Such theatrics. Farewell," Ashra said, staring into the darkness.

Alrion walked carefully, not trusting his body. His recovery had been frustrating and slow. And he could feel the Blight within him. Ashra and Certan had provided useful advice for trying to slow its spread. But he could sense the darkness within marching on regardless.

He stopped suddenly, a curious thought entering his mind. He unstrapped his sword, and looked at it carefully. The diamond embedded in the hilt let off a faint but noticeable glow.

"Don't worry, there's still time," Vincent said.

Alrion nodded and put the sword away. At least he had a way of judging how far he had gone. He knew how bright the diamond had been when encountering Wraith.

That detestable monster. How do I defeat him now, when I have no access to my power? Alrion thought. His recent mastery of Will didn't seem like it would be enough by itself. The monks had not fared particularly well. He could almost hear Wraith laughing, in that strange and strained Shade voice.

"It's not your imagination. We are linked now," Wraith said in Alrion's mind.

The hideous laughter returned, much louder now.